‘Screenwriter and novelist Derek Haas confidently strides into espionage with his adrenaline rush *The Right Hand*. A lean, no-nonsense plot . . . the vigorous pace never slows as Haas’ sparse prose propels the plot that crisscrosses Europe.’ *South Florida Sun Sentinel*

‘Cinematic . . . *The Right Hand* never lets up.’ *Dallas Morning News*

‘A lean and mean tale laced with wit, mordant insight and, at perfectly judged moments, flashes of sharp prose. He paces his tale with crack action scenes that, however well they read on the page, may soon have film directors calling “Action!” These high-octane scenes, however, never detract from Haas’ canny plotting, which is capped by a final, unexpected twist and a poignant fade-out. It’s not the game, but how well you play it, and Haas plays it very well indeed.’ *Kirkus Reviews*

‘Haas spins a riveting page-turner with just the kind of sharp dialogue one would expect from someone who writes for the movies. Readers will want to see more of Austin Clay.’ *Booklist*

‘This hard-edged contemporary spy thriller from Haas covers a lot of ground with great narrative economy. Forceful, cinematic scenes show off the lean grace of Hass’ prose. Cleverly placed plot twists and spycraft details help make this a standout.’ *Publishers Weekly*

Also by Derek Haas

The Silver Bear

Hunt for the Bear

Dark Men

DEREK HAAS

The Right Hand

First published in Great Britain in 2012 by Mulholland Books
An imprint of Hodder & Stoughton
An Hachette UK company

First published in paperback in 2013

1

A CIP n Library

Paperback ISBN 978 1 444 72921 4
eBook ISBN 978 1 444 72920 7

Printed and bound by Clays Ltd, St Ives plc

Hodder & Stoughton policy is to use papers that are natural, renewable and recyclable products and made from wood grown in sustainable forests. The logging and manufacturing processes are expected to conform to the environmental regulations of the country of origin.

Hodder & Stoughton Ltd
338 Euston Road
London NW1 3BH

www.hodder.co.uk

For my older brother, who shaped me,
And for my younger brother, who straightened me out

The Right Hand

PROLOGUE

HE SMELLED wood burning, and also flesh, like a pig roasting on a spit, and only then did he realize he was on fire. The pain came next, searing and relentless, and it drew him out of unconsciousness like a hypnotist snapping his fingers. He jolted upright and rolled, tamping out the flames at least temporarily.

The smoke was thick and heavy and oppressive. He stayed low and glimpsed an opening, daylight filtering through the haze. Instinctively, he gritted his teeth, held his breath, and crawled toward the hole. He reached the ledge just as his lungs were bursting and leapt forward, falling five feet to the gravel below, landing awkwardly on his side.

The drop might have hurt, might have caused him to wince, except there was so much blessed air, he gulped oxygen greedily, forgetting everything else.

Vaguely, a word tickled the back of his brain. *Run*.

His head started to clear, and he blinked away tears. Heat beat the left side of his face, and from his prostrate position, he looked in that direction, taking it all in.

A train was on fire. At least five cars were ablaze, and when he looked farther down the rail line, he saw the engine and eight more cars half on, half off the tracks, capsized like a herd of dying buffalo. The back of the engine was exposed, with two tons of metal ripped asunder, blown out from underneath.

Run, the voice inside his head repeated.

He found his feet, stood upright, and fought back dizziness and nausea. In that moment, it all came back to him.

Blake Nelson had spent the last eleven years as an officer for Central Intelligence. He was the rarest of recruits, thirty-three when he joined, plucked out of a successful import-export career in which he happened to do most of his business with Moscow. He spoke fluent Russian, a by-product of his Georgian mother's mother tongue. He was a bachelor, virtually friendless, and had a placid, easygoing disposition. When they came for him, he thought it was a Moscow client playing a practical joke. When he watched his own funeral after the CIA successfully faked his death, he knew exactly how real his new life was.

And for the last five years, he had been a remarkable field asset, rewarding the risky judgment of his recruiter while making himself indispensable as the cold war cooled and then heated again. So many of the government's resources had been funneled into the Middle East after September 2001, although a few in Intelligence recognized that the Old Bear was the sole nation in the world still capable of managing a serious growl.

His current assignment involved a rail station in Omsk; he was to board a freight train, on which he was supposed to meet…

Run.

He'd been set up. There was no other explanation, none he would like. The meeting was a sham, designed to flush him, and he had walked into the trap clumsily, like a rat after cheese. The implications were staggering. It meant someone knew about Stepnoy, and if someone knew about *that,* then they knew—

A thunderous crash snapped his thoughts back to the moment at hand as the train car he had climbed out of collapsed inward. He stared at the fire for a moment, a flickering yellow-and-orange inferno, and then movement to his left caught his eye. Men were coming, silhouetted against the flames, and not just coming…sprinting.

Run! the voice screamed, and this time, he trusted it.

Nelson might have had second-degree burns on his thighs, but his legs worked. He scampered away from the train in a vague notion of north, toward a thick forest. Safety involved camouflage and quietness, he knew from his training, but it would only come if he put enough distance between his pursuers and himself.

There was another alternative. How many men had he counted against the blaze? Six? He'd had only a brief moment before he found his feet, and he hadn't had time to check his gun, and could he be sure he'd get all of them if it came to a fight? No, flight was the correct option.

The woods were thick evergreens, old growth, and were spaced out so the threat wasn't from running into a low-hanging branch but from catching a root at an ankle-snapping angle.

A foreign sensation came over him. He realized he was winded, even though he couldn't have been running for more than five minutes. Smoke inhalation must have affected his lungs, and just as this realization hit him, that he wouldn't be able to outrun them after all, wouldn't be able to make it to safety, that he would have to mount a desperate stand and fight, a bullet ripped into the back of his left leg, spinning him like a top and pitching him forward into an absurd collision with the earth.

He didn't have to block the pain because there was no pain; just a dull sense that he could not feel anything, and when he tried to sit up to move, to crane his neck so he could catch a glimpse of his enemy, his body betrayed him and remained still, defiant.

He felt hands lifting him, but all he could see was the emptiness of the night sky holding down the trees.

CHAPTER ONE

Austin Clay looked like a hiker. His beard had grown in thick and full, a slightly darker shade of brown than the wisps atop his head. His North Face backpack appeared to have accumulated years of use, although it had been purchased only a few weeks earlier.

He wound up the path where the trees thinned and the limestone boulders seemed to multiply. He had made the journey once before, a few days earlier. He would be meeting the same man now, and this time, he hoped an exchange would be forthcoming.

Clay had been an Intelligence officer for fifteen years, six of those in black ops. The last three years, he'd operated in a program consisting of exactly two members, his handler and him.

The path led to a plateau, and he made out Beto standing beside a flat rock the shape of a dining table, the chosen meeting place. It was an inspired location: no listening devices at this altitude and a clear view for miles of anyone coming. It would take Clay another ten minutes to reach him.

They spoke in Spanish, with Clay showing no fatigue from the climb and only a slight hint of an American accent.

"Good afternoon."

"Yes."

"Do you have the name for me?"

Beto coughed into his fist. He was half a head shorter than Clay, but his arms and legs were as thick as tree branches. The American knew Beto's age to be forty-one, but he also knew what this life could do to a man's features. It was a wonder Clay's own hair hadn't prematurely grayed.

Beto finished coughing and wiped his lower lip. "I've been doing some checking."

Clay waited. The conversation often turned in this direction with new contacts.

"The alias you gave me is unknown. We have sources within the intelligence community in the US, sources who have been validated on multiple occasions in the past. And no one has heard of you."

"I operate outside known circles."

"That sounds convenient for you."

"Or inconvenient, at times like this."

"Well, forgive me for being cautious, but I cannot trust a man who—"

"Then trust this. Your given name is Emilio Beto. You

were born outside Madrid forty-one years ago last week. Your mother and father were killed in a small-plane crash while flying into Zaragoza when you were fourteen. Since joining El CESID after stints with the Spanish army in the first Gulf War and with NATO in Serbia, you've tried unsuccessfully to determine whether your parents were murdered by the same government for whom you now work. Your chief officer, Fernando de Lugo, told you to drop it if you wanted to continue covert work for El CESID, and professional self-preservation won out over family bonds."

Beto stood there, eyes as wide as *tapas* plates. He started to say something, but Clay kept on, voice filled with gravel.

"When you break from professional work, you hang your backpack in an apartment in Tenerife, near Teide, so you can hike up the volcano or lie on the beach. Your apartment has only one bedroom and a small kitchen. In the freezer right now is a half-eaten bonito you caught this summer. You consider no one your friend, and you seek no female companionship."

Clay watched the other man's eyes, looking for defeat to plant its flag there. "You may trust you don't know who I am, Beto, but you can trust I know who you are. I know where to find you, and I know how to get to you, and I know what weapons you have strapped to your hip, ankle, and wrist. So let's quit running in circles. You tell me what I need to know and you can have what's in my backpack. Withhold the information or lie to me and I'll leave this spot and find you another time. And then, I assure you, you won't have a mile to see me coming."

The words had the intended effect. Beto swallowed dryly, his Adam's apple bobbing like a cork. His eyes darted, then settled as he reached his decision and found his voice.

"Gregory Molina."

Clay nodded before cracking the smallest of smiles. "Thank you. Let's hope we never see each other again."

He dropped the backpack, turned, and left the way he'd come. In the sky, a hawk circled lazily, hunting.

In Chelsea, the air smelled damp long before drops of rain would poke holes in the blanket of gray sky. Pedestrians hurried up the sidewalks, eager to get where they were going before the rain came. Clay didn't mind the weather. He liked the time right before the rain fell, when the air felt charged, volatile. He liked being reminded that whatever plans men might make, nature follows its own set of rules.

Andrew Stedding stood hunched in the doorway of a Mediterranean restaurant, closed at this early hour. He had his long raincoat pulled tight around him, the collar up and stiff, as if he were preparing to walk into a hurricane.

Clay smiled, seeing him there. Stedding never changed. They'd been together for three years, but it seemed much longer. They were opposites who somehow blended together to make a new whole, black and white mixing into a perfect shade of gray. Clay's handler was in his early fifties but knew how to play the curmudgeon as if he were near his deathbed. His face wore a permanent scowl. Clay would have sworn

Stedding took pleasure from his sour disposition, but he'd never say it to the man's face.

"Morning, Steddy...."

"Don't call me that. You know how I hate that."

"But it's apt. You're as steady as a Swiss watch."

"I do my job. My job tells me to be here to meet you, so I'm here. On time, in the rain."

"It's not raining yet."

"Give it five minutes."

"Well, I'll bring the sunshine out. I have your name."

The elevation in Stedding's mood was marked only by a slight rise of the eyebrows. His frown never lifted.

"Gregory Molina."

Stedding nodded, mulling this over. "Well, we knew it was either him or the woman, Vargas."

The name Beto had coughed up was a compromised Spanish embassy staff member in Moscow, a national who had been sharing private correspondence with certain agents of the Kremlin. Some of the information was extremely sensitive, the price of a narrowed, postmillennial world. The US shared intelligence with select allies, such as Spain, and if that information leaked, it was still up to the CIA to plug the dam.

Gregory Molina would have to die, and Austin Clay would be the man to put his thumb in the dyke. The Spanish government would never know the Americans were responsible, and the Americans would only know that their problem had evaporated, ending in the accidental death of a midlevel Spanish embassy staffer.

There has always been a need in the spy game for operations outside the boundaries of legality, for covert missions so black no one in the American government, and almost no one in Intelligence itself, knows of their existence. The left hand can't know what the right hand is doing. Most often in the last three years, Austin Clay had been the right hand.

"That's it, then," Clay said, popping his hands together. "I'll take care of it."

"No."

"No?" This was new. They'd been focused on this assignment for the better part of four months, and in Clay's experience, Stedding never pulled him off a mission until it reached its inevitable conclusion.

"We have a higher priority."

"Oh?"

"Blake Nelson."

The name rang a bell somewhere in the back of Clay's brain.

"I remember him. He started at Langley a month after me. . . ."

"Yes."

"Russian op, from what I remember."

"The last three years in the field. He's been doing some very sensitive work near the Caspian Sea."

"Oil?"

Stedding nodded. "And missiles."

"Between Iran and Russia."

"We think so, but we're not sure."

"Nelson flipped?"

"We'd like to ask him that, but he's five days late on his last contact."

"Missing, then?"

Stedding's frown threatened to pull down his entire face. "That's right. I got a personal call from the DCI. He wants Nelson back."

Clay arched his eyebrows, impressed. "The Director. Someone must've finally noticed the work we've been doing."

"There's a difference between noticing and acknowledging. They always notice; they never acknowledge."

"What if Nelson's dead?"

"The Director wants him back. He didn't say back alive."

"Where can I get the case file?"

"I've got a man working it up right now. Dead drop in Heathrow in two hours. Burn it all when you land in St. Petersburg."

The rain started to fall, pounding down all at once as if someone had turned on a faucet.

"Good seeing you, Steddy. I'll report in as soon as I have something to report."

Stedding just grimaced, pulled his collar up tight, and headed off into the rain. Clay watched him trudge away for a moment, then left in the opposite direction.

Heathrow's enormous terminal was packed with travelers, a sea of bustling, milling, shopping, eating masses, killing time while waiting for gate information, ants scurrying inside an anthill.

Austin Clay sat at the end of a row of uncomfortable seats,

dressed like any other businessman. He held the *Herald* in his lap, but his eyes were fixed on a waste bin thirty feet away.

The news of the Director's involvement intrigued him. He thought back to what he remembered of the missing officer, Blake Nelson. They'd worked together only briefly, when Clay had completed training. They both spoke Russian fluently, and that had put them around the same conference table more than once. Clay was a bit surprised that Nelson had become a field officer...he remembered a lanky, bookish type, a guy destined for years staring at a monitor in a small office as satellite data splashed across his screen. Maybe that was precisely why he'd been placed in the field; the man could certainly pass for a Russian intellectual.

In Clay's experience, though, an effective field officer needed to be both intelligent and physical. It's one thing to move pieces around a chessboard, quite another to have a gun pushed against your temple or a knife pressed to your throat and still manage to move the pieces. And now Nelson had gone missing. Maybe he should have stayed behind a desk after all.

At exactly noon, an unassuming, portly man in an ill-fitting suit approached the bin with a briefcase in one hand and a half-eaten bagel in the other. The bagel went in the can, the briefcase went beside it, and the man left.

Clay stood and collected the case in seconds, then moved toward his gate without breaking stride.

At thirty-three thousand feet, the plane leveled off and turned eastward. Clay had a pod in first class and spun his chair around so it turned inward, toward the small built-in desk. He opened the briefcase and thumbed through its contents, removing the thick Agency folder before settling in to read. Five hours in the air would give him plenty of time to catch up on Blake Nelson's recent history.

Nelson had been stationed in Moscow for the last six years, an embassy staffer who'd transitioned into a consulting gig with the Russian oil company, Rukos. This wasn't an especially clever cover for an American spy, and Clay wondered if Nelson had been compromised and tolerated for a while, or if his life in espionage had been discovered only recently.

Nelson's main contact was a handler named Nikolai Adromatov. Adromatov, a native Russian, had spent thirty years with the Agency, after being successfully doubled while the Iron Curtain remained on the shower rail. He had a life in Moscow, a family, a mistress, and a fine apartment near the Kremlin. He was former KGB and had risen to a midlevel staff position within the current government. His ability to survive the wall's coming down, regime changes, and infighting while maintaining his true loyalty to the United States made him invaluable.

Clay had met Adromatov twice before, once during a bit of nasty business involving a Georgian mole named Uznadzi, and a second time at Langley, right before Clay was assigned to his current black ops position. Clay had liked Adromatov instantly; the man was as large as a bear, with a wild, curly black beard and ruddy cheeks. His mind was like a computer, able to process reams of minutia and spit out a wise, sound plan.

According to Adromatov's report, which Clay was reading over as the plane chugged along, Nelson had been carefully building a case that Russia and Iran were exchanging more than oil, that hard-liners and throwbacks within the Russian government were engaged in providing weapons to Iran that could proliferate throughout the Middle East. It wasn't groundbreaking intelligence; the US had routinely received similar reports from other officers since the mid-nineties.

Clay tried to read between the lines, a skill honed over his fifteen-year intelligence career. More often than not, the real gems were to be found in what was left *out* of intelligence reports. But there was nothing in this dossier on Nelson that leapt out at him as extraordinary. Nothing to point to why Nelson had gone missing. Nothing to point to why the Director would personally involve himself.

If Nelson had been compromised and arrested, the Russian government would have made a big political show of it, the way they had with Cecil Roots in 2001. They would have wanted to embarrass Washington. Catching a low-level spook gathering moderately sensitive information has more utility as a political showpiece than anything else.

Between the lines. That was where the truth lay. So what had Nelson stumbled upon that was more than moderately sensitive, perhaps even outside the range of his mission? And why would the Director send in Clay? Why would the left hand not want to know what the right hand had to do to get Nelson back?

He read every page in the dossier twice more before touch-down.

Clay rode the bus from Pulkovo Airport to the city center. As always, it was numbingly cold in St. Petersburg, and there was a pervasive smell Clay always thought of as distinctly Russian. It was a mixture of charcoal and tobacco and wool, and it was as ubiquitous as the wind. The more time you spent in the country, the more your awareness of it dulled, but when you returned after an absence, it greeted you like an addled relative, at once welcoming and repellent. Clay breathed it in and headed past St. Isaac's Cathedral toward the river.

A gold-and-black Volga pulled up to where he stood. Clay looked into the driver's window, smiled, and climbed into the passenger's seat. Adromatov steered the car back into traffic, casting sidelong glances in Clay's direction. His expression was pleasant, though hard to gauge beneath the beard.

"Welcome back to Leningrad."

Clay smiled. "You're gonna get arrested for calling it that."

"Pssh. Half this city was happier before the wall came down. They worked without thinking. They were just as poor, but vodka was cheaper and their apartments were paid for."

With that, he tipped a flask to his lips and smiled broadly.

"They weren't free to—"

"To the working class, freedom is overrated."

"You sound like a revolutionary."

"The days of mass revolt died with the advent of the subsonic jet engine. Wildfires are now easily contained."

"Tell that to the Republic of Georgia."

Adromatov chortled. "I don't have to. Vladimir Putin did a long time ago."

He took another tug and waved the flask in the air as if he were erasing a blackboard. The car lurched toward the curb, then realigned.

"Enough. Discussing the shortcomings of the Russian people makes my mind atrophy. Let's get to more pressing matters."

"Blake Nelson."

"Yes. You should have received my report."

"What's not in the report?"

Adromatov's large face broadened as he smiled. "I remembered you, Austin Clay, but now I *remember* you. What's not in the report? That's it, then, isn't it?"

"That's it."

Adromatov paused for a moment, his eyes intent on the city street. His massive chest rose and fell with his breathing. "A woman. A woman is not in the report."

Clay started to open his mouth, but Adromatov waved him down with the flask. "I already know your two questions. Who is she, and why did I keep her out of the official file?"

It was Clay's turn to smile.

"The truth is, I don't know if she exists. I certainly would not commit ink to what is no more than a rumor."

"Then tell me the rumor and leave the ink in the pen."

The Russian laughed, and the baritone sound reminded

Clay of a department store Santa. "Yes. The rumor, then. We have a bit of a drive before we reach our destination, and as you know, Russians don't talk conversationally, they give speeches. So I will give you the speech, or—how do you say it? Tell you the story? Yes, I will tell you the story of this girl.

"Do you know the name Alexi Benidrov?"

Clay searched his memory but came up blank and shrugged.

"Why would you know it? Alexi Benidrov is a midlevel bureaucrat serving as a minister under Igor Zechin."

"That name I know."

"Yes. Deputy Prime Minister of Defense. Well, Benidrov was a man who used other men's backs as though they were rungs in a ladder, yes? He destroyed careers and trampled anyone who stood in his way as he rose inside the Defense Ministry. He was ruthless and cunning, and as you might expect, became a favorite of President Sobyanin."

"A man carved in his own image."

"Precisely."

"And yet you keep referring to Benidrov in the past tense."

Adromatov laughed again, and this time, his whole body shook. *Like a bowl full of jelly,* Clay thought.

"Yes, past tense. Let a man tell his story the proper way, with the gruesome details spared for the grand finale, yes? Americans just love to get everything right out front and forgo the surprise."

Clay nodded and the Russian continued, absently watching the road. Somehow, the Volga avoided careening into any number of trucks and sedans.

"So Benidrov finds his way into the Defense Ministry, and his eye is on Zechin's post. He is careful in everything while inside the Kremlin—careful to flatter whoever needs flattering, careful to crush whoever needs crushing—all without splattering any blood on his hands. As he becomes more and more relevant in the ministry, he is entrusted with more and more, let's say, sensitive state materials, yes? Weapons deals, oil-for-cash deals, nuclear armament information, proliferation, too? Yes? And as I say, he's careful, because the cost of being unstable is..." Adromatov drew his finger across his throat, crossed his eyes, and stuck out his tongue. Then he pointed his finger in the air. "Except Alexi Benidrov is not as careful as I have described.

"Yes, careful at work, in public. But at home? You see, Benidrov had a baby girl and a baby boy—twins, yes? His wife was weak from the pregnancy and her health failed and became... what is this word? Chronic? Yes? Because of this, Benidrov started to employ nurse care...."

"Nannies."

"What is this?"

"A nanny. A full-time babysitter."

"Yes, precisely. A nanny. And Benidrov liked to hire Hungarian women. They speak no Russian, they can't know his business, they stay out of his way, they keep to themselves in uneducated oblivion. He can work late; his wife is infirm, after all, but the twins are looked after, and this continues for some time. The agency sends over various Hungarian women, and I don't have to tell you that these ladies are built like blocks of cement, all broad shoulders and thick faces and arms like bags of flour. Benidrov barely notices them, this succession of Hungarian cattle—just enough to mutter a curt hello and a kiss-kiss to the little darlings and he's on his way.

"In the meantime, the pressure is building for him at work as he climbs closer to the top echelon of the Kremlin, and like a kettle of tea, he needs to release steam or he'll explode.

"Enter Marika Csontos, a breathtaking eighteen-year-old beauty with—according to accounts—a perfect pair of pouty lips and a face that radiated innocence. I mean, after the parade of bovine babysitters marching through that house, any girl with youth and a figure would have allure, yes? So maybe she was a great beauty, maybe she wasn't, but the story is better for it. Anyway, Benidrov takes notice, this we know.

"And here he is, a top deputy minister with no one to whom he can pour out his secrets as that pressure builds, no one who can listen and understand and nod encouragement and withhold judgment…except…here's the cream in the pie…except this Hungarian girl who speaks no Russian and can't understand a word he says. This is like an angel from heaven, a gift from the Almighty…someone up there recognized his unique problem and said, 'Here's the solution, my child.' Benidrov tells her everything. I mean everything. Who, what, where, when…all the state secrets, everything he's working on, everything. It's as if he's using her as his living journal."

Adromatov grinned, as satisfied with his story as if he'd just devoured a hearty meal. "Can you see where this is going?"

"Marika could speak Russian."

"Yes! Precisely! Russian and Hungarian. She lied to the

hiring agency because she needed the work. So she pretended not to understand a word he said, all the while hearing and retaining it all."

Outside, the city turned industrial as they crossed the Tuchkov Bridge and moved inland.

"So what happened?"

"Pah. I wish I had an ending. Maybe it has yet to be told. But here are the only facts I know. A deputy minister named Benidrov was found dead in his office in the Kremlin, apparently a suicide, but as you know, 'apparently' is relative in the Russian government. A young Hungarian girl named Marika Csontos did work as his nanny for a month, until she vanished two weeks prior to Benidrov's last day on earth."

"Vanished?"

"Like a specter in the mists of a moor." Adromatov waggled his finger and mimicked the hollow howl of a ghost, then burst into his now-familiar chortle. "No one knows where she went or why or how. But the story I've told you is the story that arose from the ashes of Deputy Minister Benidrov's death, and that is why I'm relating it to you. And yet as to how much of the story is fact and how much is fancy, I can scarcely offer an opinion. Russians love their folktales, and this has the ring of the Brothers Grimm all over it. It even has a moral: Don't spill state secrets to anyone or it will be your neck in a rope!"

Clay nodded. "Nelson believed it."

"You are astute, Austin Clay. Very astute. I bet it would have been difficult to be your parents on Christmas morning. You had already figured out all the presents under the tree just by the size of the box."

Clay's mouth disappeared into a thin line. "I wouldn't know."

Adromatov swallowed and frowned for just a moment, sure he had made a gaffe, though unsure how it had happened when things had been going so well. Like a ship correcting its course, he deftly pulled the conversation back on track. "Yes, Nelson confided in me that he believed the story and he wanted to pursue finding this girl, this Marika Csontos. I counseled him to forget it, that it was a fool's task and he had more important concerns on which to focus his attention. I believe he ignored my advice and spent the last several months doing his best to find the missing Marika. If he located her, I don't know it. He disappeared from a train traveling between Perm and Omsk."

"There's something between Perm and Omsk?"

"Ha. Miles and miles of forest and beet fields."

"Don't forget cabbage."

"How could I?" Adromatov was delighted that his gaffe didn't seem to be casting any lingering shadows over his time with the agent. He told himself not to bring up anything involving Clay's childhood, however innocently or indirectly.

"The train he was on exploded and derailed."

"I read about that in your report. A freight train."

Adromatov shrugged. "Not uncommon for a spy to travel this way."

Their car pulled up to a blocky, windowless building that looked like so many other Iron Curtain–era edifices in Russia: sexless and stale. Adromatov turned the key and silenced the Volga's whine.

"Nelson's office."

"The Russians already pick it over?"

"The one he uses as a front in downtown St. Petersburg, yes. But they don't know about this one."

Clay liked Adromatov. He wore the spook life as comfortably as broken-in shoes and managed to do it without its seeming like an illusion, a façade. The Russian actually enjoyed it, and Clay wondered if maybe they shared the same secret, the same antidote to fear. Clay was a good spy because he never rattled. And he never rattled because he simply didn't care whether he lived or died.

CHAPTER TWO

HE AWOKE not in a jail cell, nor a bunker, nor a hospital bed, but convalescing in a posh hotel suite. He had been drugged; his cotton mouth and throbbing headache made that clear. He turned his head and saw onion domes out the window, an elevated view of the Kremlin. A glass of water awaited his lips on a stand next to the bed. He knew he shouldn't drink it...had no idea what was in it...but his thirst overwhelmed him. He emptied the glass in two gulps.

His left leg had been operated upon and was in a cast from his hip to his ankle. Pain emanated from a spot behind his thigh every time his muscles contracted or expanded, which meant always.

He tried to remember what had happened after he'd spilled out of the burning train car—running, trees, gunshots, falling—but the images were fuzzy, the way the world had warped when he tried on his father's glasses as a little boy. He knew the essentials, though: he'd been tricked, trapped, shot, and captured. What would come next? Torture? Then why was he in this hotel room?

He thought about trying to get out of bed. Could he? Pain shot through his leg as he tensed just to make the effort to roll it over to the edge of the bed. Nausea made the room swim in front of his eyes, and words somehow spoke inside his brain...

Quit. Just quit and wait.

...but he swept that exhortation aside. The human brain was a wondrous thing, and somehow the concept of mettle, of indomitability, of valor, had arisen when people had tuned out the brain's warnings. He could make his legs do this.

Sweat popped out on his forehead, and it evaporated just as quickly, like water sprayed on a hot pan. He suppressed a scream as his legs finally did as they were told and swung out and over the edge of the bed. He was in a seated position, and he rested a moment with one hand on the wooden headboard.

Nelson took a few quick breaths, building up oxygen in his lungs for the effort, and then pushed up with his hand. He put all of his weight on his right leg, using the casted left only for balance. A new wave of vertigo hit him, but he held the position until it passed. Could he get to the bathroom? The window?

He did neither and was standing there stupidly when he heard clapping behind him.

A fat-faced man with a shaggy white beard spoke in Russian. "Awake and upright, I see. Good, good."

Nelson started to talk, then just fell backward onto the bed.

The Russian clucked his tongue. "Too much too soon, Mr. Nelson. There's no need to overexert yourself. Where could you possibly go?"

Nelson answered in English. "I won't belittle you by saying there's been a misunderstanding."

In his peripheral vision, he could vaguely see the Russian smile.

"I assume negotiations have begun."

"To the contrary," the man said in husky English. "Why don't we just talk for a bit first?"

The smile widened and the man approached the bed, staring down at Nelson the way a father gazes down on a baby in a crib—but that wasn't right. The stare was more like the look of an exterminator who finally catches a rat in his trap.

"I need to use the—" But Nelson didn't get the words out before the smiling man pushed down with the palms of both hands on his cast.

He might have screamed, but the blackness rose quickly to cover him.

Michael Adams parked his Range Rover on the street and rose from the driver's seat. He looked over the field and saw the team with the lime-green uniforms, the fierce name MERMAIDS printed on the front. They were just getting into their starting positions; the referee hadn't yet blown his whistle, and he could see both of his daughters, Kate and Grace, set in their positions on either side of the ball at the center line. They were a year and a half apart, eight and seven, but Michael had requested they play on the same team to avoid doubling the drives to soccer fields every Saturday.

He nodded at a couple he recognized but whose names he couldn't remember, climbed the stands, and sat down next to his wife. She leaned in for a kiss and took his hand just as the whistle sounded and the game began.

"Let's go, Kate and Grace!" he bellowed at the top of his lungs, and both girls looked up and beamed.

"Sorry I'm late."

"I'm just glad you made it at all. This is a nice surprise." He'd first met his wife, Laura, in college when they were both nineteen and she drew eyes in any crowd. Twenty-six years later, she still did.

"They got you working this weekend, Michael?" The question came from a guy who lived five houses over from theirs on Las Palmas in Hancock Park. What was his name? Chris? Craig?

Laura turned and answered for him, smiling. "They have him working *every* weekend."

"I'm not complaining," Michael added. "It's good to be busy." He didn't feel that way at all, but it seemed necessary to say.

On the field, the Mermaids were successfully attacking but couldn't seem to put the ball in the net. Michael stopped for a moment and thought, *When did they get good?* It seemed like yesterday when they would cluster in circles around the ball until it would suddenly shoot out from the pack like an escaping animal. Now they were passing, moving, setting up plays. And his daughters seemed to be leading the charge.

Laura leaned her head on his shoulder. "The girls have next Thursday and Friday off."

"Why?"

"Teacher work days or something like that."

"I swear they have more days out of school than they do in."

His daughters went to a pricy private school near Beverly Hills. He wouldn't have minded their going to the public school down the street, but the subject was nonnegotiable. He might run some things at his office, but Laura ran the house. He had learned to say "Yes, dear" a long time ago, and if he had to be honest, he was happy to do so.

"I thought maybe we could go somewhere...take them somewhere."

"What'd you have in mind?"

"Santa Barbara. Or Ojai. Or the other way...San Diego. Just get out of LA and get them out of the house."

"Book it, Danno."

"Really?"

"Why not?"

"I'll get online when we get home and find us a place."

"Ojai sounds good," he said, so she'd have that in mind. He was a member of Wilshire Country Club and liked to play golf; the Ojai Valley Inn had a great course. Maybe he could get out for a round while the girls lay by the pool or rode horses.

Kate deftly switched from her right foot to her left and fired an off-balance shot at the goal, just missing the crossbar. Michael started to rise from his seat but sat back down, oohing when she missed. It was Laura's turn to shout, "Great shot, Kate!" She clapped a few times, as happy as he'd ever seen her.

"Do you think..." she started to say, but his phone buzzed in his pocket and he didn't hear the end of her question.

He quickly fished the phone out, saw the number, held up a finger to his wife, and moved down the bleachers so he could stand by himself.

Pressing the Answer button, he said a curt "Hello."

"Is this line secure?" asked the caller, Warren Sumner, his assistant.

"No. I'll have to get to my briefcase in the car and call you back."

"Use the subcomp number."

"Got it." Then, "Who's calling, Warren?"

"Director Manning."

"I'll call back in less than a minute."

Adams hung up, pointed to his phone, and mouthed, "I have to take this," to his wife.

She nodded and smiled, but he could see concern on her face. He ignored it, walking briskly to his SUV. On the field, the ball finally found the back of the net, but he missed which girl had done the scoring.

CHAPTER THREE

THE INSIDE of Nelson's office was as sterile as the building outside. It contained a desk, a bank of file cabinets, and a fake banana tree in a planter in the corner, without which the room would have had no color at all. If Nelson owned a laptop, he'd moved it or taken it with him.

Clay pivoted around the room with the practiced eye of a smuggler, running his hands over the plaster walls, rapping with his fists for the telltale signs of hollow pockets, while Adromatov lit a cigarette and watched him through half-mast eyes.

"You're looking perhaps for a magician's false door, yes?"

Clay continued his careful search, then spotted what he was looking for, a slight change in paint color where two walls came together, almost covered (but not quite) by a bookshelf, barely noticeable.

"Well, I can tell you I've spent some time here and I've never—"

Adromatov's sentence was interrupted by the click and slide of a magnetic spring release. A section of the wall pushed in to reveal a tiny opening. The Russian pursed his lips, and a hint of a frown creased his face.

"How did you…?"

"You hide in plain sight, Adromatov. Men like Nelson and me, we hide by hiding." Clay took out a small penlight and shined it into the opening. It looked like close quarters, but it was hard to see how far back the room recessed into the wall.

He gestured for Adromatov to enter with him, but the Russian held up his palms and shook his head. "I'll go into a tomb when I'm dead, Austin Clay. Not before." In fairness, he did look too fat to fit through the opening.

"Suit yourself." Clay ducked and squeezed himself into the space. The entrance ran parallel to the wall, and if he eased himself down the strut line to the right, he could see the space widening. He reached a compartment about the size of a walk-in closet and shined the penlight over shelves of binders—some with dates, some with Russian names written in the Cyrillic alphabet, some with nonsense words that must've meant something to Nelson. Clay tucked the penlight in his mouth and pulled out the binder in front of him marked JUNE. Inside was a collage of printed emails, Internet site pages, maps, journal entries—all collected schizophrenically, with no piece of information appearing to be more important than any other. Still, the binder was thick, and there was a distinct possibility of gold among the silt. Quickly, he ran his fingers over the other binders, the light bouncing off their spines, and he scanned them so hastily that he almost missed the one titled MARIKA. Almost.

He was halfway through the first page in the file when he heard a bump through the wall, then the distinctive sound a rubber-soled shoe makes as it skids across cement. He tensed, cocked his ear, but couldn't make out anything else. An inexperienced man would have called out, "Adromatov?," giving himself away, but Clay knew better. Binder in one hand and penlight in the other, he made his way back to the opening behind the bookshelf, then peeked out to see Adromatov down on the floor, his face painted in blood, a tall, clean-shaven Russian in a dark suit standing with one heel on Adromatov's flabby neck. Two more Russians flanked him with pistols out but held near their sides, eyes fixed on the pummeled man on the floor. They looked younger, new FSB men, both sporting dark mustaches. Adromatov must've told these agents he was alone when they showed up unannounced. It was inevitable they'd find the place, but why did it have to be right fucking now?

The three agents of the Kremlin swung their heads around at the same time, like a herd of deer that hear a hunter cock his rifle in the forest. At least, that was the way Clay liked to think of them.

He moved quickly; this was always one of Clay's greatest weapons. Enemies were so surprised by his adroitness, by the way his body moved, that even a moment's hesitation gave him all the advantage he needed.

He launched himself like a missile at the nearest guy, the one who was too busy gawking to get his gun up. The pen-light connected with the fleshy part of the agent's neck, driven there by Clay's arcing fist. The man choked and gurgled before he knew what had happened, his neck lit up like an airport runway. Before he could fall, Clay's right hand clasped around his wrist and wrenched his weapon away.

The second Russian—the other mustachioed one—had the time to respond, get his gun up, get a shot off, but he was so distracted by his partner's strange death, not to mention the sheer speed with which this battle had gone from offense to defense, that his last thought was *What happened?* before Clay shot him from two feet away.

The third man, the big one, the one with his heel on Adromatov's neck, must have foreseen the inevitable. Even in the blur of ferocious activity, he made the decision that if he was going to die, he would take one traitor with him. He raised his boot and drove his heel into Adromatov's neck with the entire weight of his body, snapping the poor man's spine and ending his thirty-year career as a double agent. The lone Russian standing then turned toward Clay and let out an animalistic cry, as centuries of battlefield warriors had done before him—right before Clay raised the PYa and shut his mouth.

The Volga eased out into the light St. Petersburg traffic. He had worked quickly. Russians are meticulous by nature, especially government officials. They love their stamps on documents—stamps for CLASSIFIED, stamps for APPROVED, stamps for DENIED, stamps for CHECKING IN, for CHECKING OUT. He was sure these three FSB officers would have kept detailed records of where they were going and what their mission entailed, and soon they would be stamped MISSING. Clay dragged the bodies, all four of them, into the hidden room and then performed a cursory sweep of the place to clean up the blood and brain and body fluids. It wasn't a thorough sanitizing, but it might buy him an extra day or two as the first wave of investigators inspected the empty location. At least, until the bodies started to smell.

Still, Clay was in the positive column of the ledger. That was how he tended to think of every mission...a ledger book with markings in the plus column and others in the minus column. Losing Adromatov was a negative, yes, but he had gained Nelson's binder on Marika Csontos, and that sent the bottom line, for now, back into the black. As long as he stayed in the black, he had a chance. The black ink was life, was success—the red ink, well, that meant blood.

The binder sat in the passenger seat, virginal. He'd only skimmed its contents while in the secret chamber—just enough to know that somewhere inside it was the answer to finding Marika Csontos. Clay had snapped the binder shut and headed back out, and it was a good thing he hadn't sat down to read more of it or maybe he'd have been the one surprised in that office.

One thing troubled him about the encounter, and the more he thought about it, the more certain he was his assumptions were correct. Nelson was alive, in custody, and giving up information. Clay didn't begrudge his counterpart this; from what he remembered about the guy, it wasn't a matter of *if* he would crack but *when,* and it was impressive that he'd held out long enough to give Clay first look at his info dump, even if it was only moments ahead of the Russians. They might have fucked up a lot of things in their country, but the one thing Russians had always done well—to the point of perfection—was extract information out of hostiles.

It was a good sign that the FSB goons had shown up there, because it meant Nelson hadn't spilled a bigger secret—where the girl was hiding. Otherwise, the Russians would've skipped to the end of the story and gone straight for her. Nelson would assuredly squawk about that soon enough, Clay supposed. He hoped he could stay a step ahead.

The first thing he needed was a place to hole up. Whatever plans Adromatov had made for him were null now. Clay had no way of knowing what tracks Adromatov had left behind, so best to shift off-grid for a while. He'd have to call Stedding soon and download what he'd learned so far, but not until he'd had a chance to sift through the binder and maybe, just maybe, discover what information would lead him to the nanny.

Clay took a room in the Oktiabrskaya Hotel—a big, unattractive economy job on the Ligovsky Prospekt that catered to backpackers and tourists who wanted to pop for a place one notch above a hostel. The hotel room was bigger than the room he grew up in—not too many places were quite that cramped. That fucking boat. Every now and then, Clay would see or smell something—a seashell, a whiff of sandalwood—and he would be back in that tiny cabin, bobbing on the fucking ocean like a bottle holding the message: *Get me the hell out of here*. The size and shape of this hotel room reminded him of that place, that coffin, and the ocean air outside didn't help. Fuck. Bury it.

He opened the binder to close off that part of his mind. Nelson had been thorough in his notes; little wonder he'd built a safe room to house his papers. Upon closer inspection, the binder read like a journal, with Nelson using abbreviations and shorthand for contacts and calls and locations but not exerting too much effort to obfuscate his meaning through code. Clay grinned—it was amazing how often trained officers, both ours and theirs, junked their training after a few years and grew comfortable, sloppy. An extended period of leading a double life plays tricks on the brain. You fool people for so long, you start fooling yourself: that you're infallible, invincible. And then a train derails between Perm and Omsk and the glass house you've built shatters to the ground. Clay wondered if he had built one of his own, if he was as guilty as Nelson of buying into his own mythology. He knew the Agency referred to him as the Right Hand—ostensibly because they wanted plausible deniability of his methods. The left hand doesn't know what the right hand is doing. But he'd heard whispers of a different interpretation:

that he was the Right Hand of Zeus, the one that hurled thunderbolts and cracked worlds. Let 'em think what they wanted. Just keep your eyes open and your emotions in check and let the storytellers write the stories. His reputation could be used to his advantage, but he wouldn't buy into the myths as anything more than fiction.

What would the storytellers within the Agency write about this mission? *A shift*. That would be the noted thing here: a shift in the objective. His mission was clear—to bring back Nelson. So why had he already changed the objective from finding Nelson to locating the girl? He told himself she was the key to finding Nelson, but every way he turned it over in his mind, it was the other way around: Nelson was the key to finding her. She was what was not in the report—and two American officers were dead or captured because of her, a young Hungarian nanny who happened to speak Russian. No one, not even Clay's handler, Stedding, knew that the mission had changed, the objective was different. The Left Hand didn't know what the Right Hand was doing, and Austin Clay, at this moment, liked it that way.

Nelson had been set up. He had concluded that Marika was in one of two places—through a series of phone records, he had figured out that she had a twenty-five-year-old stepbrother who was attending school at Far Eastern Federal University in Vladivostok, where he was studying biotechnology. This option was interesting in its locale—certainly a train going to

Omsk might be heading on to Vladivostok, but the binder seemed to indicate that Nelson had shied away from the choice. If he'd spoken to the stepbrother, he didn't mention it. Something had turned his head to the second option: that perhaps Marika Csontos was being harbored by the man who ran the placement service, the company that helped get child-care workers into the homes of government officials.

That man was a middle-aged Armenian male with no children of his own, and he had parlayed his position as head of an orphanage under the Soviet regime to a shrewd business in postwall Russia. His service was located in a little town east of Moscow…along the train route to Omsk. Nelson had contacted him fourteen times on the phone in the last six months. The content of their conversations was not recorded, but Nelson had convinced the man—Viktor Zhedenko—to meet him face to face. An exchange was to be made. Based on some of Nelson's records in the binder, Clay surmised quickly that the trade was to be money for the girl. Nelson had set out on a train to meet Zhedenko and had never come back.

Stepnoy is a mining town in the pocket of Ural Russia not too far, relatively speaking, from the northeast border of Kazakhstan. Clay had never been there—and after this particular piece of business was finished, he hoped never to return. Whatever the mines threw up into the air cast a filter over the sky so the city had a consistent gray pall covering it, as though it were in perpetual mourning. The people were hard as rock, forged of hopelessness and medicated with vodka. It was a cruel life, living in Stepnoy.

Clay's beard had grown in thick and dark, obscuring his

features and camouflaging him among the town's denizens. They all looked the way he did: unkempt and unruly. He elicited no stares when he parked his truck and walked up a street named Chelyabinskaya in the middle of the industrialized section of the city.

Zhedenko's office was in a corner of what had formerly been a finance ministry outpost that serviced the mines during the Soviet era. Most of the office remained unrented and unoccupied, another dying monument to Communism—except for the five hundred or so square meters Zhedenko utilized. A desk, a middle-aged secretary who looked as though she hadn't moved since 1975, a phone, and a computer were all Zhedenko needed to keep his business prosperous.

Clay gleaned all this from Nelson's file combined with two days of covert observation. It wasn't difficult to track his subject. The man moved in that sleepy, almost inanimate way that seemed indigenous to Stepnoyans, as though the same perpetual fog that covered the area covered their heads as well.

Clay decided to confront the man in his office, in front of his secretary. There are many ways to gain the advantage in an argument, and most have the common denominator of making your opponent uncomfortable. If you can do this in his territory, where he's most at ease, all the better.

Clay shuffled into the room, his eyes stern, his expression annoyed. His Russian had always been flawless, and his meticulous pronunciation had the desired effect in rural areas; it made him sound officious.

"You are Zhedenko?"

The middle-aged man eyed him as though a wolf had just entered the room and he was a rabbit with nowhere to hide.

"I am Zhedenko, yes."

"Vladimir Zhedenko?"

"Yes, yes, Vladimir Zhedenko."

The secretary looked up from her desk, shock on her face. Clay guessed she wasn't used to receiving too many walk-ins here at the office.

"I am Boris Antopov, with Central Ministry. Forgive me for the unannounced arrival."

The secretary stood and began to gather her things.

"Please stay, Marta."

She started at the sound of her name. It was like this all over Russia for men and women over forty. It was as though they expected the government to roar back into their lives at any minute. They were perpetually waiting for the other shoe to drop. Marta looked as though that day had just arrived. She sat quietly and stared with cow eyes.

Before Zhedenko could collect his wits, Clay continued, raising his voice and clipping his enunciation to sound even more obnoxious. "I understand you provide service for government?"

"Yes, Mr. Antopov. I—"

"And I understand you do so for ministries throughout Russia?"

"Yes, Mr. Antopov."

"This service is for exchange of care, yes?"

"I do not—"

"You facilitate child care service, yes?"

"I...yes..."

"You use girls for other service?"

"What? No! Now, I—"

"Where do the girls come from?"

"I—"

"Where do they come from, Mr. Zhedenko!"

Clay pounded the nearest table, causing Marta to jump as though a gun had gone off in the room. Zhedenko looked as though he might burst into tears.

"I don't understand the question, Mr. Antopov. I find the child care workers through referrals and recommendations, and sometimes they phone me directly."

"And you interview the girls yourself?"

"Yes, I—"

"Speak up!"

"Yes, Mr. Antopov."

"You do a thorough job of interviewing?"

"I try to be thorough, yes."

"You sleep with these girls?"

"No! I—"

"It doesn't matter. Let's talk about one girl. Marika Csontos."

The trapped expression on Zhedenko's face intensified. "As I explained to your colleague—"

"*Colleague?* What is this *colleague?*"

Zhedenko looked confused. "Mr. Uh...Mr....I forgot his name. Your colleague from Central Ministry—"

"Remember!" Clay demanded.

Zhedenko searched his memory while each tick of the wall

clock sounded like bullets from a firing squad. *Tick, tick, tick*... Suddenly, Zhedenko's finger punctured the air as he remembered. "Mr. Petrasky. That was it."

Clay would have to check to see if that name was real, but he had a sense it was fake and a strong idea who had used it.

"What did this Petrasky say?"

"He asked if I could facilitate a meeting between himself and Marika Csontos."

"What did you tell him?"

"I said I did not know where the girl was."

"You're lying!" Clay roared at him, the sound echoing through the room. Clay was practiced in adding a level of bass to his voice when he needed it. Zhedenko took a step back as though he'd been struck. The secretary, Marta, looked as if she were shrinking, trying to make herself invisible.

"I'm not," the Armenian offered weakly.

"Mr. Zhedenko, let me tell you a story. Would you like to hear it?"

Russians and their stories. Zhedenko nodded as though grateful he'd been granted a reprieve from talking. Clay slowly crossed the room toward the Armenian as he spoke.

"When I was a young man growing up in the North Caucasus, my father would return from his job as a truck driver, his breath stinking of tobacco. It was as though he had smoked the entire Bialowieza Forest on his way home. His clothes reeked of it, his beard, his hair. My mother would ask him if he had been drinking, too, if he had nipped vodka on his driving route, which as I'm sure you know is strictly forbidden for mountain drivers. 'No,' he would tell her. 'No, my darling. I only smoke to stay awake, but I would never jeopardize my detail by drinking vodka in the truck.' You see, even as a young man I knew he was lying. I could see it by the way he lowered his eyes, by the way his voice inflected higher as he protested. 'No, my darling.' I knew the excessive use of tobacco was to mask the distilled smell of homemade vodka. She believed him, but I knew."

He had only a few more feet until he was standing directly in front of Zhedenko, their noses only inches apart.

"My father wrapped his truck around a needleleaf tree that winter, drunk as a degenerate. His face penetrated the front windshield and a shard of glass punctured his neck until he bled to death. My mother couldn't afford to shelter my brothers and me, and we became children of the state. So don't tell me I don't know when someone is lying, Mr. Zhedenko! I have experience with liars! All my life, I have experience with liars!"

Clay let his voice really boom on the final word, and spittle flew from his mouth as he stressed the hard Russian consonants.

"I... I did tell him I did not know where the girl was...."

"What else?"

"I—"

"He contacted you fourteen times!"

"Yes. It is coming back to me now...."

"I'm pleased it is coming back to you," Clay deadpanned.

"Yes, I remember now. When he called back, I said I could arrange a meeting with him. That Marika Csontos was afraid but she would trust me. You see, I had heard about Marika and her troubles."

"You had heard?"

"Yes, that maybe she had...maybe there were relations between Marika and one of her...one of the officials who—"

"Relations?"

"Is that what this is about?"

"Yes, of course, curse you. Speak no more of it. You arranged a meeting?"

"I...attempted to."

"Attempted?"

"I truly do not know where Marika Csontos had gone."

Clay realized quickly where this was going. "But you pretended you did."

"Innocently. I thought I could find her easily enough by the time he arrived in Stepnoy."

"For a fee."

"Yes. We're new capitalists, right?"

Clay had heard this notion before. The new capitalism of Russia meant that whoever had the deepest pockets could acquire whatever he wanted, laws be damned. It was a corrupt notion of a pure idea.

The Armenian continued, "Except Mr. Petransky never arrived. I swear it's true. I thought perhaps that was the end of it and I would never hear any more of this business, but now I see I am mistaken."

Clay knew the answer to the next question, though he felt compelled to ask anyway. "Did you ever locate the girl?"

Zhedenko's eyes shone with the truth. "No, I swear it. She disappeared, and the few records she gave me appear to be, well, invented."

Clay lowered his eyes for the first time. If there was disappointment or relief in them, he didn't show it. "Thank you, Mr. Zhedenko. I have learned all I needed to learn. I will ask that you forget this affair quickly if you value your business."

The Armenian stammered, "Of—of course, of course. It is forgotten."

"You as well, Marta."

She jumped again at the sound of her name, then nodded vigorously.

Before Clay could leave, Zhedenko stopped him. "I met her, I want you to know. She is a very smart girl. And very pretty. I was surprised and disappointed she compromised herself in that way."

Clay kept his face expressionless and his eyes hard, spun on his heels, and left. Better to keep the man off-balance than to let him unload his heavy heart, thinking he'd made a connection with a concerned official.

Zhedenko had told the truth; Clay was sure of it. He still had not seen a picture of Marika Csontos, but the Armenian had described her as pretty and intelligent—and Clay couldn't help picturing the young Hungarian girl in his mind's eye—thin; long, dark hair; curls; glasses. He wondered if he'd be disappointed when he actually saw her in the flesh. That was the plan—to find her alive, not after…

The air smelled like sulfur, that acrid nostril-singeing smell unique to mining towns. Somewhere, an impact drill was spiraling into rock, and the piercing whine of steel on stone penetrated the air. Clay was so distracted—thinking of the girl, her hair, her glasses; smart, Zhedenko had said—as he walked toward his truck that he barely registered the two men shuffling toward him.

They should've struck while he was preoccupied with his thoughts, while he was adding the details to the girl's face—thin eyebrows, a slightly upturned nose—but they made the mistake of speaking first, and in doing so, snapped Clay back to the present.

"You have a smoke?" the tall one asked. This is a tactic akin to starting a chess match with an e4–e5 opening. It has been done for so long that it is only effective against amateurs. The idea behind asking for a smoke is simple: to get the opponent reaching into his pocket for a pack of cigs or a lighter, exposing his face with his hands lowered, and then *bam, bam,* one-two, it's over.

Clay looked up with a smile and took in the significant details of the two men in less than five seconds. The taller one was slouched on his right side, which meant he favored it. His hands were out and his fingers were flexed, though not balled. He'd be throwing the first punch. The shorter man had a few scars on his face—the bridge of his nose, his left cheek—and so had been in some nasty scrapes. His left hand was in his jacket pocket, but only pushed in up to the wrist, rather than stuffed inside the way you would if you were resting your hands. The point at the end of the pocket indicated he was concealing a knife instead of a gun. He was the dangerous one.

Clay coughed—a big phlegmy bark that startled the men and had them involuntarily reeling backward, a natural reaction. Many casual observers think the shouts that martial arts masters scream before they throw a punch or kick is window dressing, a show, a Bruce Lee Hollywood affectation. In reality, voice is a weapon, too, designed to throw your enemy off-balance, to have him on his heels when he should be leaning forward. Sun Tzu–type shit. Clay's cough achieved the same effect as a warrior's *"Ki-ay"*...it was so surprising and disgusting that the moment the tall one stepped backward, Clay swung a haymaker that came almost from the ground and caught the man flush in his temple. He spilled backward but didn't fall.

The shorter one had the knife out of his pocket in an inspired pull, and as Clay clamped one of his massive hands around the wrist holding the knife, the scrapper head-butted him backward. He came in for a second butt, emboldened by the success of the first, but that was a mistake. Clay slipped it and used the momentum to push the guy forward, off-balance, taking the knife from him before he fell. *These guys made another mistake,* Clay thought as he felt the weight of the tempered steel. They'd come here to capture him instead of kill him, and the guy who is willing to take a fight to its most savage conclusion always holds the advantage.

The tall man stepped forward to throw a wild punch, and Clay ducked it and buried the knife up to the handle in the guy's throat. The man fell backward, freeing the blade but unleashing a dam-break of blood, and his comrade, starting to rise from the ground, never had a chance. He died when the knife drove straight through his chest and caught the fleshy tissue of his heart. His eyes reminded Clay of a small spot of light in a Coleman lantern as you turn off the propane...the little bit of residual orange light tries to hold on, hold on, hold on before it finally succumbs to darkness.

Clay gathered himself and checked his periphery. The street was silent, empty. He rifled through the men's pockets but found nothing—no identification, no papers, no badges. They had sent two agents, presumably FSB, to pick him up, and those two men would soon be missed. It would do Clay no good to try to stash them or bury them or burn their corpses. The men would not report when they were supposed to report, and the hunt would begin again. If they'd tracked him from St. Petersburg to Stepnoy, they must've been on him from the start. Maybe that fat conversationalist Adromatov was playing both sides or wasn't quite as stealthy as he let on. FSB must've been watching Adromatov even before he picked Clay up at the airport, and he'd led them right to him like a baying hound dog. Clay knew one thing: he needed to get to a secure phone.

He stopped at the first dacha that had a satellite dish affixed to the roof—probably the country home of one of the mining officials, or at least an upper-level employee. Even before the fall of Communism, many Russian officials were granted these country retreats, temporary respites from the bustle of the Kremlin. This one would do.

A quick survey of the area made him confident no one was home. The place probably had a caretaker this time of year, but it was still too chilly to live here full-time. If the caretaker had visited recently, it was hard to tell. There wasn't much care to the taking.

Clay picked the back lock absently, the work beneath his skills. Inside, the dacha was dusty and empty and looked as though the air hadn't been disturbed in months. It took him only a moment to find what he was looking for.

In the popular imagination, spooks carry suitcases filled with sophisticated technology and can encrypt a phone call while sending pursuers and would-be eavesdroppers on wild-goose chases as to the source of the call. *He's calling from Geneva—no, Prague! No, London, confound him!* In reality, the best way to make a secure call is to break into a random house and place it from a stranger's phone. Trying to track a call from an arbitrarily chosen phone is akin to counting the fish in the Atlantic. There might technically be a way to do it, but the sheer number of possibilities makes it impossibly impractical.

"Finnegan's Irish Pub?" came a pleasant female voice with a hint of an Irish lilt.

"Stedding—four, two, seven, four, two, one, one," Clay answered.

He waited for the inevitable clicks and pulses that turned the line secure on the other end. Thirty seconds later, Stedding's gruff voice filled his ear.

"I was wondering if you might remember to check in this time."

"How you doing, Steddy?"

Clay wasn't sure what Stedding said in response to that, but it sounded like *"Psssh."* Clay could feel the frown seeping through the line. "Get on with it, then."

"Oh, did I catch you at a bad time? I do apologize, boss."

"I'm not your boss, and it's invariably a bad time to catch me. So do me a favor and give me your report."

"Right, boss, right. Here's what I know and here's what I need. Adromatov is dead. The three guys who killed him are dead. And the two guys who tailed me from there are dead."

Clay pictured Stedding rubbing his temples.

"Maybe it'd be easier to tell me who's alive."

"Ahh, Steddy. You have a sense of humor after all."

"Psssh." That sound again.

"I think Nelson's alive, but I'm not sure how long that will be true. The girl he was trying to find is alive. I'm pretty sure of that."

"What girl?"

"Eighteen-year-old Hungarian nanny named Marika Csontos."

"The nanny story, huh? Nelson thought it was real?"

"I do, too. I'm going to find her."

"Your assignment is to find Nelson and bring him back."

"If Nelson was closing in on Csontos and he went missing, doesn't it follow logically that she might be worth something?"

There was a pause, and Clay hoped it indicated that Stedding was thinking about it and wasn't just involved in more temple rubbing. A Skype account would sure have come in handy, but Stedding wouldn't be caught dead on a camera that could be recorded.

"You want to change the goal of your mission, that it?"

"I want to add a goal to my mission. Find the girl, find Nelson, bring 'em both in from the cold."

"Why do I get the feeling you're not asking permission?"

"Let the record show I went through proper channels."

"What record? There are no records with us, Clay."

"Even better."

"Take care of yourself and report back in twenty-four."

"Ahh, you care about me, Steddy. That's so—"

But the line went dead in his hand.

In the garage behind the dacha, he struck gold. He was hoping for a truck or at least a compact car, but he knew these would be easier to track if their theft happened to be discovered by the caretaker. Instead, he found better: an old motorcycle, a Spoykin, twenty years past its manufacturing date, under a dust-covered sheet. The bike hadn't been touched since at least the previous summer. And if he replaced the general shape of it under the sheet, it would be a long time before it was missed.

A gas can on the floor of the garage provided a full tank. The key had been left carelessly in the ignition, and when Clay turned it, the engine sputtered to life.

After the excitement of the morning, it was this kind of luck Clay needed.

The rain bit into him, spitefully cold and as relentless as a conquering enemy. Fuck. Why'd he have to find a motorcycle? A fucking motorcycle? There couldn't have been a goddamn Mercedes in the garage? A Lifan? A truck? Anything with windows and a roof?

He had been on the road traveling east for five hours. His tank was disturbingly close to empty and he hadn't seen a petrol station for hours. And yet the sameness of the cold, of the evergreens lining the road, of his single headlight beam illuminating a yellow cone of pavement in front of him, settled his mind and allowed him to think.

The stepbrother had to be the answer. Marika Csontos had a stepbrother who was attending Far Eastern Federal University in Vladivostok—as far away from Moscow as was geographically possible inside the country. She had heard what she'd heard and knew she needed to flee without looking suspicious before her secret was discovered. She would've been terrified, hearing this official pour out his state secrets as if he were sitting in a confessional, terrified he would look into her eyes and know her secret—that she understood everything coming out of his mouth. Maybe she'd called her stepbrother and he'd told her to come. She certainly hadn't called the agency she worked for. That much had been made clear in Zhedenko's office. Maybe Benidrov, the loose-lipped Kremlin official, had caught wind of her phone call and put two and two together and she'd fled before he could correct his mistake.

Clay's clothes were soaked and heavy, and only the chattering of his teeth broke up his thoughts. The route was endless country, and his only company on the road was an occasional big rig lumbering to some factory or mine or farm. The motorcycle's needle was now on empty; if it gave out he would have to continue on foot for as many miles as it took to steal a car. He almost welcomed the obstacle, anything to break up the whine of the bike, the vibration of his seat, his stiff legs and arms and neck, the pinprick bites of the implacable rain on his face. All that was missing was the salt spray in his mouth and he would've been right back on the bow of that goddamn boat thirty years ago.

A hazy light on the horizon drew him forward like a moth to a candle. He throttled the bike up a hill, and as he crested it, a small town spread before him. A snippet of a poem lit the edge of his brain like light under a closet door. *Much have I traveled in these realms of gold*... or something like that. What the hell was that from? And why did he keep flashing to his childhood? What was it about this mission that kept churning up those muddy waters? And did he really want to dig deep enough to find out?

It was too early for any shops to be open, but he could find a place to lie down under some cover until the sun rose.

He found an awning behind a garage, pulled the motorcycle over, cut the engine, and lay down on the stoop, using his soaked jacket for a pillow. He'd always been good at falling asleep.

At least the rain had stopped. The sky remained dark and gray, though, and seemed to press down, like a trap closing. Clay opened his eyes, blinking away crust.

Two Russian police officers stood over him. The nearest one nudged Clay in the ribs with his boots. Clay climbed to his feet quickly and put what he hoped was the proper amount of deference on his face. When dealing with law enforcement the world over, it's always a good idea to be respectful, humble, sheepish. He gauged quickly that they didn't know who he was or why he was there. Otherwise, there certainly would have been a much larger police presence. They wouldn't have tapped him awake with their boots; instead, he'd have opened his eyes to assault rifle barrels.

"You sleep where you like, is that it?" the boot-nudger asked in a somewhat feminine voice. He wore a beard that looked as if it had been carefully plucked and trimmed. Clay thought of Curly's glove from *Of Mice and Men* and then pushed the thought aside. He was turning into a goddamn library reference desk when he needed to be concentrating on extricating himself from trouble.

He tried to speak with a bit of a country accent, flattening his vowels and stepping hard on the *z*s and *v*s so common in Russian.

"I apologize, friends. I drove in late last night in the rain."

"You didn't want to stop at a hotel?"

"I didn't see one. Forgive me. I was tired and soaked to the bone."

"Are you a vagrant?"

"No, Officer. I am on my way to Omsk from Moscow."

"Long way on a motorbike."

"True."

"What is your business?"

"I am a writer."

"A what?"

"I write plays. Dramas."

"What is your name?"

"Parinshka."

The effeminate one was nodding now. "Parinshka, yes."

His partner eyed him with suspicion. "You have heard this name, Vlad?"

Clay waded in. "Perhaps you saw my play, *Caretaker of Stepnoy*? We held the Belanshky Theater in Moscow for eleven months last year."

The one named Vlad searched his memory and then nodded. "I have not seen it, but I understand it is wonderful."

"Thank you, friend. I have been called eccentric, as you can guess by my appearance and my strange idea to drive a motorbike from Moscow to Omsk." The power of suggestion was a favorite tool of Clay's.

"Ha! It is good for Russians to remember culture."

"The very premise of *Caretaker of Stepnoy*!"

Vlad beamed. "Will you have breakfast here, then?"

"If you will point me to the nearest petrol station, I would be much in your debt, Officer Vlad. But I will forgo eating this morning, because I slept longer than I meant and would like to continue my journey."

For the first time, Vlad's partner spoke directly to Clay. "May I see your papers, Mr. Parinshka?"

Clay shifted his eyes to the shorter officer and forced a smile.

"Why do you ask this, Gregor?" Vlad demanded.

"This man is guilty of vagrancy, is he not?"

"He is one of Moscow's great playwrights."

"Hmm...even still, your papers."

Old habits died hard in the Russian countryside. Whereas much of Moscow and St. Petersburg had embraced the rough sort of capitalism that marks the birth of a nation, the further east a man traveled, the more "old regime" Russia seemed. A mentality that still prompted officers to ask for papers.

Clay made a show of searching his pockets for his identification while Vlad apologized and Gregor's watchful eyes never left his face. After a moment, Clay produced a small billfold and extracted a laminated card.

Sure enough, it was an up-to-date ID with his picture and the name Ivan Parinshka printed on it.

"You see," Vlad said.

Gregor frowned. "Just a minute." He moved a few steps away and withdrew a smartphone from his pocket. Clay eyed him and tried to show only a proper amount of anxiety. He had little doubt he could kill these two officers, but the body count on the road from Stepnoy would give away his direction of travel and might lead others to identify the purpose of his mission.

Vlad looked with trepidation from Clay to his partner. "What are you doing, Gregor?"

"I am using Google to see if this man is a great playwright or a great liar."

"You're— This is terribly embarrassing to me, Mr. Parinshka. You see, my partner's father was high-ranking KGB, and Gregor wishes to be considered for FSB and so takes work very seriously. I am red with shame."

Clay waited for what seemed an hour. The wireless connection out here in the sticks must have been as slow as an invalid.

Vlad shifted his weight from foot to foot like a schoolkid anxious to find a restroom. "You have a new play you are writing, then, yes?"

"I'm gathering ideas as we speak."

"Oh! Ha. Hahahah. Yes."

Finally, Gregor lowered the phone, grave disappointment on his face. "It seems your plays are better known in Moscow than out here, Mr. Parinshka. I apologize for detaining you."

"It seems there are two Russias," Clay said, dusting off his pants before throwing one leg over his motorcycle. "Good day, Officers."

The playwright cover had been Clay's idea after reading an article in the *New York Times* a few years earlier about the revival of the Moscow theater district. Russians had a proud history of literary greats, and despite generations of Communism, it was a source of national pride that had resurfaced. In the new Russia's infant stage, the hint of celebrity shone brightly in the people's eyes. Stedding had been against it, wanting Clay's cover to be less flashy—a low-level government official or a shipping contractor—but Clay had held firm and had even had Stedding create websites and fictitious reviews dedicated to the emerging fame of one Ivan Parinshka. The ruse worked better than he had hoped. Never underestimate the blindness of people with stars in their eyes.

With a fresh tank of gas, thanks to a nearby petrol station, the motorcycle hummed along, settling again into the rhythm of the road. It reminded Clay of that boat again, that goddamn boat, and the endless lapping of the ocean on the hull outside his cabin's porthole. Nine years he had spent on that boat with his uncle, from age six until his escape at fifteen. He was a strong swimmer by then, and when he had the chance, he took it. He hadn't had much of a choice, what with the fire engulfing—

He was awakened from his reverie by a gunshot. His initial thought that his motorcycle had backfired was quickly erased by a second shot, which somehow missed his shoulder but shattered the glass of the right rearview mirror. He jerked his head around to see a pair of black Mercedes sedans closing on him, followed by a boxy Russian police sedan, a Volkswagen from the looks of it, struggling to keep up. *Shit.* That little ferret cop Gregor must've made some calls instead of letting it go...or more likely, the FSB was on the trail Clay had left from Zhedenko's office and had put out a call for anyone suspicious, and Gregor had been alert enough to make the connection.

Clay cranked his wrist and pinned the throttle to its maximum point while he lowered his head and zigzagged back and forth across the road like a boxer trying to duck a cross.

If they were going to shoot first and ask questions later, he wasn't going to give them a clear target to hit.

The Mercedes pressed forward and his goddamn Spoykin couldn't hold the distance. Why couldn't it have been a Ducati? This assignment's ledger was quickly dropping into the red. He pinned his knee almost to the ground and pivoted the bike off the road and into the forest. The pines were thick, but not that thick, and both Mercedes skidded into turns and followed, undaunted.

Clay bounced over loose needles, tightened his jaw, and hoped against hope that a rotting branch wouldn't send him sliding sideways. One mistake and he'd be having his next conversation cuffed to a chair.

The sun was high in the sky now, so the shadows clung tightly to the trees. Visibility was good. Clay dipped his knee again and aimed for a tight pattern of trees, something he could squeeze through. The twin Mercedes had to give ground now, had to pick their way carefully through the trees like moose trying to keep up with a fox.

Clay shot out onto a small walking trail and crested a hill. He had a minute, maybe less.

In the animal kingdom, there are a few creatures that instinctively know the art of the ambush. They don't stalk like lions, they don't group hunt like chimpanzees, they don't rely on speed or strength like hawks. They lie still, in wait, and when opportunity arises, they pounce. A crocodile beneath the water, a stonefish on a rocky sea bottom, an African bush viper on a tree branch.

Clay thought his pursuers should have spent less time taking potshots while speeding down a highway and more time learning the way nature worked. He intended to teach them the last lesson of their lives.

The first of the two Mercedes crested the hill and nearly ran over the capsized Spoykin. The Mercedes abruptly parked and the doors popped open, two FSB agents climbing out like synchronized swimmers with pistols drawn. They had only a second to realize they'd made a mistake by stepping out of the car before Clay was on them. He flew out from behind a tree and blitzed into the nearest agent, smashing him into the side of the car and wrestling his gun away in the blink of an eye. He shot the agent as he crumpled to the ground, directly through the top of his head, a kill shot. The second agent dove, but Clay anticipated the defensive move and dropped to the ground at the same time. He fired under the car and caught the second agent in the back before he could get into a seated position and gain his bearings. The agent fell over sideways and watched his own blood seep into the forest floor, unsure how he'd been killed right up to the moment his synapses stopped firing.

Clay quickly climbed behind the wheel of the Mercedes and piloted it into a three-point turn, just as the other Mercedes approached. He honked and signaled with his hand out the window for the second car to pull alongside. With the tinted windows so many European departments insisted upon, the men in the other car couldn't see a thing inside his sedan. They drew even with his driver's-side door, and the driver rolled down his window. Two bullets greeted him and his partner. Hello and good-bye.

The police sedan was the final puzzle piece in this bloody contest. It did not turn into the woods to follow, Gregor and Vlad content to lead the big dogs to the hunt and then sit back and collect whatever commendations were headed their way for their role in recognizing the fugitive.

Clay steered the Mercedes back onto the road but emerged from the woods a hundred yards in front of the cruiser. He turned to face it. No other traffic appeared on the road, and he couldn't help thinking they looked like two gunslingers facing off in an Old West town, except surrounded by chrome, steel, and glass instead of perched on horses.

He rolled down his window and waved the police cruiser forward.

The Volkswagen started his way and then stopped again, like a distrustful dog. His radio crackled and a Russian voice barked, "Report!"

Must be Gregor, though Clay couldn't see through the windshield with the sun bouncing off it. He thought about replying but decided to try the arm one more time rather than allow his voice to give anything away. He waved more vigorously. Maybe they'd think he had engine trouble or was wounded.

The radio chirped again, "Report!"

Clay shook his head and picked up the receiver. In his most neutral Russian, he tried, "We're hurt."

The cruiser in front of him didn't respond, and the radio remained silent for a good twenty seconds.

Then the police car gunned into a sharp turn, tires peeling out on the asphalt so it could head back toward town.

Clay reacted immediately, stamping his foot on the accelerator. The Mercedes charged forward, loping after the sedan like a wolf after a chicken. Thankfully, the cruiser was an older make and was no match for the diesel engine of the FSB Mercedes.

The easiest way to take out a lead vehicle is to tag the bumper from behind, forcing it into a slide, a tactic seen on the five o'clock news at least once a week in every big city in America. But the cops utilized that maneuver for a reason: they cared whether the driver lived or died at the end of the pursuit.

Clay chose a more effective route. He pulled even with the driver's back tire and then emptied into it the entire contents of the Grach he'd taken from the hand of the dead FSB agent. The tire exploded and the cruiser leapt into the air like a startled rabbit, then rolled eleven times before flipping off the road like a bowling pin.

Clay immediately parked and hurried out of his car. No time to let Gregor recover and get his bearings if he'd survived the crash. Clay didn't stalk his enemies, didn't toy with them—he moved in swiftly and shot them before they could shoot back. This wasn't sport.

He descended on the smoking cruiser, which had ended up on its back, tires up, a turtle on its shell. He quickly hit his belly and aimed into the driver's window, but stopped, surprised to see Vlad behind the wheel, alone.

"Where's Gregor?"

Vlad looked disoriented, strapped in upside down, bleeding from the chin. He turned and tried to focus on Clay.

"The Belanshky Theater closed."

"What?"

"You said you held the Belanshky Theater for eleven months. But it closed two years ago. I knew you were lying."

Clay nodded. He had misjudged which cop was the more ambitious. Vlad wanted the acclaim for himself.

"I called FSB. They're looking for you. Said you were dangerous."

Clay shot him then, thinking the FSB was right.

CHAPTER FOUR

HE WASN'T sure what he had told them. Nelson remembered the pain, the hunger, the thirst, and the fear, all with unkind clarity, but of what he had told them, he wasn't sure. Central Intelligence had trained him to withstand torture, but those efforts had proved woefully inadequate. If he had wondered during those sessions at the Farm how long he could hold out, he had his answer. Not long.

His leg was healing. The cast was off and the pain had subsided. He might walk unassisted soon, but for now, he relied on a cane. They had provided one made of hard plastic, the kind found in hospitals. Leaving him with a stick he could conceivably wield as a weapon told him everything he needed to know: they had broken him and they weren't worried.

He rose from his bed and made his way over to the window

facing the Kremlin. He had tried to open it once, but that had brought punishment. He hadn't tried again. He was sure it wouldn't open, anyway, and the glass was reinforced and unbreakable. Even if he hurled his body against it in order to jump, it wouldn't give. He was sure of that. The window was a torture in and of itself; he could see people scurrying about their business, driving cars, drinking coffee, commuting, smoking, talking, unaware of the prisoner thirty stories above them.

They'd kept him alive and treated his gunshot wound, and that meant something. He was now a pawn on a chessboard; he would be traded so the Russians could collect a piece of their own.

The fat-faced man with the gray beard entered. He'd had it trimmed sometime in the last few days, and it made him appear younger. His name was Egorov, Nelson had learned in one of the cycles when the man was nice to him. A smile formed inside the beard. This was one of those times, it appeared.

"Ahh, you're up."

"You knew that before you walked in." There were cameras in three of the corners of the room, covering it with constant surveillance. Nelson didn't even bother nodding at them to make the point.

Egorov clucked his tongue, an affectation Nelson had come to despise. "You seem irritated."

Nelson closed his eyes, then turned from the window. He forced a tight smile. "I'm fine."

"How's your leg?"

"Better, thank you."

"We're going to have another session about Marika."

The smile disappeared. Nelson wished his hand wouldn't tremble on the cane's handle, but the tremor came involuntarily. He tried saying, "I've told you everything I know."

"You've told us the answers to everything we've asked, but perhaps we weren't asking the right questions."

"What could I possibly have left to say?"

"Who might be completing your work?"

"I'm sorry?"

"Who might your brothers at Central Intelligence have sent to take your place?"

Nelson covered his right hand with his left, trying to force the trembling to subside. It was no use. He searched his brain for an answer, but only the worst one would come to him. "I don't know."

Egorov frowned, crow's-feet appearing next to his eyes. "Like I said, we weren't asking the right questions."

"Dear God, don't you think I'd tell you if I knew?"

"Maybe you need help thinking."

A couple of large Russians wearing blue rubber gloves entered the suite behind Egorov.

Nelson dropped the cane and sat down heavily on the carpet. His knee had buckled. Then he had an idea, and his face momentarily lit up. "Kespy! Kespy out of our Turkish bureau! They'd send Kespy!"

"We have Kespy under surveillance in Istanbul. He hasn't moved."

Nelson dropped his chin, defeated. He wished tears wouldn't

spring to his eyes, he wished he didn't have to fight off a sob, but he did.

Michael Adams drove himself toward downtown Los Angeles. Traffic was light on Olympic this time of night, and he picked his way through Koreatown, only braking for an occasional red light. He liked to listen to Classic Radio on his SiriusXM player, and the host, Greg Bell, was spinning back-to-back episodes of *Suspense,* his favorite old-timey show. Agnes Moorehead was in the middle of a panic attack, unable to get her husband on the telephone, when Adams reached the garage of his office building. He thought about sitting in his car until the episode ended, but time wasn't on his side. It was already late on the East Coast.

His parking space was closest to the door, and he crossed the garage, entered the seven-digit code into the keypad, and arrived in the vestibule, closing the door behind him. No signs marked the building, the garage, the vestibule, or the elevator.

Adams pulled out his key card and slid it into the slot next to the elevator. The elevator car arrived in moments and whisked him up to the seventh floor.

When most Americans think of Central Intelligence offices, they think of Langley on the East Coast, the George Bush Center for Intelligence, and men in suits shuffling past marines to get to conference rooms featuring wall-to-wall computers loaded with the latest technology. In reality, there are seven of these domestic district offices spread out across the United States; besides Virginia, there are offices in Miami, Dallas, New York, Chicago, Seattle, and Los Angeles. They look like accounting firms, with ten-years-out-of-date furniture, bland cubicles, and cream-colored walls. *At least the computers are fairly new,* Adams thought; they did run Echelon programs with the latest encryption software. Resources went into technology, not feng shui furniture.

Staffers worked the phones. There were no weekends in Intelligence, no holidays. These men and women were among those who had sewn the very fabric of this country but would go forever unrecognized. Adams admired the hell out of them. Hell, he was one of 'em.

He had climbed the ranks from a junior analyst position when he'd joined the CIA to a case officer—a handler, in popular parlance—with a stable of five field operatives under his direction, to case supervisor, where the number of field operatives quintupled to twenty-five, and here he was at age forty-five, heading the second-largest district in the Agency. Only Laura knew what he really did for a living; everyone else thought he was in risk management. Coming up on the analyst side instead of the field side, he'd been able to marry his college sweetheart and have a family. Though one or two analysts in the course of the sixty-five-year history of the Agency had been caught stealing sensitive documents, they weren't targeted by foreign intelligence the way field officers were. They could lead normal lives, as long as they didn't mind the fluctuating hours.

He stopped at the desk of Warren Sumner, a recent Princeton graduate he had pulled out of Washington to be his assistant.

"How we doing?" Adams asked as he approached.

"Hovering right around fine, sir." *Why can't Warren just answer a question like a normal person?* Adams thought, but he said nothing, only smiled. Warren continued, "DCI just called... I said to hold, you were in the elevator on the way up, but he said call back when you got behind your desk."

Adams grimaced. "Thanks, Warren," he said as he headed into his office.

"One more thing." Warren held up a finger, and Adams waited, half in and half out of his doorway. His demeanor said that his assistant had better get on with it.

"I received a sit-com report from Eppie in Havana. I went ahead and gave him the parameters you described at the debriefing Wednesday. If I overstepped..."

Adams frowned and shook his head. "No, it's fine."

"I would've waited for you personally, but I knew you had this Director call...."

"It's fine, Warren. Good job." Adams's assistant beamed. Adams had told Warren a long time ago he was looking for an assistant who would step up, would reach further than his grasp, would be able to anticipate needs and fulfill requests before he was asked. Warren Sumner had exceeded even these lofty expectations. Adams prided himself on his ability to find good people, raise smart, qualified lieutenants, and Sumner would undoubtedly make a good case officer in the near future. Still, there was something a tiny bit off-putting about his obsequiousness; he was like a dog you like having around but wish wouldn't lick the dirt off your toes.

"Anything else?"

"That's it. Getting the Director now."

Warren reached for his phone, and Adams shut his door.

A minute later, he heard Director Manning's voice on the other end of a secure line.

"Howdy, Michael."

"How are you, Andrew?"

"All right. How's the family?"

"Everyone's great. Thanks for asking."

"I heard you got away to Ojai for a few days?"

"I did."

"You have to recharge your batteries every now and then or this job'll eat you alive."

"Yes, sir." Adams wondered if the Director was in one of his talkative moods or if there was a point to this call. He got his answer.

"Tell me what you know of a field officer named Austin Clay."

"One of the best I ever supervised. I mean, I was a new case officer at the time...."

"You ever get a disloyal vibe off him?"

The Director was asking if Adams thought this officer could be turned. They had ways of making euphemisms out of everything in the intelligence game...no one ever wanted to be on the record for anything, even the Director.

"Never once. What happened to him? I heard he—"

"Thanks, Michael. When are you headed to Prague?"

"Next week."

"Right. Have your man schedule it so you get a day in DC. I want to talk to you in person before you go."

"Yes, sir."

"Talk to you soon."

The phone went dead in Adams's hand.

He returned the receiver to its cradle, and Warren almost immediately knocked on his door. "Come in."

"You want to go over your calendar, sir?"

Adams didn't immediately answer. Austin Clay. Clay had worked the field all over Europe and the Middle East and in those early days had been Adams's go-to hot spot guy. Langley had moved the officer out from under him a long time ago, and he hadn't heard the name in years.

"Your calendar, sir?"

Adams snapped back to the present. His calendar. Prague. That was going to be a hell of a meeting...the other district office heads jockeying for a European appointment.

"Yes. The Director wants me for a day in DC on the front end of it."

"On it," Warren said, and headed for the door.

CHAPTER FIVE

CLAY DROVE the commandeered Mercedes to the nearest parking lot—at some sort of factory in a town with too many consonants in its name—and stole a nondescript gray van. He drove it to the next parking lot and repeated the process twice more in a shell game meant to buy him a day or two of anonymity, if he was lucky. Stealing a plane would have been nice, but piloting one was always something he thought he'd learn to do someday in the future. Why did Russia have to be some damn massive?

He got lucky with his last steal—a fairly new Lada hatchback with a Russian road map in the glove box. If he pushed, he could make it to Vladivostok in three days while keeping off the main highways, at least for the next thousand miles. He hoped for a bit of leeway as new agents were brought up to speed on him—this man who kept dispatching his pursuers. He hoped they wouldn't figure out where he was going. He hoped Nelson hadn't yet confessed to the existence or location of the stepbrother.

Off the main motorway, rural Russia might as well have been trapped in the nineteenth century. Roads weren't paved, endless farms rolled by the window, and towns were little more than a couple of communal buildings. If he was lucky, he'd find a gas pump, if not a station. He located shady, secluded spots where he could sleep for a few hours during the day and tried to drive mostly at night, pinching just enough petrol and food to avoid attracting attention.

Traffic was minimal during the night. He stumbled upon an unmarked military base of some kind, and congestion picked up as he negotiated his way around jeeps, trucks, and transports, but if he looked suspicious in his little beige Lada, no one seemed to notice. At least the excitement temporarily broke up the road's relentless monotony. Soon the military machinery faded behind him and he was back alone on the road. Once he misjudged his spot on the map by a good thirty kilometers, but he kept the dash pointed east and soon picked his way back to a listed road. He knew he needed to report in to Stedding at some point, but he felt he was making progress without sounding any alarms, and he didn't want to risk a break-in if he didn't have to. His scent, he hoped, had disappeared from the hounds charged with hunting him.

After three days of bumping along back roads, praying that a sudden storm wouldn't muddy things up, he jogged back to the main motorway that headed into Vladivostok. The sun was out and felt warm on his face.

Clay's stomach cramped, and he realized he hadn't eaten in twenty-four hours. He was narrowing in on Vladivostok from the north but wasn't sure how far he had to go. When he saw a small motel with a few cars in front, he eased into the lot. Smoke was curling up from a stovepipe affixed to the roof, and he could smell meat cooking. His stomach made some noise, presumably to voice its approval.

Inside, the motel was dark, with a low wooden ceiling that barely cleared his head. A small desk to the right must have been for reception, but it was unmanned. Two long wooden tables stood a little farther into the room, with benches on either side, occupied by simply, inelegantly dressed customers. The smells of eggs, potatoes, butter, and roasted beef mingled with cigarette smoke and formed a wreath around his head.

An overweight man wearing what looked like a smock gestured from a kitchen door to a seat at the end of the second table. The man spoke Russian with a flat, hollow accent and said something along the lines of "Please, sit," but Clay wasn't sure he'd interpreted it correctly. He moved to the indicated seat and sat down heavily. A plastic bowl was immediately filled with soup, and Clay nodded at the family staring at him before digging in. He was expecting something bland and was surprised by the flavor; extreme hunger has a way of making everything taste gourmet.

A girl of no more than six sat closest to him. She stared brazenly, watching as he dipped his spoon again and again into the bowl. Her mother pulled her in tight to her side, a hen protecting her chick. Her father sat across from her; he was a big man with a curly black beard and eyes spaced too far apart.

"You're a traveler?"

Clay nodded as he scooped up another bite of the soup. "Driving to Vladivostok." He could feel two tables' worth of diners straining to hear what he had to say.

"Wonderful. It is nice to see men traveling these roads again. We live in Ussuriysk."

Clay kept shoveling the soup into his mouth. He didn't want to be impolite, but he wasn't keen to make conversation, either. His soup bowl was whisked away when he finished, and a plate of meat and potatoes replaced it. There was not a green vegetable or a ripe piece of fruit in sight, but he didn't mind.

"We grow wheat. This is my wife, Dina. Our daughters are Oksana, and Lidya is the one who hasn't stopped staring. My name is Pavel."

"Ivan," Clay said, and tore into the meat. The potatoes tasted more of butter than of well, potato, but he couldn't bring the food into his face fast enough.

"What brings you to Vladivostok?" Pavel asked happily. He shook out a cigarette and lit the end.

Clay stopped eating long enough to put a smile on his face and say, "I am a playwright, Ivan Parinshka. Just visiting the university."

Pavel beamed. "Oleg works at the university!"

Clay felt his throat tighten, but he kept his face blank. All eyes turned to the man seated one table over, directly behind Pavel. Pavel turned and clapped the man on the back warmly. "Oleg, say hello to Ivan. He is coming to visit your university!"

The man named Oleg spun on his bench, wiped his mustache with his napkin, cleaned his hands, then stuck one out to Clay. "Pleased to meet you."

"And you," Clay said, and returned the handshake. He was suddenly full and put his fork down.

"Did I hear you say you are a playwright?" Oleg asked. He had dark brown eyes that shone with intelligence, a sharp contrast with Pavel's vacant expression.

"I am. From Moscow."

"Will you be speaking at the linguistics—?"

Clay interrupted before he could finish the question. "In what department do you teach, Oleg?"

Oleg smiled. "International Relations."

"Fascinating. You must spend much time traveling, then?"

"Oh, yes. I stayed a few months last year on the Korean peninsula. I will be spending another few months in Japan next year on an exchange with Waseda University."

"Wonderful," Clay said, standing up abruptly. "I would love to talk more with you, but I must be on my way. Perhaps if I find myself with a minute, I can stop in and see you in your office, Oleg."

Oleg looked mystified to discover that the conversation was ending and that this man could have finished his plate so quickly. Clay found the cook with his eyes and gestured for the check. The man grunted something about four hundred rubles.

Pavel stood and shook his hand. "Must you be leaving so quickly?"

"I am very tired and would like to get on with my travel. How much farther is it?"

"No more than one hour twenty minutes straight down the M60."

Clay fished some money out of his pocket and put the bills on the table next to his plate.

"You didn't tell me where you are speaking at the university. Perhaps I can come hear you speak?" Oleg said just as Clay began to move away.

Clay stopped and turned back to the professor. "I'm attending incognito, I'm afraid. I am writing a new play about a student. I am just attending to observe student life."

"I see," Oleg said. "Well, please stop in to say hello to my colleague Sergei Trushin in the journalism school. He would be delighted to interview a playwright from Moscow."

"Sergei Trushin," Clay repeated, pretending to commit the name to memory. "I will certainly do that, Oleg. Thank you."

"With pleasure," Oleg said, and turned back to his dish. Clay nodded at the family and headed for the door, ducking his head to avoid bumping the ceiling. He replayed the conversation in his mind all the way to his car but couldn't see any mistakes in it. Still, he cursed his stomach for speaking up when he only had an hour and twenty minutes to go before reaching the university.

The stepbrother was named David Czabo. Clay hoped the difference in the surnames—Czabo and Csontos—had thrown FSB off his trail and they hadn't found the connection Nelson had found.

He entered the biotechnology building and passed the classrooms in search of the faculty offices. The university felt modern and clean, a stark contrast to his last week out in the backwoods of Mother Russia. He was clean, too. He had called Stedding as soon as he'd found a phone on the outskirts of town. Within three hours, Stedding had gotten him a room at the fine Azimut Hotel and a closet full of clothes his size. Every now and then, Steddy liked to remind Clay how resourceful a handler he could be, and how fortunate Clay was to work with the best.

He passed several closed office doors and arrived at an open one, inside which a bearded academic sat over papers. The name on the door read *Zagrevsky.*

"Professor Zagrevsky?" Clay asked as he knocked and entered.

"Yes." The man looked up and then back down at his work immediately.

"I am Boris Antopov, with Central Ministry."

As expected, the professor looked up. His fingers went to his beard and scratched nervously.

Clay put on his warmest smile. "Biotech division."

"Yes?"

"You have a student here named David Czabo."

"Yes, yes. Fine student, David."

"I wish to speak with him, but my assistant did not give me his living address and the office is closed in Moscow due to scheduled renovation."

"To speak with him? What is this concerning?"

Clay's smile spread. "Concerning ministry business."

The academic frowned. "I see. Well, you are in luck with your timing. I have class with David Czabo in just over an hour. I will introduce you upon his arrival, yes?"

"Thank you, Professor Zagrevsky."

The academic nodded and returned to his paperwork as though the intrusion had never occurred.

Often, Clay's missions involved stalking prey. He could wait patiently for hours, days, weeks, hiding in the shadows, as undetectable as the proverbial white spider on a white flower. He could observe and make notes, search for weaknesses and defenses, plot the best way to intercept, confront, or control his target. Patience was never a problem for him; it was a component of his childhood, long hours looking at an endless roll of waves on that damn boat.

But stalking wasn't an option here. There was simply no time. He hoped he had beaten FSB to Vladivostok, but he couldn't be sure. So he had spoken to Professor Zagrevsky for a specific reason: he wanted to frighten his quarry. More often than not, frightened quarry scuttles back to its nest.

It didn't take long to prove this theory correct. David

Czabo ran like a spooked squirrel as soon as the professor opened his mouth, bursting from the utilitarian classroom corridor and out the nearest door.

Clay sprang after him, marginally concerned about the way this incident looked in front of dozens of faculty and students, but Russians come from a long tradition of keeping their eyes shut and mouths closed. The professor would tell everyone that Czabo had "government trouble" and probably leave it at that.

The kid was agile. He darted across the campus, leapt a bicycle rack like an Olympic hurdler, and stole between cars into the street. Clay wasn't concerned. Pursuit wasn't always about overtaking prey.

Clay hung back just far enough to let Czabo think he had lost him. It wasn't fair, like putting an amateur into the ring with Ali. The kid tried to execute a couple of evasive maneuvers, doubling back on his trail, darting into a shoe store to watch across the street, but Clay tailed him as easily as if he'd planted a GPS chip in his backpack. After a half hour, the kid poked his head out into the street, now wearing his jacket inside out. It almost made Clay snicker. Almost.

Czabo crossed the street, ducked down an alley, and headed into one of the commonplace gunmetal-gray apartment buildings that made up this port city.

If Marika happened to be out, this plan was going to go sideways fast. Clay had been thinking about her so much since he'd left St. Petersburg, he wondered how blurry his mental picture would prove to be. It was like reading a book and having a character in your head, so real you could recognize her in a crowd, and then discovering that the actress picked to play the part in the film version is nothing close to your image. Everything you had in mind before is lost forever after seeing a new face in the part. Would he be disappointed? Would he be shocked? Would she be as plain as wallpaper? He took the stairs two at a time and then leaned back to set himself outside her door.

She was hastily packing a bag when Clay kicked the door in.

One thing registered as he first laid eyes upon her: his mental image was indeed inaccurate. She was astonishingly beautiful, even more so than he had imagined. She had wide, impossible eyes, a shade of blue that seemed to absorb light. Her hair was long and black and wild, and her lips were full and intense. Goddamn, she was stunning.

The second thing he noticed was her stepbrother lunging at him with a knife. The girl's pulchritude threw him off his game, and he reacted too slowly. The blade caught a piece of his forearm as he defended a second late.

"Hey!" he shouted in Russian, now angry. Czabo lunged again, and this time Clay met him before he could bring the knife around, popped his wrist, and Czabo's grip wasn't professional enough to hang on. While the kid watched the knife sail, Clay grabbed his arm, pulled him in, and held him tight.

"I'm not here to harm you. I'm here to help!" he grunted. Clay's arm was bleeding more than he would have liked.

Marika's face flashed emotion: terror, anger, hope.

Czabo struggled, and Clay bent his arm a little farther, until he stopped struggling.

"Who are you?"

"American," Clay said, dropping the accent. "There are people coming for your sister. I can get her to a safe place."

"Why should I believe you?"

"You...you shouldn't." Clay let him go, and he stumbled back toward his stepsister. "But I'm all you have right now. If I'd been sent to kill you, there wouldn't have been talking. I would have put bullets in both of you in the time it took to raise that knife."

The stepbrother held her defensively behind him, an instinctive protective stance Clay found admirable.

"What do you want?"

"Only to help her. If I found you, they'll find you."

"She doesn't know anything."

"I can see that isn't true."

"It's not her fault. She didn't want any of this."

"I believe that, but it doesn't change what is."

Clay lowered his arms and assumed his most unthreatening position. He moved his eyes to lock on to hers. He could feel his heart beat faster. Maybe it was the chase, the excitement a hunter feels when finding his target. Maybe...His arm continued to drip blood, but he ignored the pain. "Now, look. I don't know when they're coming, but they *will* come. I can get you both out of here...out of the country...someplace safe."

"I have my studies."

"Not anymore."

He could see the stepbrother wince as he worked this out in his mind, all of his best-laid plans shattered.

For the first time, she spoke, and her voice matched her

appearance. It wasn't the gruff Hungarian of government agents; it was smooth and soft and guileless. "I'm so sorry, David."

His eyes softened for just a moment, like the moon popping out of a dull sky. He looked on the verge of tears, a young man tossed in a world he didn't understand, as though he'd thought maybe he could hide her here in this distant city on the edge of Russia and no one would come looking for them and everything would stay the same. He could be a professor or a scientist and they could have a life together. And then Clay had shown up, carrying a stark dose of reality. They were both soft, disoriented, fragile. Clay knew to keep them talking, moving.

"Do you have a car?"

Czabo shook his head, but Marika nodded. It would've been comical in another circumstance.

"I know I haven't earned it yet, but you're going to have to put your trust in me if you want to live."

Marika spoke. "I have a cheap Volga."

"It'll have to do. Leave everything here, lock your door, and let's go."

"Can we confer for a moment?"

Clay swallowed, then nodded. "Yes, but hurry, please."

They moved to the window to huddle together as Clay stepped toward their kitchenette. He grabbed a hand towel and tied it over his wound as he watched them. There wasn't much privacy to be had in this tiny apartment.

The siblings spoke in low tones, and though Clay couldn't make out the words, he understood the meaning. They were trying to assure each other that everything was going to be okay if they just stayed together. Sunlight filtered through the window, stirring the motes in the air, and the cone of light, falling right on them, reminded Clay of his porthole. He had been in his cabin, praying to a God he didn't know to deliver him from this, to give him some kind of sign, and a beam of sunlight had broken through the clouds, penetrated his cabin, and shone down on his desk. It was jumbled in his mind now—had he prayed for the sign first, or had the sign come first and understanding later? The sunlight settled on a wood carving of Belenus he had picked up in Dublin, a carving he had stuck in a drawer years ago and only recently rediscovered. Had he left it on his desk? Had the sunlight really illuminated it or had it just missed the carving? Had he left it out in just the right place, manufacturing a divine sign? He was just a kid, he told himself, just a kid imagining a world without—

A green light shone through the window and lit Marika's cheek.

"Down!"

She didn't move, didn't get down, but her stepbrother did. He lurched forward as though propelled by some invisible force and shielded his stepsister from the window, drawing the laser sight from her to him, and when the bullet came, it hit him square between the shoulders. She stumbled back as his weight fell on her, and her eyes widened in shock and bewilderment. The green laser found her again, running up her face and settling on her forehead. She dropped David, unable to support his weight anymore, and Clay showed his professional skills by darting to her and pulling her back toward the shadows only a half second before fresh gunfire split the window and ripped into the room.

"David," she whimpered, her voice choked, her eyes fixed to his body.

"We have to move."

"David," she protested.

"Look at me, Marika." Clay spoke in Russian, grave, hardening his words. "He's dead. You'll die, too, if you don't keep up with me, yes?"

His words jolted her as though he had tossed a bucket of ice water in her face.

"Your car, where is it?"

"Parking lot."

"This building?"

"Behind it."

"Keys?"

"I...I don't..." Her hand absently searched her pocket and came up with a set of keys. He took them from her, then squeezed her hand. He hoped the contact was enough. He tried to will trust through it.

"Okay, then...run with me."

She took one last look at her stepbrother, and the pain in her eyes was enough to take Clay's breath away. He couldn't have any more of that.

"Now!" he screamed as bullets crashed once more into the room, splintering the wooden floorboards.

When he bolted for the door, she followed.

—

They tried to hit him in the stairwell, and it might have worked, except for his downward momentum. They opened the door on the lobby landing and swung inside, automatic weapons shouldered, but he was already halfway down that flight and he launched himself from six steps above them, hurling his full weight into them before they could pop off a shot. Marika screamed, and her cry echoed in the enclosed chamber so the sound of it masked the collision of elbows with noses, of knees with throats, of fists with temples, of heels with necks, until the echo of the scream died at the same time as the two assailants dropped.

Clay looked up at her, now with blood literally on his hands and speckled across his cheek. "Keep moving," he growled. He thought he saw appreciation in her eyes, but maybe he was just flushed from the kill and imagined it.

They made it to the Volga before the next wave hit. How many fucking guys had they brought?

"Get in the back and lie down!"

She obeyed. He threw the car into reverse just as the rear windshield exploded.

A car roared forward and tried to box them in, but Clay stamped the accelerator in reverse and the tires held, driving the attacker backward and giving Clay just enough room to throw the Volga in drive and launch it forward between parked cars. He might not have known how to pilot a plane, but damn, could Austin Clay drive anything with tires.

He squeezed between two approaching black SUVs. They

threatened to pinch him between them but chickened out at the last moment, and that told Clay he might just have a chance. Drivers afraid to wreck their government-issued vehicles would always be at a disadvantage to a man with nothing to lose.

The Volga spun out of the parking lot and slid across the asphalt like a speed skater swinging wide into a turn, until the tire treads again found purchase and the car corrected from sideways to forward. Only the sea was to his right, while the city lay to his left, and three SUVs fell in behind him as three more whipped out in front of him, closing like medieval jousters. If they had failed to bring adequate forces to take him before, they appeared determined not to underestimate him again. Well, he'd dispatched every last son of a bitch who'd tried before, so could he blame them for switching to a strength-in-numbers assault?

He set his jaw, lowered his head, and mashed the accelerator, vaulting the Volga at the trio of trucks that wished to drive him from the road.

Marika's head peeked out like a prairie dog's, and she let out an eardrum-shattering shriek as she saw the SUVs closing the distance in front of them.

"Down!" he snapped for the second time that day, and this time she obeyed.

He twirled the wheel at the last possible moment, and his side-view mirrors popped like balloons as he judged correctly and squeezed the Volga between two of the SUVs as they shot past him, two bullets with a hairsbreadth of space between them. The paint on the Volga's doors might need retouching when this was over.

Nelson. Everything Nelson suspected about the girl must've been true. The Russians hadn't sent a sniper after her; they'd sent a goddamn division.

As if to accentuate the point, the familiar *wut-wut-wut* of a helicopter's rotors overpowered the whine of his sedan's engine moments before the black beast buzzed overhead and burst out in front of him.

Well, that complicated things. The ledger was starting to bleed red, and Clay doubted it would ever return to black. If he'd thought he could outrun or outduel them, that notion went out the window now that they had eyes in the sky. No, this account had gone belly-up quickly, but Clay would be damned if he was going to cut his losses and run.

He threw up the hand brake, spun the wheel, and skidded up on two tires as he took a turn back toward the city while keeping the accelerator mashed to the floorboard. The helicopter banked and turned after him, while behind him, two of the six SUVs overshot the turn and smashed into each other. The remaining four filed in line behind him.

"You have a parking garage here? Any place I can hide from the chopper?"

"Fortress museum," came the reply from the backseat.

She was right. Vladivostok was teeming with sprawling, unique subterranean forts built in the late nineteenth century to fend off a Japanese invasion. Later, they'd been expanded right through the cold war to house Soviet platoons and matériel. They were extensive, empty, interconnected, and everywhere under the city.

"Which way?"

She poked her head up again and did a quick scan of their position. The noise of the chopper's rotors beat down on them like a machine gun.

"Ul Zapadnaya!" she screamed, and cowered back down, covering her ears with her hands.

He cut through the city, left, then left again, angling for the water once more. Every time an SUV attempted to slide in behind him, he cut off the angle.

The sun hit the water with a glancing blow as it descended, throwing harsh light into his eyes, and he squinted to fight off the glare. He dodged through light traffic like a mouse in a maze and then ducked left onto the wider Ul Zapadnaya. *Wider* is relative in Russia: this street managed to have two lanes going in the same direction. The chopper overhead swung low and practically filled his front windshield. He braked sharply, spun the Volga up on the curb, and cut over a grassy knoll toward the entrance to the fortress. Tourists were mostly absent at this hour, as the museum was thirty minutes from closing. Clay honked and snaked past a couple of bicyclists, then drove the sedan up the sidewalk bordering the fortress's entry point, almost losing control as his tires hugged the curb that protected the shrubbery along the fortress's side. As the SUVs swarmed behind, attempting to keep pace, Clay gritted his teeth and gunned the car for the glass doors of the tunnel entrance.

A sleepy ticket-taker barely managed to pivot out of the way as the Volga took out the glass and frame like a passing hurricane. Clay thought he heard Marika scream again, but it all got mixed up in the glass and debris and mayhem echoing inside the stone corridor.

One good thing about the fortress museum: they had left the tunnels intact, preserved, untouched. Two of the SUVs had overcome their reticence and barreled into the opening behind him, but the other two hung back with the helicopter, presumably to guard the exit if he should somehow manage to storm back out.

Inside, the tunnels featured curved stone ceilings and were narrow enough that only one vehicle could fit. The floor was uneven, marked with ruts, and Clay was jostled in the front seat like a lottery ball. He hoped the tires would hold.

Perpendicular tunnels opened to his right every hundred meters. If he could anticipate the pattern, then maybe he could—

Bam! He was bumped from behind, and then *bam!* Bumped again. Fifty feet to the next opening. Forty-five. Gunfire poured through the back windshield. Thirty-five, thirty. He spotted the pattern. He was sure of it. Right? Twenty-five. Twenty. If he hadn't got the pattern right, if he had measured incorrectly, it would end here, in this tunnel, with more questions than answers, and no one would know why he'd died or for whom. A bullet whistled past his shoulder, close enough to bury itself in the steering wheel. Ten, five.

He pulled the wheel down with all his strength, and the Volga was up to the challenge. It T-turned into an open tunnel, and the SUVs' inertia was too strong to make the same turn. They blundered past the entrance, then tangled as they realized the vehicle they were pursuing was no longer in their crosshairs. They wouldn't be untangling anytime soon.

Clay drove straight ahead for a good fifteen minutes before his tires blew.

They ditched the car and set off on foot, until they heard voices. Someone was calling the time, five-thirty, and announcing that Fort Seven was closing. They mingled with two dozen tourists and emerged fifteen kilometers north of downtown, without having to tussle with any security.

CHAPTER SIX

THE TRUTH lies in the darkness.

A man can move about during the day and fill his mind with decisions and conversations and busywork so he doesn't have to focus inward. When he crawls into bed at night, however, when it is just him and the blackness, he is forced to grow introspective. After the denials, after the protestations, after the justifications, the truth will creep in and plant its flag.

Nelson had failed his country. First, he had compromised himself by chasing an unsanctioned mission. Then he had botched that mission by getting caught. Then he had broken under torture and confessed to everything, offering every detail about who he was, how he worked, and what he had done since settling in St. Petersburg years ago. He had told them about his research into the life of Marika Csontos, and where he thought she might be hiding.

Was that somehow worse? Was throwing a young girl to the wolves even a greater betrayal than confessing state secrets? Somehow, it was. The Russians most likely knew most of what he'd told them about the way the CIA worked. He'd probably offered very few classified bits they weren't already privy to. He didn't even know the real names of other CIA officers. His confessions were probably typed up in a memo that sat on some low-ranking FSB official's computer. But Marika? He had given them a road map. If she wasn't in Stepnoy, then she was most likely with her stepbrother in Vladivostok.

Tears burned the corners of his eyes, here in the dark, with only his thoughts to sting him. The three omnipresent cameras would record his every move, but were they even watching him anymore?

He reached out and felt in the darkness for his cane where it leaned against the wall. He brought it back under the covers and rested it across his body. If his movements were noted by some sort of infrared camera, no one entered to let him know.

He felt around to the base of the cane and removed the rubber gripper. The cane was made of hard plastic, and originally, the end had been rounded off to form a knob. But Nelson had found that if he scraped it against a screw protruding from the back of his bed's headboard, he could start to shape it into a fine point. He worked for only about fifteen minutes each night, lest he make too much noise or movement. Afterward, he would put the rubber gripper back over the point and return the cane to its position against the wall before the sun shone through the curtains.

The first few nights, he was terrified he would wake to find the cane removed and Egorov standing in its place, that half smile disappearing behind his beard as he summoned the large men with gloves. But no one had punished him yet, and still his cane remained where he left it.

Scrape. Scrape. The point was growing sharp. He would work at it for a few minutes more, alone, with just his thoughts in the darkness to keep him company.

Adams stood in the lobby of the Renaissance hotel on Dupont Circle, waiting for the black Lincoln. He checked himself in the glass next to the elevator. Laura had bought him a new suit and picked out a matching tie and shirt. With so much going on in his head, he fired few neurons thinking about the way he dressed. This was what a great wife did—picked up his slack without asking. If he wasn't going to put any effort into the way he looked, she would make sure he dressed the part of a confident Central Intelligence district chief.

Right on time, a dark Lincoln pulled up to the curb and a young black officer ducked out of the driver's door and opened the rear door for him. Adams slid into the backseat and shook hands with Director Manning.

Contrary to expectations, Manning was a garrulous, warm personality with razor instincts and a gambler's guts. He'd survived two administrations by knowing which cards to lay down and which to keep tucked under the table.

He smiled at Adams. "Thanks for pit stopping in DC, Michael. How was the flight?"

"I can't complain."

"You never do."

The driver eased the car into the soup of traffic and headed toward the highway.

"The reason I wanted to grab you on your way to Prague... Michael, I'm gonna ask a favor."

"Name it."

"I'm gonna ask you to step up for me and run European Ops."

Adams tried to keep emotion off his face but wasn't sure he succeeded. Manning gave him a break by keeping his eyes forward.

"Now, I know it's a bit of an uproot, but I gotta put a man on that horse I know can ride it without getting tossed to the ground, understand?"

Adams spread his hands. "I'd say I'd think about it but you aren't going to let me, are you?"

"No, sir, I'm not."

"Then I accept."

"Good man. I wanted to get this in so you could announce it at the district head meeting and start to plan your transfer while you're there."

"You haven't told Dan?"

Dan Clausen was the head of the New York district office and had made no bones about his interest in taking over EurOps.

"If he wants to talk after, I'm all ears, but he's doing a fine job in New York and that's just the right size sandbox for him."

Clausen was not going to take this well, but it was part of the game and he'd have to lick his wounds and wait for the next opportunity. Adams wondered about the other district heads...what would their eyes look like when he announced the Director's decision? He had to admire Manning's tact: implying that this promotion would be doing him a favor instead of the other way around.

The car eased onto the beltway and headed toward Virginia.

What the hell is Laura going to say? Adams thought. But he knew the answer. *She's going to take up the slack like she always does.*

He smiled to himself and turned his eyes out the window as they passed the Jefferson Memorial, lit up bright against the soft purple of the evening sky.

Later, Adams stood along the Mall about halfway between the Washington and Lincoln Monuments. The moon was out and the park was well lit, but only a few tourists mingled on the far side of the reflecting pool. Adams liked it here. It might have been sentimental or saccharine, but he always felt a swell of patriotism when he visited the park. *Reflecting Pool* was an appropriate name; he caught his image in the still water and his thoughts turned to the telephone call that had changed his life.

Unlike many of his peers, Adams had sought out employment in Central Intelligence, rather than the other way around. He was a mathematics major at Princeton, had stayed there to receive his master's, and was staring down a long ivy-covered corridor at a career in academics. In the course of doing a spot of background work for his thesis, he'd stumbled across an obscure reference in the *Journal of Mathematics Research*. It pointed to an intelligence report that cited the burgeoning recruitment of young mathematicians into the CIA. He went to the library and read up all he could on American intelligence in the late twentieth century, contacted the placement office in Langley, and on a whim, filled out an application, stuck a stamp on it, and mailed it in.

Two months later, he had forgotten all about it, had defended his thesis and passed his oral exams, and had grown serious about asking Laura to marry him. He still couldn't believe that of all the men falling over her on that campus, she had chosen him. Each day, he felt sure she would stop seeing him, would laugh, explain it was all a joke, but that day never came.

The phone rang one night as they sat on his couch, watching a David Lynch movie on his secondhand VCR. "Mr. Adams?"

"Yes. This is Michael Adams."

"This is Kandus Simpson with the Central Intelligence Agency. We'd like you to travel to Virginia tomorrow morning for a formal interview."

He hung up, his throat dry. When he told Laura, she beamed and hugged him. He proposed marriage that night.

Whatever was going to happen to him, it would happen to them together.

The interview lasted nearly a week. It was unlike any corporate interview he'd ever heard of. It started with the basics—discussion of his goals and merits, where he'd worked, attended school, his family life, where he'd traveled, any extracurricular activities in which he'd participated. That first round concluded after a few pleasant hours in a few different offices.

At the end of that day, they asked him if he'd stay the night in Virginia; they might want to speak to him further. They put him up at a Doubletree and he slept uncomfortably, analyzing and reanalyzing the answers he'd given until they were all jumbled and he couldn't remember anything, even the questions.

The next morning, they added a lie detector to the mix. He was grilled about the European travels he had gone on during the summer after his sophomore year, a summer backpacking adventure that was so innocent as to be laughable, only no one in the room was laughing. They knew everywhere he'd been, everywhere he'd used his parents' credit card, every train ticket he'd bought. He tried to answer in as careful and considered a manner as he could, but he simply couldn't remember all the details. The dates when he'd visited Prague, the date when he'd missed his train in Berlin, the night he'd spent in a hospital in Paris. They knew more than he did. He tried to find some meaning, any meaning, in the examiner's expression, but he was at a loss. He asked for a break and they denied him one. At that point, he realized that they were testing more than his answers, maybe they were testing the *way* he responded, the *way* he handled the process as a whole. He was determined not to give them a single reason to doubt him. He had always been good at concentration, and he focused like a laser. When later they asked if he would like some water, he politely declined and told them to keep going.

Again they put him up in the Doubletree, and again he barely slept. He wanted to call Laura, but something told him maybe they were still watching him, even in this hotel room, and he would give them no arrows in their quill with which to shoot down his application.

The following two days were filled with math examinations. The exams started out easily enough, advanced algebra, spatial relationships, programming basics, but then they made the examinations progressively tougher. They introduced outside elements, like loud music and flashing lights, and still made him fill out paperwork, or move puzzle pieces around, or decode difficult ciphers. His concentration never flagged.

On the fifth day, he was seated with three other mathematicians and they were given a complex problem to solve. One man in the group, an older man with hard eyes and a clean-shaven face, insisted on his way of doing things, even though Adams could clearly see he was leading them down the wrong path. Adams started to interrupt him, but the man was insistent to the point of belligerence. They had been working half a day when the man suddenly erased half of their whiteboard and insisted they start over.

Adams had had enough. To the surprise of the other two younger men, who were frustrated but resigned that they wouldn't be able to solve the problem with the third man making it so difficult, Adams stood up and told the angry man to leave. The man stared at him incredulously with those hard eyes, but Adams folded his arms across his chest and stood his ground.

In an even voice that never rose, Adams dressed him down while outlining why he was wrong, why he was a bully, why he was actually retarding the process instead of moving it forward, and why, as a team, they wouldn't solve the problem while he remained in the room.

The man started to protest again, and Adams just shook his head, pointed to the door, and said, "Leave." The man approached Adams as if he were going to hit him in the face, but instead handed him his erasable marker and left.

"Now, let's get to it," Adams said to the other two, and they redoubled their efforts, solving the problem with only a few minutes to spare before their time was up.

For the fifth straight night, Adams was asked to stay in Virginia, and this time, he called Laura from the hotel phone, told her he was okay and that he loved her, and that he had no idea whether he was going to have a career in intelligence or she was going to be a professor's wife. Her voice was strong and supportive on the other end of the line. "All I want is for you to do what you love, and for us to be together." He hung up, feeling as refreshed as if he'd taken a shower. That night, he had his first good night's sleep since he'd arrived.

On the sixth day, he sat in a waiting room, staring at a clock on the wall. They had always come for him within a minute of 8 a.m., and here it was already ten till nine, and no one had checked to see if he was in the room. After an eternity, a door opened and a woman he hadn't met before ushered him down a corridor.

At the end stood a door with a nameplate: DEPUTY DIRECTOR OF CENTRAL INTELLIGENCE ANDREW MANNING. The woman opened the door and Adams walked inside. A man stood up from behind the desk and crossed toward him. Adams was shocked. It was the man from the fifth day, the one who had been so disruptive, the man Adams had forced to leave.

He smiled, his eyes much softer than they had been before, and stuck out his hand. "Welcome to Central Intelligence, Michael. I'm Deputy Director Manning. I must say, you've impressed the hell out of me."

For the first time in nearly a week, Adams was flustered. "Thank you."

"We're expecting great things from you," Manning said, draped his arm over Adams's shoulder, and guided him to a chair.

All these years later, Adams believed he had finally exceeded those expectations. His reflection in the pool hadn't changed; not even an insect had landed on the water to upset its smoothness.

His phone rang and he retrieved it from his pocket.

"Sir?"

"Hello, Warren. Are we on a secure line?"

He waited a few seconds, then heard the familiar clicks and beeps. "We are now."

"I have some news, and I expect you to be discreet."

"Of course." He could hear the tremor in Warren's voice, and it pleased him. His wife might have to fake her enthusiasm for this promotion, but Warren would barely be able to contain his glee. Adams realized that was probably why he wanted to tell Warren first but pushed that thought from his mind.

"The DCI asked me to head EurOps. It won't be announced until the district heads' meeting in Prague, but I want you to start thinking about the transition."

"Yes, of course. Discreetly, of course. Yes. I'm on it. Right away."

"I knew you would be, Warren." Adams hesitated for a second, then proceeded. "I'm going to promote you to case officer after I settle in. You've proven to me you're ready."

"I appreciate that, sir. Nothing would please me more."

"I know. I'll talk to you after I land in Europe."

"Yes, sir. And thank you for your faith in me."

"You've earned it."

Adams hung up and smiled. He felt a paternal pride, and maybe that was why he had risen as far and as fast as he had: because he felt as if the Agency were a family. His family.

A couple passed him on their way toward the Washington Monument, and he watched their hands clasp in the reflection of the pool.

CHAPTER SEVEN

HE LET her cry.

Two hours directly north of Vladivostok, they found an empty country house, not much more than a log cabin that would've made Huckleberry Finn feel right at home. It stood alone, deep off a crooked dirt road, surrounded by old-growth forest and so dusty as to cause clouds to rise from their footsteps. In the years since Communism, so many of these dachas had simply been abandoned. With a confusion of property rights, elderly owners found it easier to just jettison a property than to fill out the mounds of requisite paperwork. Of course, many of these citizens had died, and the records of the houses' existence had died with them.

Clay didn't interrupt her sobbing, didn't offer a handkerchief, didn't rest his hand on her shoulder. Her stepbrother had died, her world had crumbled, and every dream she had held for her life had evaporated. She had learned one of life's cruelest lessons: sometimes you pay for other people's mistakes.

So he let her cry and he did not hold it against her. He had learned that lesson many years before, a different life ago.

Austin Clay was born to Craig and Melissa Clay under a blisteringly hot Louisiana sun. His father had waited too late to drive his mother to the hospital, and she had given birth to Austin pulled to the side of the road, his father stooped half in and half out of the passenger seat. Austin was the city in which he had been conceived. Although his parents remembered the location, the night itself was a little fuzzy. That town did three things right—barbecue, beer, and music—and the Clays partook of all three over the course of that weekend.

Austin was loved. That had been clear to him from the time before he could consciously remember. It was a feeling; it was images: his father's arms, his mother's hair, the toys, the crib, a laugh, a kiss, friends, a blanket, a bear, sunshine, a fire, a song, bare feet, warmth, laughter. They were there, with him, part of him, real, as real as he made them.

His father worked for a candymaker and smelled of sugar. His mother worked in the front office of a car dealership but took a leave of absence to have him and never went back. They lived in a house on a street lined with houses just like theirs, where wooden fences marked the property lines but all the neighbors knew each other by first name. He remembered that his mom made costumes for him: a pirate with a paper beard one day and a cowboy with a gold star pinned to his shirt the next. He was loved; she loved him; she told him every morning, whispered it to him every night. He could climb into her voice and take a nap.

They died with their names on a police report but not in the paper. They had hired a babysitter to give them a night out, a respite, an evening for themselves. When they stopped at the grocery store, it had been because of a joke. He pretended he was going to take her to the deli counter, but he really had reservations at the French restaurant downtown. It was their sixth anniversary.

A former employee named Larry Blank walked into the store holding an automatic pistol. He had been fired three days earlier, when it was discovered he had drilled a hole into the women's bathroom and he was caught with his pants down in the adjacent broom closet. When his wife learned of the circumstances surrounding his sudden dismissal, she absconded with their two children. Blank thought the manager of the store, Steve Latier, must've told her the details of his sudden ouster. Latier was a gossip who liked to flap his gums and had ogled Blank's wife on more than one occasion when she came in to buy diapers. The disgraced employee didn't have much of a plan except to kill that prissy asshole, but—as he admitted to the court-appointed psychiatrist later—when he psyched himself up to walk into the store and shoot, he saw only red, bright red, went through the automatic doors, and started firing. He remembered nothing from there, not how many times he pulled the trigger, not how long it all took—just red, and then he was knocked off his feet by the same officious son of a bitch he had walked in to kill. When he later learned he had ended the lives of seven people, including a state senator, his response had been "No," as if they were telling him something that had happened to someone else. "No, that couldn't be right."

The state senator, a popular Mormon who had served three terms and was short-listed for a congressional run, received all the press, of course. Clay's mother and father were always included within the phrase *and six others*.

They left no wills. They weren't yet in their thirties and thought they had all the time in the world. Wills, trusts—those were for old people, for sick people. What did they have to bequeath, anyway? They were just getting started.

Craig Clay had a brother named Bobby. A court investigator found him on a sailboat docked in San Diego. He was the only living relative of the six-year-old boy left behind when his parents were murdered simply for walking into the wrong grocery store at the wrong time.

Bobby cleaned himself up, put on a button-down shirt, clean jeans, and socks, flew halfway across the country, and appeared in court to claim the boy and the two-hundred-and-eighty-seven-thousand-dollar life insurance payout. Forty-eight hours later, Austin Clay stepped onto his uncle's boat for the first time. He would rarely step off it for the next nine years.

The abuse was never sexual. With the hefty insurance claim, Uncle Bobby loaded up with liquor, pulled anchor, and set sail for open water. He had a vague notion—maybe the only romantic notion he'd ever had—that he would sail around the world, teaching the boy about life, about sailing, about travel, about women, and would give him a real education, not the kind they taught you in brick-and-mortar schools. He had always kept his drinking in check before; he'd been responsible enough to support himself chartering out to tourists from Baja to Santa Barbara. But something about the open water, about the financial windfall, about the plentiful supply of liquor in the stores, loosened his will, and he found himself nipping more from the bottles each day.

Any plans he had to teach the boy died in the first three months at sea. Austin discovered a survival instinct that was innate—if he was going to live, he would have to teach himself every inch of that boat. He'd have to know how to tie the knots, how to jib, how to tack, how to adjust the boom, how to keep the engine tuned, how to keep the oil out of the bilge, how to fish, how to cook, how to clean, and how to make himself small when his uncle balled his fists.

He woke to see Marika staring at him. She had pulled all the curtains across the windows so the only light inside the cabin came from a dusty floor lamp. Her hands were in her lap and her eyes were wide, like a naturalist observing a wild animal.

Clay sat up and rubbed his temples. Truth be told, his head was pounding. He didn't get headaches often, but when they came, they were beasts. He stood up, and she flinched. He thought about ignoring it, but something made him hold his palms up and say to her, "It's okay. I'm on your side."

She nodded but kept her expression neutral, closed.

"Is there clean water here?"

She nodded and pointed to a tiny kitchenette.

He returned in a few moments with two full glasses and set one in front of her. He gestured for her to drink and she complied.

"None of this is your fault. I want you to know that."

She nodded and then said, "It doesn't matter."

Well, that is good, Clay thought. *She's rational about it, which means she's not in shock*. He wondered how long he'd slept. His headache was easing. He fought the urge to go over and open the curtain, gauge where the sun stood in the sky, but the next few minutes would go a long way toward establishing trust, and Marika wasn't ready to be exposed to windows anytime soon.

"Do you know if there's a phone here?"

"Next to the bed in the bathroom. I did not try it."

"Okay, listen. I'm going to make a call to a man in the United States. He is going to arrange for us to leave the country and go where no one can harm you, where no one will find you, yes?"

"How do you know?"

"Because this is what I do. I promise I'll keep you safe if you'll do as I say when I say it."

"You didn't keep David safe."

"No, I didn't. I'm not infallible. But I am very good at my job and I hate to say it, but David was not my mission.

You were my mission. And now my job is to get you out of here. You have my word that I'm going to successfully do that."

She nodded again, but he wasn't sure whether it indicated acceptance or was just to get him to stop talking.

He stood and finished his water. She stared down at her half-filled glass. He wanted to hold her, to hug her, to protect her with his arms, but he didn't.

Stedding's voice was gruffer than usual.

"They want an exchange."

"What?"

"Nelson for the girl."

"How did you— Who wants an exchange?"

"Both sides. Deliver Marika Csontos to the embassy in Moscow, then check in when you're out of the country. I'll meet you in Europe for a debriefing and we'll discuss your next assignment."

"I'm afraid I don't understand, Stedding."

He waited a moment, unsure if his handler was still on the line. Finally, the voice came through, strained as tight as a guitar string. "What don't you understand?"

"I found her just as an elite FSB team was trying to put an end to her. Now you're asking me to turn her over so they can...what? Finish the job?"

"Wrong. I'm not asking you to do anything. I'm commanding you. These marching orders are directly from the DCI, and you will follow them. There's a shitstorm brewing between Moscow and DC right now, and you're at the heart of it. Getting Nelson back was the mission; it still is the mission. The key, as you said, was finding the girl, and you did that. Now dropping her off will get our asset back, and you'll get to keep working autonomously and anonymously, and some secret commendation will go in some secret file in the basement of Langley and you'll be on to the next thing."

The dull ache in Clay's head was back.

"All right, Stedding."

"Now I'm worried. Where's the wise-ass response?"

"My head's pounding. I'll work up some barbs later."

"When can you get to Moscow?"

"Three days."

"Talk to you then."

The line clicked and buzzed and fell silent.

He waited a few minutes, then returned to the big room. Marika had not stirred from her spot.

"If you want to clean up or rinse off or do whatever you need to do to get ready, we're leaving in ten minutes."

"Where are we going?"

"Moscow."

She whitened, so he added, "The American embassy there," but he kept his eyes lowered. He knew what he had to do, so he had already thrown a mental switch. She was not a *she* anymore, not to him. She was a folder, a file, a pack—something he had acquired and now needed to turn over to his own government. It had to be this way. He had a job to do, and this assignment ended in Moscow, and it didn't matter what happened after that because she would be somebody else's problem. There it was again. Not *she*. It.

She watched him, unblinking, but didn't say anything. It was as though she'd been reading his thoughts and now didn't know how to handle him, as if she couldn't keep up with the shaking sand underneath her feet. After a minute, she rose, went into the bathroom, and shut the door. Soon after, he heard the water in the shower running. It would be cold but clean.

The water in Brazil was warm. His uncle had guided them to Paraty to stock up on gas, food, and most importantly, liquor. It was January, so the weather was sunny, and they had hugged the Brazilian coast for more than a month, parked outside Ilha Grande, fishing and keeping to themselves. Occasionally a yacht would sail close. His uncle would be awkward on good days and rude when he was drunk, and the chance for human contact would evaporate like a mirage. Every now and then, Clay would spot a child on board one of these cruisers and they would stare at each other, but they might as well have had the entire ocean between them.

"Check on the bilge," his uncle would say. Or just "Head below," and he would enter his tiny cabin, lie on his bunk, and stare at the ceiling until his vision blurred.

Run.

He couldn't say when the idea first crept into his thoughts, but it had seemed to possess him from the time he was seven.

Run.

He had been through kindergarten before his parents died, and he had been one of the early readers in Ms. Britton's class. He had learned all the sight words—*the, a, into, but, and, go,* a hundred others—and he had the foundation for putting sounds to letters. Blessedly, his uncle liked to read while he drank and had a collection of historical and crime fiction Clay could pinch. Books like *Eye of the Needle* and *The Eagle Has Landed* became his elementary school primers.

The book that saved him, though, was *The Mouse That Roared.* He picked it up thinking maybe he'd finally found a book written for him, for his age, but though it turned out to have been written for adults, it was different from anything else he'd read. The book centered on a tiny forgotten pissant country that stole an atom bomb out of New York City and brought the world's powers to their knees. It was hilarious and ludicrous and satirical, but an idea was planted in his mind and took shape. The mouse *could* roar.

Run.

Two girls with long legs and short bikinis told his uncle about Paraty. If he docked there, he could load up on everything he needed, *anything* he needed. Clay was ten, but even he knew what they meant.

He was only allowed off the boat to help load supplies, and this time would be no exception. A few bruises under his shirt and a cigarette burn on his side let him know the price of trying to talk to anyone while they were docked.

Run.

He would wait until his uncle had been gone an hour and

then he would do it. Any shorter than an hour and he risked that the bastard would have stopped at the nearest bar with a clear view of the port. Any longer and maybe his uncle would stumble home early after annoying the wrong bartender. One hour and then he'd take off.

When he heard his uncle's heavy footsteps lift from the deck onto the dock, he started the count, but every minute burned away as hot and slow as roasting embers. He could feel his heart racing and he tried his best to calm it, but that only made the beating worse. He couldn't sit still for the full hour. After twenty-seven minutes, when it felt as if the walls of his cabin were going to press him flat, he stuck his head out of the hatch and looked around. The sun was down and the docks appeared empty. Laughter drifted over from somewhere to his left, and the sound buoyed him. He breathed once, choked down a stomach spasm, and made his move.

No one stopped him.

The street at the end of the dock twisted up toward an old mission and was lined with souvenir shops. Christmas lights blinked over the shop fronts, and multicolored flags and pennants crisscrossed above the street. Was it Christmas already? Had it passed? He couldn't remember.

His legs felt wobbly and the horizon seemed to roll as if the earth were made of water. He didn't know if that was from being at sea for so long or from his heart exploding inside his chest. A screen door slammed to his right and he jumped. A couple stumbled out, hands all over each other, but the man was too tall to be his uncle. Some kids a little older than him moved his way, kicking a soccer ball, and they stared at him as if he were in an aquarium. One called to him in a language he didn't understand. The smile on the kid's face conveyed the opposite of what that expression generally intends.

Clay turned on his heels just as a pair of military police officers stepped out of an apartment doorway. The kid said something to him again and took a step forward, holding his hands up while his friends laughed.

Clay shook his head and hurried over to the officers.

"You must help me."

The first officer stepped aside so his partner could stoop down. The man had soft eyes and a kind face. "English?" he asked gently.

"American."

"Are you hurt?"

"No. Yes... I—"

"What're you doing there?" Uncle Bobby's voice erupted just behind him. Clay catapulted behind the officers, tucking in behind their legs.

"This boy is yours?"

"I'm his uncle. We're Americans."

Clay could see his chance evaporating. He made a decision to lay everything on the table. "He kidnapped me! He beats me! Look! Look!"

Clay pulled up his shirt and showed the purple bruises in clear relief against his skin. The kind officer ran his fingers over the splotches, then wheeled on his uncle.

"This is a serious thing."

His uncle's nostrils flared and he glared fire at the boy. *Just walk away,* Clay thought. *Just walk away and sail away and leave me here. I'm not worth the trouble.*

A kind of grudging resolve replaced the anger on his uncle's face. He reached into his back pocket, fished out his wallet, and withdrew a fistful of bills.

"All right, Officers. Sorry to inconvenience you. Here's a bonus to the Federale fund." He thrust the bills forward while Clay watched, his stomach lurching. The two officers stared at the proffered bills but didn't take them. Clay's uncle sighed, licked his thumb, and counted out five more bills. This time he pressed them into the kind-looking officer's hand. His fingers then circled Clay's small wrist and jerked him away from the apartment's stoop, back toward the dock. Clay dug his heels in like a dog fighting a leash.

"No!" he screamed, and reached back for the Brazilian officers, but they stood there dumb, immobile. With every bit of his strength, Clay wrenched his wrist down, freeing himself. Surprised, he spun like a top and began to run for the streets.

He made it only two steps before he felt the wind knocked out of his stomach as a foot flew out of nowhere to catch him flush in the gut. He crumpled over from the kick as the kind-faced police officer pulled his foot back. Then he felt himself picked up by the collar and handed back over to his uncle, who nodded appreciatively.

That was the day Clay learned that all men had a price, some cheaper than others. It was a lesson he would keep at the forefront of his mind until he was dead.

They dumped the car for a truck and the truck for a van as they headed west. She slept most of the first day, and he preferred it that way. Sleeping meant not talking, and not talking meant he could keep on thinking of her as an object. He had sacked the pantry of a tiny restaurant on the outskirts of Khabarovsk and taken cans of beans and boxes of crackers from the backs of shelves. The theft would go unnoticed, at least for a little while. Russian agents would be scouring all the police reports around Vladivostok for any signs of the fugitives. He hoped they would believe he'd keep heading east, catch a freighter over to Japan, out of the country, as soon as he had the girl. Instead, he followed a northern route through Siberia, swinging up through the plains, though not so high up as to hit snow.

He looked over and the girl was staring at him. He grimaced, looked away, and when he looked again, she was still watching his face. If she weren't so goddamn stunning, this would be—

"You never told me your name," she said.

He ran through the checklist of his thoughts—*Don't tell her, use a cover name*—and then, for some reason he couldn't explain, crossed them off and said, "Austin."

She repeated it, and it sounded funny in her pronunciation. For the first time, a smile broke across her face and lit up the car. He was glad he had told her his name.

"Have you been to Los Angeles?" she asked.

He thought the question funny but didn't want to embarrass her. "Once or twice."

"It is my dream to go there."

"You want to be discovered?"

"Discovered?"

"Act in movies?"

"Oh, no. I have no talent for it. I want to see Mickey Mouse."

"Ahhh..."

"Do you think they will let me do that?"

A twinge of pain rippled through Clay, but he kept it off his face. "I'm sure they will."

She folded her hands in her lap, pleased. "Are there many Hungarians in Los Angeles?"

"There are many everything there."

She laughed. "When you came through the door, I thought you were the most frightening man I'd ever seen. I am pleased to know you are funny."

He should just stop, stop talking, stop engaging, and drive on, keep the conversation short, trifling, but he seemed powerless to check himself. The snowball was already rolling downhill, and an avalanche seemed inevitable. What was it about this girl?

"Do you have children?"

"No."

"Wife?"

He shook his head. "No."

"It is forbidden?"

"It's just too hard in this line of work. I have to..." He searched for the correct Russian term. "Keep secrets? Leave for a new destination at any time. Sometimes for months...

years. It would be difficult...very difficult for a wife. It would be unfair of me to put anyone through that. Selfish, yes?"

She nodded. "I would like to be married someday. There was a boy on my street named Jani I thought would marry me."

"Yes?"

"His parents moved away. I don't know where they went. One day he was my neighbor and the next he was gone. It was a long time ago." She wiped her hands on her pants leg as though she were wiping away the memory.

"I'm sure you'll find many willing suitors in California."

"I'll have to learn English."

"Yes."

"Can you teach me?"

"I don't—"

"How do you say *chicken*?"

He laughed. "Why *chicken*?"

"I like chicken."

He told her how to say it in English and she did her best to repeat it.

A new thought occurred to him. What if she was on to him, had observed his change in demeanor and concluded he was not willing to help her anymore? What if this conversation in the car was an act, a way to humanize her in his mind, a way to get him to connect with her, care for her? Was she that calculating? Was it an innate survival mechanism? That smile? The warmth, the honesty of her voice? The sensitivity in her eyes?

My God, he thought. *If this is all a scheme, it's working.*

"What did you hear?"

Her smile faded. "Hear?"

"The Kremlin official. Your employer. Benidrov. What did he tell you that put you in so much danger?"

She turned her eyes to the window. A vast plain stretched out to the horizon. Theirs was the only vehicle for twenty miles in either direction.

Her voice cracked as she spoke. "He told me so many things that didn't make sense—names, people, departments within the government—I had never heard of them. It was all meaningless to me. It was all so stupid. Meaningless and stupid. I didn't ask him to tell me these things."

"If it was all meaningless, why did you run?"

"He frightened me. He would say things." She lowered her voice to imitate him. "'You don't understand what I'm telling you, my little flower, and that is good. If you did I'd have to pluck out all your petals.' Every day, he'd say this to me. Vomit out his nonsense and then brag about me not knowing what he was saying while threatening me at the same time. The tension built and built until I couldn't take it anymore. How he learned I knew Russian I don't know, but he came home and tried to strangle me. But he couldn't even do that right. I managed to get my knee into him and ran off with nothing but the clothes on my back. I heard he killed himself after that. I knew I had to disappear, but all I can tell you is I don't remember anything he told me. Not one word of it."

She was lying about the last part. He could tell by the way her eyes darted down and to the left—a giveaway so common it was referred to as the Liar's Look at Langley. So she did remember something Benidrov had told her, but Clay knew better than to press right now. She was frightened and vulnerable and defensive, and if he played this poorly, she might retreat.

"I said it before. It's not your fault. None of it is your fault."

"Yes. You said it. And I wish to believe it. But if I hadn't run to David, if I had just vanished, then he would still be alive."

"And you'd be dead and they still would have targeted your family because they would want to be sure you hadn't told them anything." He could see on her face that she hadn't thought of that. "You did the right thing under extraordinary pressure."

She nodded and then, as if to reassure herself, nodded again. "Thank you."

"Thank me when you're at Disneyland."

"I will."

She grinned and turned again to the window. A few minutes later, he heard her breathing grow steady as she drifted to sleep.

What does she know? he thought. *What's important enough that they sent an army to kill her?*

The sun dropped behind them, and only the hum of the van's engine kept his thoughts company.

CHAPTER EIGHT

It was dumb and it was dangerous and it was so unlike Clay's modus operandi as to have no precedent. There would be no ledger for this side excursion; he couldn't think in those terms, because he knew it would bankrupt the mission ten times over.

They would be watching her, he was sure of it, and that made the stop ridiculous. Still, Marika had asked him if a visit would be possible, had said that the woman had offered them a chance for a meal and a bath before they ventured into Moscow, and it was the urgency of the way she asked that pierced his defenses. The woman was named Natasha Chkeidze and had been a maid in Benidrov's house at the same time that Marika had worked as a nanny. Natasha had selflessly harbored Marika in those first twenty-four hours when the young woman fled—she had given Marika money and food and bought her some clothes, and if she was alive and unharmed, she had most certainly withstood FSB interrogation in the aftermath of Benidrov's suicide. Marika owed her life to this woman and wanted to thank her. Clay and she understood it would be Marika's last chance to do so, though they expected it to be for different reasons.

Natasha lived in a twenty-story apartment building in a southeastern suburb of Moscow near the Promzona metro station. This section of the city was mostly industrial, and the citizens who lived here weren't quite as prosperous as the ones in the southwest, near the university.

Clay parked in a garage two blocks away.

"Wait here. Don't leave the car. Keep your head down. I'll be back in two hours."

"And if you don't return?"

"Then get yourself to the US embassy any way you can, understand?"

She nodded.

He took the full two hours. She looked as relieved to see him as if he had just saved her from drowning.

"The building looks clear. If FSB visited your friend, it was a while ago and they didn't leave a permanent surveillance team to watch the building. They didn't know we'd come to Moscow. They have to believe we're out of the country, so we have surprise on our side, too. On top of all that, it's a dumb move for us to make, and I don't think they're expecting me to make a dumb move."

"So dumb is good?"

"I wouldn't go that far. Come... let's make this quick."

"She's there? My friend?"

"Yeah. I saw her check her mail and return to her apartment."

Clay helped Marika out of the van and they crossed a congested street to enter an alley. The smog was as thick as fog here. No wonder so many people living in this city had bronchial asthma.

"We go in the back and up the service elevator. If I catch wind of anything odd, I yank you out of there and you follow as fast as those legs will carry you, yes? No good-byes, no hugs, no tears... we run for the car and don't look back."

"I understand. And thank you. I promise not to burden you for much longer."

"What makes you think stopping at your friend's apartment in the middle of a national manhunt is a burden?"

She punched Clay in the shoulder playfully, and he feigned a wince. It was good to see her act like a teenager instead of a woman who had seen and heard too much over the last month. They approached the building, and Clay swept the alley with practiced eyes. Nothing. If someone was watching, then they were better at this than him.

The pair of fugitives popped inside a brown steel door that led to the building's furnace room. Six old-fashioned boilers with Cyrillic lettering made a hissing sound as they passed.

They forwent the elevator for the stairs and soon stood outside Natasha's seventh-floor apartment door. Marika balled a fist, but Clay stayed her hand, then easily picked the lock, allowing them both to slip inside. They could hear chopping in the kitchen; it sounded like someone dicing a vegetable on a cutting board.

"Natasha?" Marika called softly, and the dicing immediately stopped.

Clay's antennae went up and he tensed but didn't pull out his weapon. The last thing he needed was a hysterical woman screaming her head off in a cramped apartment.

Natasha appeared in the kitchen entrance, her hair covered in a scarf, her cheeks red and her eyes already wet.

"Marika? Is it really you, *solnyshko*?" She looked back and forth between them as if she thought she might be having a hallucination.

"Yes, it's me." The large woman opened her arms and Marika bounded across the distance between them, burying herself in the woman's ample bosom.

"Shhh. Shhh, *solnyshko*. Shhh, little sun. It's all right," the woman cooed, and Clay realized Marika was sobbing. He excused himself and headed to the bathroom, leaving Marika to explain who he was. He'd seen more emotion over the last few weeks than he had in the previous few years. He didn't need to see any more.

They sipped black tea in glass mugs while Marika laid out the events that had led her back to Moscow. Natasha patted her knee and refilled her mug when the level of the tea neared the bottom. The woman could make damn good tea, Clay had to admit.

When Marika concluded her tale, Natasha clucked and said, "When masters are fighting, the servants' forelocks are creaking." Marika nodded, but Clay could tell she didn't quite understand the expression.

"It's an old Russian proverb... it means when powerful people fight, it is the commoners who suffer."

"Yes, I see what you mean," Marika offered to her friend.

"You must stay the night," Natasha insisted.

Clay began to protest, but the big woman would not be dissuaded. "Look at you two. You both look like you haven't slept in months. Your eyes are as red as the devil. And you smell like a barn. Bathe, then sleep, then be on your way."

"Please," Marika importuned softly, afraid of his answer.

Clay shook his head but was surprised to hear himself say, "Okay."

He grew older and the beatings worsened. His uncle was like a lion that worries about a cub growing strong enough to challenge him so wounds it while he can.

He hectored Clay constantly, the criticisms and jabs becoming so commonplace as to fail to even register. The boy didn't respond, didn't give his uncle further provocation.

At first, he started swimming just to get away. An hour in the water meant an hour alone, no voices, no complaints, no pain. He waited until Uncle Bobby had drunk himself absent, then stripped down, lowered the ladder, looped a line to his ankle, and dove in, no matter where they were or what the ocean was like. It was dark and dangerous and lonely and empty and he could easily have been swept away from the boat, but the truth was, he didn't care. If he died, he died. If the ocean took him, then so be it. There were times when he felt like pulling free the tether, spreading his arms and just fading to the bottom. His uncle would wake from his stupor and call out and there would be no one to answer, and he would shout more loudly, more angrily, and only then would he realize the kid was gone, baby, gone. Or maybe Clay should cut himself and dangle from the line like chum and wait for something large and massive to strike him. What would he feel in that last moment? Pain? Or relief? Instead, he just drifted, weightless, and opened his mind, cleared his mind, and found what all humans seek, even young men: peace. He grew more empowered as his body grew stronger, and his stays in the water lasted longer and longer, until he was swimming twenty minutes, thirty, an hour. Once, he did dive in without the rope linking him back to the boat, and he was shocked at how quickly the distance widened between them. He'd been in the water for less than a minute and the boat seemed a mile away. His heart raced and panic filled his head. A new feeling spread over him, one he didn't know he possessed: strength. He kicked and dug his hands into the ocean and ignored the current, ignored the salt spray licking his face, ignored the wall of blackness that seemed to cover the ocean surface like a blanket each time a wave rolled between him and the boat. He was tired, he was out of oxygen, but he found that strength growing deep inside him, and before he knew it, he was at the ladder again, standing in the vastness with no one to acknowledge his accomplishment. His uncle hadn't stirred.

And that was when his idea metastasized.

It didn't happen often in open water, but occasionally they would pass another boat. Not a tanker or an enormous cruise ship, but a trawler or a sailboat or a touring yacht like theirs. The boats would pass in the night and sometimes the other vessel would flash a floodlight, but Clay's uncle was always too far in his cups to respond. Clay didn't know when the next opportunity would present itself, so he waited and watched the horizon.

Four months later, four months of nothing but emptiness and his uncle's fists and swimming in the darkness with the taste of salt on his lips, in his nostrils, and he saw it. He was nearly asleep, just about to head below deck to his cabin, when he saw a light on the horizon. His pulse quickened and he was suddenly as alert as if he'd stuck his finger in a socket. He kept watching—maybe the ship was going to veer in the wrong direction; maybe its trajectory would take it too far away. The wind was picking up, too; perhaps the sea would grow too choppy. As he watched, though, the light steadily grew larger. He found a pair of binoculars and could just make out the vague outline of a yacht, bow pointed his way.

He looked over at his uncle, snoring steadily in a hammock he'd stretched out on the deck, an empty bottle of whiskey curled under his elbow. Clay's breath quickened, like a sprinter psyching himself up before the starter's pistol fires. Could he do this?

The light kept coming. It was do it now or wait for another

opportunity, and who knew when that would present itself? He had to act; he had to do this now.

He stole one more look at the yacht's light, and yes, it would pass within a couple of miles of their position, he was sure of it, and before his doubts could paralyze him, he sprang for the hatch and practically fell down the steps.

He passed his cabin without looking inside; the room held no fuzzy feelings for him. Instead, he put his shoulder into the door of his uncle's cabin, and on the second thrust, it gave. Breathing hard, eyes raking the bed, the desk, the shelves, he stepped inside and moved toward a jar. The top wouldn't open without popping a couple of latches, but he was too worked up, too pressed for time, so he smashed the jar on the floor, then snatched up the cash lying among the shards. There must've been five hundred dollars there in various denominations. He didn't know if he'd need money, but he was thinking clearly enough to know that it might help him in a bind.

As he was reaching for the last twenty-dollar bill, he heard a rustling at the door.

"Whatchoo—whatchoo doin'?" His uncle blinked at him in a stupor, like a man waking in a front yard he doesn't recognize. Clay had panic written all over his face, and it seemed to knock some sobriety into his uncle's eyes.

The boy put his head down and decided to charge past, hoping Uncle Bobby's reflexes would be too diminished to stop him, and he had almost made it, had almost sidestepped his uncle cleanly, when he felt cold fingers close around his elbow.

"Whattiz this?"

Clay tried to wrestle his arm free, but Uncle Bobby held him in an iron grip. "Y'anssser me!" he slurred. Then his eyes lighted on the money in Clay's hands....

"Let go."

"You wuz robbing me."

"Let go!"

But Bobby's nostrils flared and his eyes disappeared into slits and he shoved Clay back hard across the galley, slamming the boy into the unyielding cabinet.

The boat, Clay thought. *The boat*.

He tried to get up, but Uncle Bobby stumbled toward him, crossing the distance in two steps. Clay kicked out with his foot, and if Bobby hadn't been drunk the kick might not have made a dent, but it caught Bobby's foot just as the heel was coming down and Bobby slipped and fell back against the oven, banging his head.

Clay stood up. Bobby didn't move. He had to step over his uncle to get to the hatch, but as he crossed, Bobby grabbed his leg, and he was still strong enough to heave the boy across the galley floor. Clay slid headfirst into the bilge room door, which smashed open from the momentum.

Clay's head felt as if someone had stuck pins in it, and he blinked blood out of his eye to see Bobby trying to rise to his feet, moving as slowly and gracelessly as a walrus. The smell of gas from the bilge hit Clay's nostrils and gave him an idea. A ludicrous idea, but he couldn't think clearly, couldn't think of consequences, as those two words echoed like a mantra in his ears...*the boat, the boat, the boat*.

He reached over and pulled the feed line out of the engine so that fuel flowed from the stripped black hose. It splattered over him, but he didn't care. He lurched up quickly and dashed back to the counter, bumping into Uncle Bobby as he did, which sent Bobby flopping onto his face. Clay flipped open the first cabinet drawer and rummaged quickly until his hands found what he was looking for, a weathered box of kitchen matches.

He backed up until his feet were near the ladder leading up to the deck. The yacht would be passing soon. He shook out a matchstick. When he struck the match, it flared, and for just a moment, he saw his uncle turn his head to look up at him from his hands and knees. What is it about fire on the tip of a match that gives us pause?

Clay returned his uncle's hard-eyed stare, threw the match toward the bilge room, and flew up the ladder. He heard the sound of the engine blowing, felt heat on the back of his neck, but he was too focused on the horizon to flinch. The yellow light was still there, glowing ever closer. Clay stripped off his shirt and his shorts, hurried quickly to the rail near the bow, snatched up a life jacket, and prepared to dive into the black water. As his legs crouched to jump, he was thrown off-balance by a hand once again seizing his arm.

Bobby's face was black, the skin on one side melted, stringy. The flames rose out of the cabin behind him and shone a bright orange in the darkness.

"You were going to kill me." He said it almost to himself, as if he were having trouble believing such a thing. Then his face twisted into an evil so stark naked that, for the first time in a long time, it truly terrified the boy. Clay reacted instinctively, throwing a punch with his free hand right into the throat of his tormentor. It was the first time he'd ever fought back, and the blow startled Uncle Bobby more than it stung him, but it was enough that he spilled backward, letting go of Clay's arm—but not before jerking him back onto the deck. Even untrained in close-quarters fighting, Clay knew he had Uncle Bobby off-balance, so he kicked him in the side and sent him flopping ass-over-teakettle onto his back like a bluegill pulled into the boat. The fire hit the reserve tank and it blew. The boat lurched up and then back down again as its stern started to take on water. Clay pirouetted and ran for the bow. Uncle Bobby flipped out a hand and caught him in the ankle, a lucky lurch, which caused Clay's two feet to bang together, and he stumbled, lost his footing, and knocked his knee into the step leading to the rail. Bobby tried to rise to his feet, the flames whipping behind him, the boat capsizing. He looked like a devil, *the* devil, his mouth twisted, his teeth bared, his hands clenched, his eyes red. Clay snuck a quick glance over his shoulder and saw that yellow light, now less than a mile away and coming closer. He looked back at his uncle and knew he couldn't just jump off, leave him to drown. No, that wouldn't be enough.

Clay launched himself through the air and met Uncle Bobby with a kick to the chest. His heel popped Bobby squarely in the breastbone, and his uncle went over backward into the hatch, right into the mouth of the fire like a pig pushed into the oven, the devil stuffed back into hell. Clay heard screams as loud as a klaxon and then took two paces, sprang to the step, and leapt over the bow, ignoring the pain in his knee. The sea rose to meet him, and only then did he realize he'd forgotten the life jacket in the fight. He hit the water and brought his head to the surface, kicking, treading, bobbing like a cork. It took only a moment for the firelight to flicker and die as the ocean overtook the boat and pulled it under.

That was it. Nine years on that boat, nine years of misery and oppression and boredom and fatigue, and it was all gone in a flash of fire and a flood of water as if it had never existed.

It hit him then—maybe it hadn't. Maybe none of it had existed, because who could witness that it did? Not his uncle. Not the ocean. Not even the boat would give up its secrets. Could he start over? Come out of the water a new person?

A jagged piece of hull floated up next to him. He latched on to it and kicked toward the yellow light.

Clay had been hearing a muffled voice, but for how long? He opened his eyes without moving his body. The room was still. He was seated in a chair next to a bed in Natasha's apartment. Marika slept silently; even her breathing was quiet. Clay had allowed himself a few hours of dreamless sleep, but even at rest, his body seemed to sense danger, the way a snake's rattle twitches a warning.

He had heard that muffled voice and then the metallic clack of a phone returned to its cradle. Dammit, how long had it taken for his sluggish mind to catch up? Five minutes? Ten? He leapt to his feet.

Clay charged out of the dark bedroom and rounded the corner into the kitchen. Natasha stiffened even though her back was to him, pulling a pot of stew off a stove burner. She turned, but her face was colorless. The burner hissed as the blue flames curled, unattended.

"Who did you call?"

Natasha's lip quivered.

Clay raised his voice, made it like stone. "Who did you call!"

The woman flung the pot at him, but he saw it coming a mile away and easily sidestepped the assault. It flew past him and crashed into the wall, and the smell of boiled stew filled the air. He was on her before the pot hit the floor, taking her throat into his thick fingers and pushing her down toward the open flame on the stove. He put his fingers to her ear and repeated, more quietly this time, full of condemnation, "Who did you call?"

Marika appeared in the kitchen, trying to understand what she was seeing. "What are you doing?" was all she could manage.

"Who did you call?" growled Clay for the fourth time, pushing Natasha's head so close to the flames that her hair threatened to catch at any moment. It worked. Her eyes rolled from his face to Marika's, looking for some sort of release.

"I…I—"

"Talk!"

"I called state police."

The words hit Marika physically. Her knees sagged and she crouched over, holding her stomach.

Clay eased his grip, and the woman went to Marika, her arms outstretched like a sinner begging for forgiveness. "They threatened my family. They already took Oskar's job. They told me I could make things easier for everyone if I let them know where you were. Oh, *solnyshko,* look at me, please." Her voice was beseeching, grief-stricken. "Please, Marika. I hadn't a choice. They'll give Oskar his work."

"We have to go."

"Marika!"

But Marika pushed Natasha away, and she crumpled onto the floor, gasping. Clay held his hand out to Marika and she took it. They headed for the door without looking back.

Natasha remained facedown on the kitchen linoleum, her chest heaving, her sobs silent.

A navy van blasted to the curb in a shriek of brakes that sounded like an animal in its final throes. Clay had just rounded the corner from the stairwell to the building's lobby when the commotion reached him. He'd thought they had more time, but the net was falling now.

"They're here." He backed Marika into the stairwell again and was surprised at the expression on her face. A ferocity there. *Good,* he thought. *She'll need it*.

She started up the stairs again, and he grabbed her by the elbow. "You go up, you get trapped." She nodded, a student ready to learn, and they plunged down a level just as four men in dark suits banged through the front door and hit the stairs. Clay pulled Marika against the wall and watched all four of the men disappear in a hailstorm of shoe soles pounding on the metal stairs, headed up to Natasha's apartment. He pulled Marika's arm and the two of them were moving again. Not down toward the boiler room, where they had entered the night before; rather, out the front door and right into that navy van with the engine still running.

Clay looked up to the seventh-floor hallway window just in time to see a Russian FSB agent's face staring back at him, red as a furnace fire. Clay thought about giving him a salute but instead threw the van into drive, buried the accelerator under his foot, and rumbled from the apartment. The nearest train station was only a mile away.

She wanted to talk, and he let her. In the back of a restaurant, over Stolichnaya salad, lamb shish kebab, smoked sturgeon, and mugs of Zhigulevskoye beer, she opened her heart and her mind and the words came out sure and strong like a canyon wind. She spoke of a shared bed and of a doll made from a torn dress and of laundry tied to a line. Of policemen at her door, of her father's funeral, of empty bottles in the sink. She spoke of blackboards and chalk and a new father and money and hope and her mother resting and a stepbrother who took up for her, and happiness, genuine happiness for the first time in her life. She spoke of the thin exhilaration of having money after never having had it before, of the fragility of hope and the reluctance to accept Fortune's smile. She spoke of a better education, of a chance to be more than her birthright, stronger than her birthright. She spoke of setting out to earn enough of her own money to pay for her secondary education, of responsibility and courage and the optimism of honest work. She spoke of child care and a big house and her friendship with Natasha, and of the time when Benidrov came to her and started speaking in Russian. And at first it was nothing to feign ignorance, but she soon realized the danger, she likened it to dangling from a rope over a pit, and the only defense was to close her eyes and smile and hope he wouldn't see comprehension in her eyes. It was a secret and it could kill her and she hadn't asked for this, but it was her lie—her lie about the language, her lie about what she did know and didn't know that had led to all these horrible things, and now David was dead and it was her lie, her lie, her lie....

He let her go on and get it out because it was the time for it, because only after she had drawn the poison from the snakebite would it heal. She might never be whole again, but he needed her on that road if he was going to do what he'd been thinking he might.

Clay left her in the restaurant, asking the bartender where he could buy cigarettes. The young man pointed out the window and said something about a smoke shop two blocks away.

Clay ducked out the door, and it took him only a few steps to find what he was looking for. Cell phones were as commonplace in Moscow as they were in every other part of the world these days, and he waited for one of the pedestrians on the sidewalk in front of him to prove incautious. The first guy kept his cell to his ear, the second was texting, his thumbs working like jackhammers, but the third—a woman—hung up and popped her phone into her coat pocket without a thought. Clay passed her, had the phone in his hand without the woman's sensing a thing, and turned a hard right away from her, down a deserted block. Another right and a left and it was as if he had disappeared.

"Where the hell are you, Clay?" Stedding's voice barked through the line as though he were standing next to him holding a bullhorn.

"I want to change the parameters."

"Oh, good lord. Here we go."

"They want to make an exchange, right? Marika Csontos for Blake Nelson?"

"Yes, and by God, we want the exchange as well. It's already been cleared through State. The Director himself has turned his watchful gaze our way, and it's a position I don't much like. Nor should you. Now, drop the girl at the embassy and let's return to obscurity, shall we?"

"We want the exchange because we want Nelson back, correct?"

"Why the hell else would we want it?"

"Good. Then I'll change the parameters back to the original mission. I'll get Nelson back and then there won't need to be an exchange."

The line fell silent. He could picture Stedding gaming it

out the way a chess player tries to map out various moves on a board before picking up his next piece. Clay decided to keep pressing. He liked dirty street chess, the kind played in Washington Square Park in New York, the kind where half the game is guff, intimidation, and smack.

"What am I missing, Steddy?"

"Don't call me that." But Stedding's voice was more resigned than upset.

"Then I'd have to find a new way to get under your skin. What am I missing?"

"What's this damned girl to you?"

"Nothing. I just don't want to sacrifice a pawn who didn't know she was on the board."

"When did you turn sentimental?"

"The first time you made love to me."

"Chh-rist."

"I deliver Nelson to the embassy, the girl can disappear."

"How much time? The Russians are expecting an exchange by the end of the week."

"Stall them. Tell them the girl is at the embassy."

"They'll want proof."

"You can fake that."

"Give me something to fake."

"Fine. But I need more than three days."

"You can have all the time you need, but after three days, when there's no exchange to be made, things will get infinitely more difficult for you. We don't want a dead spy back, Clay. The Russians aren't fucking around here; that has been made clear."

"I know they aren't, believe me. They're doing everything they can to take the bullet out of our gun before we line up across from each other. I'm going to take their bullet first."

"Report back when Nelson is in hand."

"I might need to call in some kind of military extraction. Seals."

"For somebody who's supposed to be a quiet asset, you sure are making a lot of noise."

"Just so you won't forget about me, Steddy."

He thought he heard Stedding chuckle before the line went dead, but it was probably just a chirp of the security line disconnecting.

He needed to store Marika at least for a few days, and there was no one in either government he could trust, at least no one currently on Russian soil. There was someone else, though; someone in the service industry who understood, if nothing else, capitalism.

Kitai-Gorod was half a good neighborhood and half a nightclub scene that held everything from French-style bistros to raving dance discotheques to smaller, more intimate clubs. They used to call them whorehouses, but that name had fallen out of fashion around the time Pat Garrett betrayed Billy the Kid. Now they called it the red-light district, as though everything was softened under the gentle glow of colored bulbs. Maybe it was.

Marika sniffed as she ascended the stairwell from the street and entered the small foyer. A man propped himself against a wall, reading a book without a cover. He raised his eyes enough to assess Clay and Marika—Marika longer than Clay—and then said something about not being interested. Clay asked for Katya. The man stiffened and his eyes became circles. "What do you want with Katya?"

"That's between Katya and me. Now go fetch her, and don't waste any more of my time." The man went through the back curtain without another word.

Marika was wary, but Clay knew she trusted him. She'd seen the men pursuing her; she'd witnessed what had happened when she'd chosen to contact a friend from her former life. She had only him.

It was an odd feeling for Clay—so often he was used to operating alone; if people were dependent on his actions, he didn't know them, didn't know their faces, didn't know their expectations beyond completing his mission, which he'd always done. But this girl, this fragile young woman, was as reliant on him as a cub to a wolf. He liked the feeling for a reason he couldn't quite put his finger on.

Back when Adromatov was alive, he'd introduced Clay to a particular club owner—Katya Zminsky. She was a tough woman in a man's world, a natural beauty with a shrewd mind. In the decade since he'd first met her, she had somehow found the fountain of youth, or there was a painting of an older her in an attic somewhere, because she appeared to be growing younger. If she recognized him, she didn't let on.

She sized the two of them up with a quick sweep of her eyes. "Yes?" she asked, her posture noncommittal.

"I'm not going to ask you any questions if you'll afford me the same courtesy. Here is five thousand dollars US. You will get another ten thousand US in four days if I return and my charge here is delivered back to me unharmed, well rested, and well fed."

Katya flicked her eyes from the money in Clay's hand to Marika. "May I ask just one question?"

Clay nodded.

"Will anyone come looking for her?"

"No one knows she's here."

"Come with me, kitten," Katya said, and took Marika by the hand. Before she moved behind the cloth, Marika broke free, crossed the six steps to where Clay stood, wrapped her arms around him, and buried her face in his chest.

He didn't know what to do, so he patted her back, his face reddening. Finally, she stepped away.

"Come back for me." Her body trembled.

"I will," he told her. He meant it.

He stood there for a good five minutes after she'd disappeared with Katya behind the curtain. He could smell gasoline, fire, and the salty brine of the ocean. The only water nearby was the *drip, drip, drip* of an exposed pipe.

He waited down the street from the Spanish embassy, watching the traffic flow in and out like bees in a hive. The Russians and Spanish have a tight if tenuous history, dating back to the Spanish Civil War, when Stalin sent men and munitions to

Franco's Republicans, and it has grown much more complicated since. As such, the embassy was a hub of activity, and Clay waited patiently in a stolen truck, reading *Izvestiya* and watching the cars buzz in and out of the garage. It was patient work, but Clay had learned patience from a childhood of watching endless waves pitch and roll toward his boat.

Finally, he recognized the dark-haired, dark-complexioned Spanish man driving a small sedan out of the lot, threw on his blinker, and followed. Away from Marika, his thoughts had shifted, blackened. The right hand of Zeus was back, ready to hurl a few thunderbolts.

Gregory Molina parked in a compact lot near Mayakovskaya Street and slipped over to one of the omnipresent Bavarian-style beer halls that were springing up all over Moscow like kudzu. The outside of the place looked like a Disney façade, with fake stone walls and a string of blue-and-white balloons made out of plastic lining the wooden eaves. All of this was centered in a Communist-era block building so it resembled a puff of pink bubble gum popped on an ugly face.

Clay parked nearby and followed Molina inside. The room was musty and dark and smelled of stale tobacco and embarrassed desperation. The pub looked like a blind date who was trying too hard, affecting an effusive personality so no one would notice her warts and bad teeth.

Molina took a table in the corner, ordered a beer and a roasted chicken, pulled a tablet computer out of his leather satchel, and tucked in to read while he waited for his food. Clay ordered a pint at the bar and waited to see whether Molina was meeting someone or dining alone. Normally, he would look for some sort of pattern to emerge before he made a move, wait for the best possible time to intercept his target, but he didn't have that luxury. Patience was an effective weapon if you could afford to use it; otherwise, blunt force worked well, too.

Convinced Molina was eating alone, Clay crossed to his table and sat down. Absorbed in whatever document he was reading on his tablet, Molina didn't look up, just shifted his weight and twisted in his seat while chewing absently on a morsel of bread.

"Hello, Gregory," Clay said in Spanish. The words had the intended effect: Molina's face flushed and he jerked upright.

Speaking Spanish, he said, "Yes do I know you what's this about?" in a rapid-fire, guttural voice that rose in pitch as it accelerated. Now that he looked up, Clay thought there was something a bit walrus-like about the man's features.

Switching to English, Clay said, "I was sent here to kill you."

The walrus turned green. "I don't excuse me what are you why are you what did you say—"

"Here's the way it works," Clay interrupted, if only to stop that barrage of meaningless words. "You work for Gutierrez, who serves as US-Spanish liaison sharing classified military strategy, weaponry, and technology between the two allies. You, in turn, copy these sensitive documents and sell them to Russian Intelligence at twenty-five thousand a pop, sometimes more if the information is particularly revelatory."

The walrus started to sputter again, but Clay kept the harpoon in his side. "You've gotten away with it for just under a year, and like all creatures who fall into a routine, you grew fat, complacent, and sloppy. So I was sent here to put my thumb in the dyke and stop the flood by putting a bullet in your head."

"How did you you couldn't but how could you—"

"A squat Spaniard named Beto sold you down the river for a fistful of silver."

Clay watched Molina's face shake as though he had palsy. His tongue actually flicked out to moisten his lips, but no moisture came.

"What do you what do you how can I..." he started, and this time Clay didn't interrupt. As he suspected, Molina didn't even finish his thought. The words just dissipated in the air like puffs of smoke.

"I don't want to kill you, Gregory. I want to give you a way out."

Molina's eyes darted to Clay's, looking for a lifeline, a flash of hope.

"An American spy is being held in Moscow, awaiting an exchange. His name is Nelson. I need to know where he's being held and the route he's going to take to arrive at the exchange."

Molina sputtered again, "But how can I how would I even begin—"

"You make an exchange, but the currency is information. Then I give you forty-eight hours to disappear and I promise not to come looking for you. Otherwise, if you can't tell me what I need to know by this time tomorrow, if you run instead, or tell me you failed, then I'm going to cut you up and deliver little pieces of you to your family back in Madrid so they'll know you're alive but also know that each day when the post comes, you'll be more and more disfigured, until they won't even want you back.

"Twenty-four hours. Set out from the embassy in your car and head north. I'll flash my lights when it's safe to pull over. Don't fuck this up."

Clay got up and left before the chicken came.

He spent that night at the Vega Hotel near Izmailovsky Park, the kind of high-rise hotel built for the 1980 Olympics with so many rooms, more than seventy-five hundred, that each customer was scrutinized with the same attentiveness with which you might look at an individual blade of grass on a lawn. He stayed in the room, with the DO NOT DISTURB sign hung on the door handle, and thought of Marika. Had he been rash to dump her in such a place? Was he foolish not to keep her where he could see her? No, it was the right thing to do. The next bit was going to get messy, and if he was caught, or worse, she would have a fighting chance. He slept, and woke with muddy memories of unsettling dreams.

Molina had dark circles under his eyes when he handed over the folder. He peered at his feet and said, "It's there all of it it's there."

Clay took it from him without looking at the contents and headed back to his car.

Molina shouted, "You won't see me again thank you I'm

sorry for what I did thank you I'm—" but his words were cut off when Clay shut his car door, indifferent. Maybe his next assignment would be to track down Molina and kill him. If so, he would show no remorse, and the promise not to come looking for him would prove as empty as his mercy.

They already had Nelson in Moscow and were holding him at a well-armed, well-guarded safe house on Teatralny Porezd. The plan was to transfer him to the exchange via the popular Novoryazanskoye Highway, which would include a short trip through a double-lane tunnel. The exchange would take place on a closed runway at Domodedovo Airport. The Americans would have a G5 already parked on the tarmac, waiting to whisk Nelson away. The Russians would load Marika into the same Suburban that Nelson had just occupied, and she would evaporate from the world as quickly as dew on a meadow. They would use two black Suburbans for the transit. The entire trip, from safe house to airport, would take less than twelve minutes.

Clay made a phone call to Stedding and asked for two things, two things that gave his handler an upset stomach and little doubt as to Clay's intentions. First, he asked that the exchange be negotiated for the following afternoon at 5 p.m.—when traffic would be at its thickest—and that the US side put up every sign that they were negotiating forcefully but acquiesce as to the location and terms of the exchange.

The second thing he asked for was a car full of guns.

Sometimes things went terribly wrong. If you can plan appropriately, you can whittle chance down to a fine powder. You can fortify your position with backup plans and alternatives, with reinforcements and fallbacks, but when you try to do this shit by the seat of your pants, when time is of the essence, when the mission changes and then changes again, when you make decisions based on emotion—and how the fuck did that happen, anyway?—well, it had happened even before Clay stepped into that apartment in Vladivostok, when she had just been an image in his mind's eye and then it had solidified on the long road to Moscow, when she showed courage and depth and grit and mettle—and it wasn't reason driving him, it wasn't sense, it wasn't calculation; it was a raw, terrible hungry idea that he could prevent injustice from happening. He could act quickly, he could do the right thing, he could protect an innocent girl who had listened to a blathering dolt who should've known to keep his mouth shut. And now he had not to act but to react, not to plan but to improvise, not to think but to move. It was aleatory anarchy, a flash mob, as ugly as a blunt-force instrument when a sniper's rifle would've been so, so clean. It was out of character, but it was his character, an oxymoron that couldn't be halved, reconciled. Sometimes you lit dynamite and the fuse burned too quickly and it exploded in your face. Forget the left hand, the *right* hand wasn't quite fucking sure what the right hand was doing. And sometimes things went terribly wrong.

When attempting to intercept a target, when planning an ambush, it's best to strike while the asset is in transit. Clay knew the route they'd be coming by, thanks to Molina's file. He knew the approximate time they would take that route. He knew how many of them there would be, and he knew where they would be positioned. There was a lot he didn't know: how they were trained, how responsive they were to extreme stress, whether or not they would kill their prisoner the moment they knew they were under attack. He preferred not to think about what he didn't know, because sometimes things went terribly wrong.

Nelson wondered about the exchange. He believed they really were willing to deal him—why would they go through the motions of collecting him in a black Suburban while its twin led the way to the airport? They were incredibly advanced at psychological warfare—he had been the subject of that particular experiment for longer than he'd thought he could endure—but what more could they gain from faking his release?

No, this had the feel of a real exchange. He wondered what his side had been willing to give up to get him back. There was a famous story that King Edward III had exchanged a few horses and a trifling sum to ransom a young page named Geoffrey Chaucer back from the French after the Battle of Rheims. He wondered what captured low-level Russian agent was on his way to the scene right now.

As he rode the highway to the airport, he thought for the first time of his future. What would the CIA do with him? What do you do with compromised agents? Give him an analyst position? Let him teach a class on how *not* to stand up to torture? Egorov sat in the passenger seat, looking small in the large Suburban. Behind the wheel was a young man Nelson hadn't met before. On either side of him were the two large Russians who had put on the gloves and executed Egorov's bidding. It would all be over soon. How much would he tell his own handler of what he'd endured?

Clay spotted them creeping toward the tunnel and eased from the service road on the hill into the oncoming lanes. In about fifteen minutes, they would meet in the center of the tunnel, traveling in opposite directions, surrounded by congestion, boxed in on all sides. He would step out of his car and shoot the two drivers, then everyone else inside the Suburbans other than Nelson. He would use the inevitable commotion inside the tunnel to get back into his SUV and plow over to the emergency lane to get the hell out of there. That was the plan. It wasn't flawless; hell, it wasn't even sound, but he had surprise on his side, and he had his skills, and he hoped Nelson would pitch in, but sometimes things, well, they went terribly wrong.

He eased toward the tunnel and watched it happen. In the oncoming lane, a delivery truck clipped a Fiat and it spun like a top, popping into a tiny Niva next to it before flipping over onto its side. Several drivers exited their vehicles to see where they could help, and the already thick traffic on that side of the tunnel shut down completely.

Shit, Clay thought.

Egorov clucked his tongue just as they approached the tunnel. Nelson could see through the front windshield that an accident had brought traffic to a standstill. The driver pulled up a phone, and Nelson heard him say something about sending police to help them through the jam.

Egorov fidgeted and finally demanded they turn around and find an alternate route. The driver relayed this to the security patrol in the lead Suburban, and they banked into the emergency lane and headed into the flow.

Nelson's pulse quickened. Was this some sort of staged accident so the Americans could free him? His hand tightened around the handle of his cane, which he held absently between his knees.

Clay was already ensnared on the inside lane just outside the tunnel, and only the downslope on his side allowed him to see what the Suburbans were doing. He threw on his blinker, but there was nowhere to go. He felt like an animal in a cage, and he could feel blood rushing to his face, hot. He swiveled his head, but both sides of the traffic were equally stuck. The

Suburbans continued to move away, back against the traffic, like salmon swimming upstream.

Clay saw a flash in his side-view mirror as a motorcycle buzzed by, zipping through the spaces between cars. He switched to the rearview and saw more motorcyclists with the same idea heading his way. He reached over his shoulder, unzipped a black canvas bag, snatched up a pair of Beretta compact Cheetah .380s. Each had a clip of thirteen rounds, and he hoped it would be enough in a firefight. He didn't have time to pocket the spare clips.

His driver's-side mirror showed a Voskhod rider with a black helmet rapidly approaching. Clay eased his sedan a foot toward the center barrier to narrow the space in which the motorcycle could pass and then timed it perfectly. As the cycle went by, he put his shoulder into his door and whipped it open like a battering ram. He caught the back tire flush, and the unprepared rider somersaulted over the handlebars as the bike bucked and then fell. Clay was out of the car and throttling the bike before the rider could climb to his knees and curse him. Cruising between cars as easily as rainwater finding a rivulet, Clay pegged the Voskhod. He handled it better than the bike he'd stolen back in Stepnoy, and he was thankful he had put some miles on a two-wheeler recently. He slipped back into the balanced feel as if he were putting on comfortable shoes after a few days of hiking in work boots.

Up ahead, the traffic bottled as he neared the wreck, and he followed a few other motorcycles around a semitruck, found daylight on the other side of the tunnel, and broke into the open. The traffic behind him, he had this side of the highway more or less to himself, and he charged ahead like a bullet escaping a barrel. He could make out the black Suburbans heading up the emergency lane and thought he might get some help from a patrol car moving up the lane from the other direction. The patrol car split off, though, as if it had been summoned. Maybe it had, maybe someone inside the lead Suburban was in communication with the police—that was only going to add more to the equation, because he only had twenty-six bullets, and sometimes things went terribly wrong.

The police car sliced the traffic like Moses parting the Red Sea and let the Suburbans shoot over to the opposite side of the highway, where an exit took them away.

Clay lowered his head over the handlebars and jerked the bike to the right, crossing twin lanes and dipping down off the highway. It was one of those circular exits and Clay flew around it, using the centripetal force to slingshot himself under the highway on a crossing street.

He temporarily lost sight of the two black Suburbans as he zigzagged through slower traffic, exploding past cars and trucks like a sidewinder missile.

He cleared the other side of the highway underpass, then picked up the black Suburbans filing up a smaller, industrial street, one lined with warehouses and factories coughing turbulent smoke into the air.

Clay's mood matched the color of the exhaust as he punished the motorcycle, its engine producing a shrill whine. He swerved out into the street and chased down the Suburbans from behind. They were braking for a red light, and he might still take them by surprise. They had avoided the ambush by chance and were unaware of it, he hoped.

He slowed the bike, dropped it behind the trailing Suburban, ducked low, now fisting both handguns, scooted past the first vehicle, and crept up on the driver's side of the other to begin his work.

A mistake would've been to fire into the driver's window—the glass was surely bulletproof. Instead, he fired two quick shots into the door lock at point-blank range, disintegrating it. With the shots still ringing in his ears, he flipped up the handle and the driver's door sprang open. He had eleven shots left in this gun, thirteen in the other.

The startled driver jammed on the gas, but Clay had already climbed up into the door. He shot the driver and then the passenger, head shots, kill shots, and the Suburban jerked forward, running into the back of the police car in front of it.

Clay rode this out, half in and half out of the driver's door as if he were surfing a wave, calm and methodical. In the backseat were two men in suits, most likely diplomats, but Clay couldn't leave anything to chance, so he put them down with two more bullets.

Ahead of him, both Russian policemen had popped out of their squad car and were taking the standard cop position taught the world over, using their doors as shields. There was a flaw in this technique, though. Clay fell backward out of the Suburban, lay on his back on the pavement, and fired under both doors, first hitting the cops in their knees and then in their heads.

Gun number one was empty when he turned his attention

to the second Suburban. He hoped to find Nelson alive in there, but sometimes things went terribly wrong.

Nelson lowered his eyes. He told himself to control his emotions, to choke back the self-pity, to be glad he was still alive, but his wretched lack of character overwhelmed him. They had broken him completely. If only he had one tiny bit of—

"What's this?" he heard Egorov chirp, alarm rising in his voice, and Nelson jerked his eyes up. Beyond the front windshield, a large man was hanging outside the driver's door of the lead Suburban. Muzzle flashes were lighting up the interior, and then the vehicle leapt forward and smashed into the back of the police car.

Everyone in Nelson's Suburban leaned forward, as if they were watching a 3-D movie out the front glass and were being sucked into the action.

A smile crept across Nelson's lips. He had fucked up royally, he had spilled every secret he had ever known, he had folded like a boneless, skinless chicken when they had put him on the rack, but all of that could turn on a single word: *redemption*.

While everyone else in the truck watched the big man spill onto his back and shoot both cops out from under their defensive positions, Nelson reached down and pulled the rubber gripper off his plastic cane.

Clay chucked his spent gun and transferred the loaded one from his left hand to his right as he jumped back to his feet.

In every fight he'd ever been in, someone had made a mistake. He'd had near-misses when he had underestimated an enemy, but had been lucky enough not to fatally pay for those judgment lapses. The men in the trailing Suburban weren't so lucky. The rear doors flew open and twin behemoths stepped out of either side of the truck. Clay caught the first one in the side of his head before he put both feet on the ground.

The second fired across the hood of the Suburban and then ducked down to use the vehicle as a shield, but Clay snaked toward him and was closing the distance when the driver panicked, threw the car into reverse, and left the Russian exposed. Clay hit him in the chest three times in a tight pattern and the big man toppled backward.

Clay had dropped his motorcycle behind the Suburban for a reason; in the driver's excited attempt to reverse the hell out of there, the back tires entangled with the bike, and the result was that the vehicle floundered like a beached whale, the tires spinning without traction. The back doors were still open.

Nelson watched the men on either side of him throw open the passenger doors to help their comrades. *Big mistake,* he thought just as both men were mowed down on either side of the Suburban.

The driver turned backward to reverse the car; he hit the gas, and Nelson raised the cane and drove the sharp tip with all his force into the man's head as if he were thrusting a sword. It went in easier than he'd imagined, or maybe it just seemed that way, and the driver jiggled, surprised, and then slumped over. Nelson pulled back on the cane and withdrew the bloody tip just as Egorov spun in horror and raised a tiny 9mm Makarov pistol.

Clay reached the door just in time to see Nelson pull some sort of sword out of the driver's face. He recognized Nelson—though the man looked twenty pounds lighter than the last time he'd seen him—but for the life of him, he couldn't figure out where the hell the agent would have gotten a sword.

As these disparate thoughts rattled around his head, he saw the last man standing—sitting, actually—a bearded, gray-haired, fat-faced Russian in the passenger seat. The man swiveled with a small pistol in his hand and aimed at Nelson in the backseat. Clay hurried to shoot him before he could pop a shot off, but Nelson swung the sword more quickly, getting just enough leverage to wallop the bastard in the side of the head, just as the gun went off. The bullet nearly tore off Nelson's shoulder but buried itself in the backseat about an inch too high.

Clay made sure the Russian didn't have a chance to correct his aim.

He helped Nelson from the car, and it became apparent his cohort couldn't put any significant weight on his left leg.

"You hit?" Clay grunted, his eyes flashing over the scene.

"Before. It's healing." Nelson reached back inside the bloody Suburban and fished out his sword, which Clay could see now was a medical cane with a sharpened end.

"They thought they'd broken me," Nelson offered by way of explanation.

"Had they?"

"Not enough."

Clay hurried the agent over to the police car, whose doors were still wide open. He shouldered Nelson into the passenger seat, then slipped behind the wheel. He didn't see the Russian cop on the far side of the car, still alive when Clay stepped over him. He didn't see the cop blindly raise his side arm and fire into the passenger door. He heard the shot, knew the sound, but didn't know its origin. He didn't know the dying cop's aim was true. He didn't know the bullet had found its target.

Oblivious, Clay floored the accelerator, and the car leapt forward like a horse out of the starting gate. He swept his eyes in every direction, but no more shots came. He leaned back in his seat, momentarily relaxing. The car whipped around a corner and he pulled into an enormous parking structure adjacent to an apartment tower, then drove down to the lowest level, where only a few rusty cars sat abandoned in the poor light.

"We'll have to ditch this cop car and find a..." he started. It was then that he noticed that Nelson's face had turned chalky and his breathing shallow.

"Fuck," he spat, leaned over, and moved Nelson's hand from where it was plastered to his side. Blood had soaked his shirt, and when Clay moved the cloth out of the way, it leaked in spurts from a small hole.

"Can you move?" Clay asked.

At first, Nelson gave him a slight shake of the head, but it turned into a nod as the wounded spy's mind worked out the alternative.

Clay opened his door, then quickly moved around to the passenger side. His mind was racing…who should he call? Steddy? A doctor? He reached in and prepared Nelson to move, but the smaller man balked.

"Okay, we'll give you a minute here, but then we gotta move. That hole ain't good, and if you're dripping on the inside, this is gonna get a whole lot worse."

Nelson's eyes wandered but then cleared. He forced his lips to work, though his words sounded as if they were coming from the bottom of a well.

"Marika?"

"She's safe. I found her and she's safe."

Nelson smiled weakly. "Ask her…" He coughed and then groaned. "Ask her about atoms…ask her…" but his eyes clouded, and only one long exhale finished the sentence.

Clay sat down heavily on the pavement next to the car. He knew he should be moving, his inner voice was screaming at him to move, dammit, but he felt extremely, bone-crushingly weary all of a sudden. It was as if he'd been driving, driving, driving, full steam, pumping his legs, soundlessly, thoughtlessly, churning, grinding, pumping, and then the juice had run out and his legs had cramped up and he'd felt he could never take another step in his life.

He looked at the blood on his fingertips, and something about the color, about the texture, about the smell snapped him back to life like salts under the nose of a boxer.

Ask her about atoms...

What the fuck did that mean? A bomb? A dirty bomb?

He didn't know, but he knew the question was important. It hit him there. He had been so focused on finding the girl, on getting her to safety, on completing his mission, that he hadn't followed up on asking her what she knew. What had that Russian government bastard told her? What secret was she harboring inside?

Ask her...

He would. He would pick himself up off this cement slab before any nervous residents walked by, before the Russian police or FSB or any number of government agencies figured out which police car had been taken and located it on their GPS system like a homing beacon and snatched him before he could get back to Marika and figure out his next move. He had parked down in the basement, so GPS would be useless, but could he be sure?

Ask her...

He reached past Nelson's body and pushed in the cigarette lighter. In a few more minutes, he'd make sure this car burned so hot, they'd need weeks to identify whose body was left inside.

CHAPTER NINE

CLAY PURCHASED a cell phone from a mobile store called CRUSH on the outskirts of Moscow and hoped it had enough starter charge in the battery to connect one call. He wasn't going to sit around looking for an outlet.

He needed a shower and a shave; he was starting to stink, and he was sure he looked more like a beggar than an intellectual playwright, should someone in a uniform ask to see his identification card.

He took the metro out to Izmailovsky Park, passed the flea market with its myriad stalls of useless Communist-era crap, and headed into the park proper. He walked to a tree where he still had a bar of reception, rested his back against the trunk, and dialed a number from memory. After he got through the passwords and protections, finally Stedding came on the line, sounding as though he had just been awoken.

"You've single-handedly destroyed any goodwill the president had amassed over five-plus years of improved US-Russian relations."

"It's all hokum-smokum anyway. They never stopped hating us."

"You're right about that. But there are two dynamics going on here, reality and appearance. Unfortunately, appearance tends to be equally important these days. Where's Nelson?"

"One of those good-news, bad-news situations, Steddy."

He heard Stedding sigh. He seemed to be hearing that a lot these days. Clay continued, "I did get Nelson away from the Russians, but he's dead now."

Clay waited. Stedding took his time before answering. "His body?"

"I burned it."

"Did you, now?"

"Don't be miffed, Steddy. It's unbecoming. I tell everyone how stoic you always are, and—"

"What of the girl?"

"I have her tucked away."

"Which safe house?"

That question nettled Clay a bit. He wondered why Stedding would want to know, but his handler brushed away his own question.

"It doesn't matter. I have to check in with some people, and I will get back to you with further instructions. No more seat of your pants. No more making it up as you go along. The reins are going to be a little tighter on both of us, I'm afraid. For how long, I don't know. How will I reach you?"

"Tell me when you want me to check in."

"Eight hours from right now."

"Done."

He pressed the End Call button and glanced around. The park was starting to fill with Muscovites who looked as if they just wanted a few hours of sunlight on their faces.

He found a green metal trash can on the way out, pitched the cell phone in, and kept walking.

The nightclubs of Kitai-Gorod were buzzing and pounding and thumping like baboons sending out mating calls. Electronic music filled the air with repetitive grooves that looped endlessly. Clay thought the Russians could use some of this in their torture sessions; hell, he'd crack in minutes if he had to set foot in one of these sweat factories.

He climbed the stairs and the man in the foyer bristled when he saw him. Clay started to address him, but the man disappeared behind the curtain. An uneasy feeling washed over Clay, as though his stomach had turned to ice. Had he miscalculated this option's viability? Had Katya realized an opportunity to exploit a desperate situation? She was in the exploitation business, for Chrissakes, and Clay had delivered his charge right into the lioness's den. What the hell had he been thinking? His eyes narrowed and he balled his hands into fists. He would beat down every last son of a bitch in this stinking whorehouse and burn it to the ground if they so much as—

And then she walked through the curtain and smiled so

broadly, it damn near knocked him over. Three steps and she was in his arms. A bear hug around his chest, her face buried in his shirt, and she just repeated, "You returned, you returned, you returned," over and over.

Clay leaned down. "Did they treat you okay?"

Before she could answer, Katya's voice arrived behind him. "She was treated like a princess."

Marika nodded her agreement. "It's true. Katya fed me and drew me a warm bath with salt in it."

Katya smiled. "She is nice girl. She should not be in place like this."

Clay paid Katya and took Marika from there to the metro station, away from Kitai-Gorod. He had his choice of safe houses, but something told him to avoid them until he talked to Stedding again. It wasn't a matter of thinking his own government would turn against him; it was more nuanced than that. His government might have a different perspective on how to accomplish its goals. That perspective might not line up with his, and he had found it almost always better to ask forgiveness than permission.

He checked them into the Hotel Metropol near Red Square, paying cash and using a dummy passport and credit card he'd had made on the black market. No one, not even Stedding, knew about this identity. In the gift shop, he bought a razor, shaving cream, deodorant, a toothbrush, and when he saw a box of chocolates, he bought that, too.

Their room was small but had two beds and a nice view of Moscow. He gave her the chocolates, hoping to produce that smile of hers, and he was not disappointed.

"Do you mind if I shower?"

She wrinkled her nose. "Please. You smell like a barn."

"Will you send my clothes down to be cleaned while I bathe?"

"Gladly."

He undressed and tossed his clothes into a pile outside the door. He was glad she was in happy spirits. He knew it was a reflexive mechanism, but it beat the alternative, a sullen, sulky depressed girl. She had character, and it would serve her well if she could maintain that armor of Teflon.

He turned the water up to its hottest and let the spray pepper his skin. It felt clean and intense, as if his body were decompressing. He'd been going hard now for a long time with only troubled rest and an account bleeding red.

His mind drifted to that boat long ago, that light that had seemed a mile away, and how he had kept kicking toward it, no matter what the waves did to try to hold him at bay. At any moment he had thought that his uncle would rise up from the depth of the sea, grab his legs, and yank him down with him, but still he'd kept kicking. The light had grown brighter, bigger, and a searchlight had joined it, flashing over the water. The yacht had turned toward the dying fire behind him, the wreckage of his boat, and the sailors inside had been conducting a search-and-rescue mission. He'd found his voice then, shouted out, yelled at the top of his lungs, and kept kicking. Marika would have to find a similar strength, a similar resolve. He believed she had it in her.

The water in the shower cooled as the heater gave out. He cranked the knobs, stepped out, and began to dry himself off.

Moments later, he kept the towel on as he slipped into the twin bed. He thought Marika was asleep atop the adjacent mattress, her head on the pillow, but he was wrong.

"The hotel said your clothes would be at the door in the morning."

"Great."

She rolled over and faced him. He could just make out her silhouette in the dark.

"May I ask you a question?"

"Yes."

"Why do you do this work?"

He thought for a moment. He wanted to give her the truth, or at least a shade of it.

"I was recruited."

"Recruited how?"

"I enlisted in the military at age eighteen. The army. I had no interest in boats, so the navy and marines were out. I knew nothing about flying, so that took care of the air force. What I did know was endurance. Toughness. Pain. I could take any punishment anyone could dole out. And I knew a little about discipline, about secrecy, and about keeping my mouth shut.

"The army put a gun in my hands, and it turned out I had a knack for shooting. The world was hot, and there were plenty of places the army could send a young soldier to test his wherewithal. I must've passed those tests, because I received orders that I was going to be put into a different program. I didn't know if they meant I'd be moving into intelligence or cooking at the mess tent. I was shipped on a Chinook with two tons of cargo and dropped off on a base that could've been in any country in the world. Some men in suits picked me up and drove me to a building with no sign and no windows. That was fifteen years ago."

Then he added, "I guess that was more than you asked for."

He wasn't sure why he had said so much, but the words had come out before he could stop them.

"Do you have to do things you don't want to do?"

"I don't think too much about wanting or not wanting. I just receive my missions and complete them."

"And your mission was to find me?"

"Something like that."

"I'm glad you did."

"So am I."

"Will I learn to shoot a gun?"

"Do you want to?"

Marika shrugged.

"I don't think we have time to train, and a gun can be more dangerous to the shooter if she doesn't know what she's doing. Or her bodyguard, for that matter."

"Is that what you are? My bodyguard?"

"Something like that."

She smiled but didn't show her teeth.

"If necessity dictates, use your fingernails. Go for the eyes or the groin. Men have a hard time fighting when they can't see or can't breathe. Eyes first, then close your fist and pound him in the balls as hard as you can."

She giggled. "I'll remember that."

"I hope you won't need to fight."

"I've been fighting my entire life."

"I had a feeling we were cut from the same cloth."

Her breathing soon regulated and he sat for a minute, watching her shadow rise and fall in the darkness. He shut his eyes and dreamed of nothing.

She crawled into bed with him. He knew this was a delicate moment, and he knew he had to handle it with tact. He eased out the other side and turned on the light. She blinked and got a look on her face as if she didn't know whether she should bite the fruit or cower in fear and shame.

He kept the towel wrapped tightly around his waist.

"What's wrong?" she asked.

"Nothing. Nothing is wrong."

"You don't like me."

He shook his head. "I like you very much, Marika. You're strong and wise and more resilient than you have any right to be at your age."

"But you don't want me?" She pushed the bedspread back, revealing her naked body.

Clay sat next to her on the bed, reached down, and slowly pulled the covers back up. They had trained him for a lot of things in that windowless, signless building, but they hadn't trained him for this.

"You're a beautiful, smart girl, Marika. You have an amazing future ahead of you, one you could've only dreamed about a few years ago. You will learn a new language, decide who you want to be, who you want to be *with,* and there is a young man out there, a man your own age who will care for you and will make you laugh. He'll bring a smile to your face just by sitting down next to you. He will open up to you; you deserve that. But that's not me. It will never be me."

She sat still for a moment, and then she asked him to turn off the light. When he did, she moved out of his bed and returned to her own.

"I'm sorry," she offered in the dark. Her voice sounded small, tired.

"You have nothing to apologize for."

"I feel like a foolish girl."

"Don't."

They stopped talking then, and he wasn't sure, but he thought he fell asleep before she did. He was cold, but that was all right.

Clay looked up from his plate of boiled eggs and ham. "I'm going to ask you a question I asked you before, but this time I want you to be specific," he said over his coffee. They were in a basement restaurant adjacent to the hotel.

She set her fork down next to her plate and gave him her attention.

"What did he tell you? Benidrov?"

Her face blanched. "I told you it was nonsense. I don't remember most of it."

"What you remember, then."

"I said before. Acronyms of departments in the government

I'd never heard of. Names of rivals, many names. It meant nothing."

"I won't let anyone hurt you."

She checked herself. He saw understanding in her eyes, so he voiced her thoughts, confirmed them. "You've been holding something back so that if you are put into some sort of precarious place, you'll have something to bargain with."

She looked down, reddening. He had touched on the truth, and she was too inexperienced to know how to hide it.

"I'm telling you, you're in the precarious place right now. In fifteen minutes, I have to call my contact at Central Intelligence, and he's going to tell me what to do with you. I don't know what those orders will be, but I can guess. I need to hit him back with something, something that will get dark men to change their plans and want to help you, *need* to help you. I can't do it alone. You have to trust me with your information."

She pushed her plate to the center of the table and looked up. Her eyes were shiny, but no tears left them.

"Something about a bomb? A dirty bomb?"

She shook her head.

"Please, Marika. I have to—"

"There was nothing about a bomb."

"Atoms. Nelson told me to ask you about atoms."

"Nelson?"

"Yes."

"Blake Nelson."

"Yes."

"Where is he?"

"I didn't…I wasn't aware you'd made contact with him…."

He could see her working something out in her mind, then that moment of discovery when she realized that all the pieces fit into place.

"He…I talked to him on the phone. He said he could help me."

"I didn't know."

"He said he was coming to help me, but he never came."

"What did you tell him?"

"Adams. Not atoms. Adams."

Michael Adams landed at the Praha-Ruzyně Airport outside Prague. They touched down on a small private landing strip just west of the main terminal, which was capable of handling G5s but not bigger jets. He had traveled with three of his fellow district heads; the rest would be arriving shortly.

He had spent the entire flight on the phone with various handlers underneath him. His field agents were responsible for putting a lid on three Iranian scientists who were part of their government's plans to open nuclear power plants, which were really shells for developing all sorts of bad ideas. Many governments had a keen interest in setting that effort back a few decades, none more than England, the US, and Israel, and Adams's network was facilitating with MI6 and the Mossad. Meat in that particular hot spot was cooking, and this meeting was as much a distraction as anything, but soon nearly all of their problems would be *his* problems, too—almost every bit of US espionage filtered through European Operations at some point.

He hadn't slept. As the plane touched down, he felt the jostle of the tires hitting the runway right inside his temples. A ladder butted up to the plane, and he and the others stepped down to waiting black vans, one for the heads and the other for their aides. Adams had chosen to fly solo, leaving Warren back in LA to begin managing the transition, and maybe that was why he hadn't gotten any winks while airborne.

Contreras, the Dallas head, swiveled in his seat to face Adams. "You need to get some rest, Michael. You look like hell."

"I'll nap at the hotel. What time are we meeting Fourticq?" Fourticq was the outgoing head of EurOps. Adams knew the meeting would start at 8 p.m. local time, in a little over three hours, but he felt compelled to make small talk. He didn't listen to the answer, but his question got the other men chatting and gave him the opportunity to check out.

He looked at the back of the driver's head as they passed old factories on the outskirts of Prague. The man had a shaved pate, and a couple of scars snaked across the back of it, as if someone had attempted to knife him but had slipped. The guy must work for EurOps—if he had been assigned the job of transporting four of the CIA's most senior officers, he must've been thoroughly vetted.

Adams realized how little he thought about such things anymore. He had been hiding in plain sight for so long he almost believed his life was normal.

But something about the scars on the driver's head brought him back to reality: he knew many dark secrets that men around the world would like to know.

A bad feeling settled over him, like an omen. He told himself it was just because he was tired.

Marika sat on a bench forty meters away while Clay repeated the cell phone trick. Stedding sounded resigned.

"You're to drop Marika Csontos at the American embassy like before."

"Change of plans."

"I knew you would say something like that," his handler spat, focusing his anger through the line so it would be unmistakable. "You can't change—"

"We're leaving Russia."

"Dammit, Clay, why do you insist on getting us fired? Despite what you may think, I actually like this job."

"You should. You're good at it. But what excitement would you have if I just did everything the way it was drawn up?"

"Where are you going?"

"I can't tell you."

"Can't tell me!"

"There are bigger events going on than you or I were previously aware of. Now, I'm telling you this, Stedding, so you can plan how to sell whomever you need to sell that I'm not handing Marika over. And I'm keeping things from you because I don't know yet who is involved."

"Involved in what?"

"Don't get nervous, Stedding. I'm protecting you. When people in the Agency say I went off the deep end, you'll have recorded proof that I didn't tell you anything."

"Clay! I—"

But Clay pressed the End Call button. Marika looked up from the bench as he approached.

"You look amused."

"Do I?"

"You do."

"Sometimes this job is so absurd, all you can do is find amusement where you can. For me, it's driving my handler insane."

"I don't understand."

"I don't understand it myself. Come on—let's get out of here."

"Out of the park?"

"Out of Russia."

CHAPTER TEN

THEY HAD an advantage: no one knew their faces. Police and every other government agency would be looking for a man and a young woman traveling together, but that described every couple in the country. If they had suspicious papers, it might call attention to them as they tried to cross the border; for that reason, Clay planned to avoid customs.

There were many ways to do it, but Clay preferred the one involving the smallest number of people.

They split, bought tickets separately, and took a train from Moscow to Smolensk. The train would continue to Prague, but they would not be on it. They met every couple of hours in the dining car, though they didn't speak or make eye contact. It wasn't ideal, but Clay told her how it had to be and she handled it artfully. Every time he thought she might show her age, turn into a rebellious or petulant girl, she surprised him. He had a feeling she would be tested a few more times before this mission ended, and he wondered how many taps her shell could take before the egg cracked. He wouldn't blame her if it did.

They arrived without incident and took separate *marshrutkas* from the kelly-green-painted Smolensk station. From his vantage point behind a cement column, he watched her hire the passenger van, and he didn't make out anyone tailing her as she drove away. There were a few Russian police officers loitering around the station, but none seemed eager to move too far from the snack counter.

He waited another ten minutes and walked to the taxi line.

An uneventful ride later—the cabdriver barked on his cell phone at someone named Nadia for the duration—he arrived at a petrol station adjacent to the M1 highway.

There are many ways to sneak into and out of a country, even ones whose borders are shut tighter than a vault. He had placed a phone call to a contact he'd cultivated years before, and they were to meet at this rest stop at noon. Marika was already seated at a small bar the station provided for coffee drinkers and smokers. She looked confident, but with the slightest rattle around the edges, like the creak a pipe gives long before it bursts.

Clay moved next to her, hoping to soften that rattle. "We're going to make it." He didn't know why he said it, but he felt it might help.

"Should we be talking together?"

"We're not out of the woods, but we're at least near the edge."

"I do not understand."

"Nothing. It's an American expression that I— Nothing."

She smiled at him, and it almost made him glad he'd attempted the joke.

The air stirred, and Clay looked up to see the man he recognized, a pale Ukrainian named Uri Bezlo, enter the station and beeline his way.

"Hello, Ivan," Bezlo said softly as he approached and shook hands. If Marika was surprised by Clay's alias, she didn't show it.

Uri was a small, imposing man with terrier-like features and shiny, pointed teeth. Clay noted the shoulder holster ballooning the breast of his jacket. He was wearing it wrong; his concealed pistol was about as concealed as a leg cast.

Clay pressed cash into his hand as they shook, and Uri did not look down to count it, just put his hand back in his pocket.

"Truck will be here in half hour. Exporting chemicals to Slovakia. You will go south through Belarus and Ukraine, yes?"

"How long?"

"Fifteen hundred kilometers. But you and girl will be comfortable. Much comfortable."

"If we're not..."

"Yes, yes. I'd have no business if you were not comfortable."

In the spy game, by necessity, Clay had to deal with men who turned his stomach. He had to compartmentalize his feelings, lie down with dogs and ignore the fleas. Uri was in the human trafficking business. He ran girls from Russia to all points inside the former Soviet bloc: Poland, Belarus, Czech Republic, Germany. He was despicable, but useful.

"Look for Averbuch Chemical truck. When driver exits to use bathroom, climb in passenger door, slip to back of cab, and open hatch. If cabin is not to your satisfaction, you knock on door, and I will take care of it."

He saw the concern on Clay's face and quickly held up both hands. "It will be right. This is excellent driver and special truck. I've known driver twelve years. Fine, fine, yes."

"Yes?"

"Yes. How much do you weigh?"

Clay told him.

"And the girl?"

Clay guessed, and Uri nodded. "I will leave you now. But I will personally accompany you on this trip, riding in cab with driver, yes. I have business in Ukraine and I will make sure you are comfortable."

Clay wasn't sorry to see him walk off. He could tell Marika had the same reaction, as if she might catch a disease just from standing next to the man.

The hatch opened to a small cabin, not unlike the one Clay grew up inside on his uncle's boat. It was about fifteen feet by fifteen feet, with a bed, a stuffed chair, a desk with an office chair, and even a small water closet separated by a partitioned door.

"Amazing!" Marika exclaimed.

It was. Uri had come through. They must've used this truck, or ones like it, for smuggling important people into or out of Russia, because Clay doubted they wasted such comfort on the poor women transported from brothel to brothel.

After a moment, they heard the driver's door open and shut and then felt the movement as they drifted from the station to the M1. The truck must've had a container full of chemicals on the other side of the wall, so any border agents opening the back doors would only see the designated material. Making the truck transport chemicals was a stroke of genius; no border agents wanted to search too thoroughly through poison. Uri had asked for Clay's and Marika's weights so the driver could take out a similar weight from the back before they left, in case they were directed to stop at a weigh station. It wasn't an airplane ride, but it was a well-planned and well-executed smuggling operation.

The vibration under their feet was strangely relaxing. Clay took the chair and gestured to the bed. "Might as well settle in. It's going to be a long drive."

Marika fell on top of the bed. "Better than a sleeping car on a train."

"And no one to check our passports or tickets."

Marika smiled and closed her eyes. Her voice came as though it were detached from her body. "I visited Prague once when I was very young. Before my father died. Before my mother remarried. Before David."

"Oh?"

"I don't remember much. I remember the spires in the city. It looked like a fairy tale. I remember my dad smiling, and I don't remember seeing that often. I remember he took us to an enormous castle with a green dome, and inside was a cathedral. I had never seen anything like it. It seemed old, like it would have taken lifetimes to build; I remember thinking this even as a small child. There was an enormous stained-glass window, with pictures of various religious scenes I didn't understand, but the bottom one I noticed because there was a name printed there, Elisabeth, and that was my mother's name. I remember thinking this woman in the glass looked like my mother, except this woman looked calm, unworried, and my mother always had worry on her face. I stared at this stained glass so long that my parents continued their tour without me, not realizing I had stopped. Through the years, I watched my mother, but she never achieved the peace of that depiction in the glass. I don't remember much, but I have a distinct memory of that Elisabeth, and looking for that expression on my own mother's face."

The truck had not been traveling long, maybe two hours, when Clay opened his eyes. He felt the vibrations slow and then stop as the truck braked and sat idle.

He heard the hatch open and tensed. Uri ducked his head inside and smiled wanly. "Engine trouble. We're on a deserted bit of highway, if you care to stretch your legs. We'll be here awhile as Sergei solves the problem."

Marika looked up at Clay and nodded, asking without using her voice if it was okay. Clay frowned but nodded back.

Uri clapped his hands together once, as if it was no problem, nothing to worry about, a minor inconvenience. Clay somehow missed what it really was: a signal. He should have been on alert, should have been tensed and ready as soon as their schedule was interrupted with "engine trouble," should have seen through the façade, but he was tired and sluggish and wasn't thinking clearly.

He stepped down from the eighteen-wheeler's cab to find five Russian police officers and two FSB agents with guns pointed his way. The truck's hood was up and smoke poured from it—he had to give them credit for selling the ruse. One of the officers already had Marika by the arm.

Uri grinned, showing those sharp incisors. "I'm sorry, friend. I can't do what I do and not cut in the Russian police. It seems they are looking for an American man and a young woman. And then you called..." He shrugged as if it were was the simplest choice in the world. Clay clamped his anger. He glared over at the driver, who was stoically closing the truck's hood. Then he looked at Marika, who was watching him with feral eyes, as if she was waiting for him to do something.

The truck's hood slammed, making a sound like a gunshot, and all eyes left him for only a moment. It was a professional's moment, experience's moment, when lesser men would have let their concentration flag. The only way to stay alive and free in the spy world is to recognize the tiniest of moments when you are ready and your enemy is not.

The semi's hood slammed, their eyes strayed, and Clay leapt on Uri. He had the pistol out of the Ukrainian's chest holster while the surprise was still on his face. The vile man died without changing expression.

Marika spun and clawed at the face of the officer who held her, and when he raised his hands, she drove a fist into his groin with all the force she could muster. Good girl. She *had* been paying attention.

Clay started shooting then, and the police reacted like a covey of quail, dispersing in different directions with varied flutters of fear.

The FSB agents knew better and charged, firing too. Clay reached for Marika and kicked the doubled-over police officer at the same moment, sending him directly into the path of the storming agents. Clay then flung Marika back, and she practically sailed through the air, landing on the ground and rolling under the eighteen-wheeler.

Then he heard the truck's engine crank and turn over, the driver getting the idea to flee. Clay shot one of the FSB agents as he tried to disentangle himself from his comrade. Then he retreated toward the truck. Out of the corner of his eye, he saw the remaining FSB agent hightail it to his sedan. The ambush was out of control and growing worse by the second.

The truck started to move, and Clay dove under the carriage, rolling and pulling Marika with him just as she was about to be flattened by the second set of tires.

He sprang up on the other side of the semi, and the driver made a mistake, tried to turn into him to get back to the M1 instead of heading straight to plow up onto the road. Clay cut the distance, leapt onto the running board, opened the door, but was not expecting the driver to be armed. A Fort-12 pistol swung his way, but in his haste, the driver had forgotten to fasten his seat belt. Clay reached in and yanked his gun arm as the pistol fired and the driver tumbled out. Nose met earth. The truck was still turning, and all eighty thousand pounds of it rolled over him, crushing bones and pancaking skin.

"Get in!" Clay bellowed at Marika, and she ran to his side. He knew she was stricken by what she had seen today, but he didn't have time to calm her. He wasn't sure he'd ever be able to remove that last image from her mind. She hurdled over to the passenger seat, and he took the driver's wheel and turned the semi just in time to see the one sedan move from the cluster of cars that had arrived to execute the ambush. In the passenger seat sat the only policeman alive, and behind the wheel was the agent from the FSB. They were flooring the sedan, angling for the highway, and it took a second—but only a second—for Clay to realize they weren't attacking but fleeing. He had one chance, but he didn't know if the semi would respond in time.

He gunned the truck in first gear and climbed it into second, almost sputtering the engine, but it held. The sedan was blitzing forward now; he wouldn't have the angle, wouldn't have the speed, but at the last moment, he tipped the wheel and clipped the back of the sedan with enough of his bumper to cause it to fishtail as it hit the highway. Tires caught on pavement and it barrel-rolled like a bowling pin.

Clay braked the truck and looked out at the smoking sedan, which came to rest on its top, tires spinning, a beetle on its back.

"Turn your head away from this," he said, opened his door, and dropped down onto the highway. He crossed to the sedan, stooped, and fired twice.

He was back in the cab a few seconds later. He pulled the lever into gear, pushed on the accelerator, eased back on the clutch, and moved the truck onto the M1.

We're going to need some luck now, he thought and maybe said aloud. He didn't know whether Marika had watched him execute the wounded men while they were at their most vulnerable.

He calculated they were only thirty minutes from the border with Belarus. He hoped no one would discover the carnage before they reached it. The sun would be rising soon, and though the wreckage was all on the side of the road, with little light to illuminate it, it wouldn't be long, perhaps minutes, before someone traveling this remote stretch of the M1 found it. Soon after, the police would be called, and he didn't know how long after that they would put two and two together and close the border.

He was driving blind—no map and no GPS—and he just hoped at each rise of the highway that he would see some sign of the border. He might be driving into a hornets' nest, but it would be better than this part—the not knowing. It was his greatest enemy, not knowing. He tried to defeat it on every mission, he tried to take it out of the equation, but there it was, appearing to taunt him, not knowing. The enemy of spies, not knowing. The harbinger of death and pain. Not knowing. It could smile on you or it could bare its teeth.

They crested another slight rise and he saw two twinkling

lights that made up the border between Belarus and Russia, a couple of checkpoint stations and old wooden gates. This was not modern border security—telephones instead of satellites, Barney Fife instead of Robocop. Yet Clay kept his guard up, his senses alert, because he was in the throes of not knowing.

"Back to the hatch for you, Marika."

She nodded and disappeared behind him.

He pulled into the designated lane, and a green-camouflaged border guard approached, an assault rifle strapped to his chest.

"Freight and transit report."

Clay looked in the glove box. Nothing. He checked the center console. Nothing. Then he spotted a blue folder tucked between his seat and the console. He gave it a quick glance—it seemed official—and handed it over.

The guard opened the folder and looked at it for less than a second. Clay started to hand over his passport—the one whose name would appear nowhere in the file—but the guard just pursed his lips, clucked, and handed the file back.

The gate swung open and Clay drove the truck into Belarus. Sometimes it could pat you on the back, not knowing. Sometimes it took pity on you and focused its attention on your enemies.

Adams walked the city square in Prague at six in the morning. He always loved this city in first light, as it awoke. He had heard a rumor that Hitler thought the city so beautiful, he forbade the Luftwaffe to bomb it. He also heard that Walt Disney had borrowed the architecture of the Church of Our Lady Before Tyn for the steeples on Sleeping Beauty's castle. Apocryphal stories or not, the city's charm was undeniable.

The sun hadn't yet shown its face, and the air held its chill. He found one coffeehouse opening its doors and ordered an espresso. His clock was off from the jet lag, so he might as well hit the caffeine and fight the long day. God knew he needed it.

He wondered again if Laura and the girls would accept the news. It might catch them off-guard, but they would warm to it, he was confident. There was more education in travel than in school, and as the world grew continuously smaller, his girls would hold an advantage from having lived abroad. He was already rehearsing what to say.

A shadow fell across his back, and he saw a dull reflection in the polished wood of the long bar.

"Hello, Michael."

Adams turned, his expression fixed. "Alan."

"You found the one espresso in Prague worth a damn."

Alan Fourticq had been in charge of EurOps for the last fifteen years. He had grown up in Manhattan, attended Yale undergrad, then Harvard Law, and had worked for the CIA as an analyst on the team that helped bring down Slobodan Milošević. He had a full head of silver hair and eyes that spoke of a lifetime of intrigue. His smile pulled the corners of his mouth up reluctantly.

"Did I?"

"I guess you'll be a regular here before long."

Adams sized up his predecessor. "You've heard, then?"

"I've spent thirty years in espionage. I have a knack for discovering secrets. Congratulations, Michael. Truly."

He offered his hand, and Adams shook it. If there was warmth in the gesture, the younger man had a hard time detecting it.

"I've been so preoccupied with this damn news and how the other directors were going to take it, I didn't ask about you.... What are the Agency's plans for you, Alan?"

"Is there a glue factory for retired spooks?"

Adams chuckled in a way he hoped sounded natural and anticipated more. Fourticq obliged. "I've put away some money, built a house in a remote corner of the world where I can take a step back for a while."

"Hmm. I guess I thought you'd plant in Virginia and consult with the Director."

"I thought I'd run EurOps until I decided to retire, but like Mick Jagger sang, you can't always get what you want."

There it was, the truth dropping on the floor and stinking up the room. Adams didn't know what to say in response, but he hadn't risen this far without being able to think on his feet.

"Sorry it didn't end on your terms. It rarely does in this line of work."

"No, it doesn't, does it? How'd your family take the news? Eager to live overseas for a while?"

Had he told Fourticq he had a family? Spooks had a general rule that they kept conversation on the professional level, never personal. Mention of his family was like hearing a false note out of a trumpet. Still, he managed to keep his smile, though it felt unnatural on his face.

"I haven't told them yet."

Fourticq winked. "Ah, well. I'm sure they'll enjoy the surprise. Never had kids myself, but Prague has an excellent American school, you'll soon discover."

Adams was eager to steer the conversation away from his family. "I'll need your help transitioning; I'd be disappointed and at a disadvantage if you didn't give me a few extra months of your time."

Fourticq measured him, then nodded. "Of course."

Adams nodded back, sipped his espresso, and started for the door.

"One other thing," Fourticq said. "Watch out for Dan Clausen. He made no effort to hide that he was gunning for this job. He's not going to take the news of your promotion lying down."

"I'll watch him," Adams said, and headed out across the square. The sun was just beginning to rise on the other side of the St. Charles Bridge, but a ribbon of clouds threatened to push it back out of sight before it could make its climb.

They ditched the semi at a train station parking lot outside Minsk, then walked into town, ate chicken and potatoes cooked together in a pot, and stole a tiny car from behind an apartment in the dead of night, but not before exchanging the plates with a car on a street two blocks away. The way to keep the little red ball undetected was to continuously move the shells.

A CIA division director named Adams was to be assassinated in Prague in less than a week. Marika had a strong memory for names and dates, and the level of detail she revealed was remarkable. Layered as it was with precise recollections regarding the inner workings of the CIA, her information was actionable. Someone senior inside the Agency was a longtime conspirator with Russian FSB, but Marika didn't know who. The name was never mentioned, just the code name: Snow Wolf. Over the last decade, Snow Wolf had handed over technology, operations, and strategy intel in exchange for the most American of reasons to be a traitor to one's country: cold hard cash. Adams, it turned out, threatened that traitor's power and therefore had been set up for elimination. When Clay had first started, he'd had a handler named Adams, whom he'd met only a few times. When he was transferred to black ops, he'd forgotten about him. He suspected that the Adams he knew and the Adams scheduled to die might be the same person. He remembered the man as being sharp and fair, and it was little wonder he had risen up the ranks on the analyst side.

Now Clay understood why so many people wanted Marika killed. Power and information were resources to be cultivated at great cost and to be protected at great sacrifice. Her knowledge would expose not just an assassination plot but a traitor. The life hanging in the balance—Adams's—was just collateral damage to the bigger target, the extent of FSB's infiltration into US intelligence via Snow Wolf.

Since the time he had orchestrated the burning, drowning death of his uncle, Clay had learned a detached stoicism in his work. He got an assignment, dispassionately executed it, and moved on to the next. But this one had fanned his inner fire, and he felt emotion brewing inside him: anger, hatred, retribution. These men played their games, they moved their pieces, and they minded losing a pawn or rook or queen only if it affected their hold on money or power. He hated them. They passed secrets and lies as easily as if they'd been dollar bills; they counted lives as though they were debits and credits, black and red ink on either side of the ledger. He hated them. They held on to their power with viselike grips and cut down threats to that power as easily as rotor blades cutting dry grass. He hated them. He had bled for his country on countless occasions, and he wondered if any of those assignments had been for Snow Wolf's gain. His hatred grew, and for the first time since he'd joined the Agency, he had no plans to check it.

The coffee outside Warsaw was strong and warmed his mind as much as his throat. They had crossed into Poland through back roads under the cover of darkness. He preferred to press on, but they needed to eat.

Marika observed him as she blew on her own cup. "You look upset," she said.

"I guess I am."

"I worry that what I told you will get you killed by your own countrymen."

"It won't."

"I am the worst thing that's happened to you."

"No. Trust me when I tell you I've lived through far worse than this."

"When my mind tries to think of David, a darkness falls over him so I can't see his face. It was only last week and I can't see his face."

"It's normal. The mind has its own set of defense mechanisms, like a porcupine's quills."

"That man yesterday. The truck driver..." She shuddered.

"He ran girls from Russia to brothels in Eastern Europe. It was just a matter of time before he got what was coming to him."

Marika fell silent. A plate of eggs and sausages was brought to their table, and she pushed them around with her fork. He hadn't seen her smile in so long. He wanted to see her smile.

"Did you know they have a nickname for me inside the Agency?"

She looked up and shook her head.

"They call me the Right Hand."

She pointed to her right hand and wriggled the fingers. "The Right Hand?"

"That's right."

"Why?"

"I will tell you, but you have to promise me that you won't laugh."

Her eyes softened and she took a bite of her eggs. She didn't know where he was going with this, and that suited him. He had heard a comedian once say that the first rule of comedy was surprise.

"It was my first job in the field. Intelligence indicated that

Iran's energy council was secretly hiring German scientists to assist them in enriching uranium at their facility in Natanz. Secret delegates from Iran's nuclear program were to meet with a leading physicist under the guise of attending a conference in Abu Dhabi in the UAE. My mission was to intercept this scientist, named Tomas Zimmermann, and persuade him to discontinue his relationship with the Iranians."

"Persuade him how?"

"That was left to my discretion."

She drew a finger across her throat and made a questioning face.

"I hoped that wouldn't be necessary, but I wasn't going to rule anything out."

She opened her mouth again, but he interrupted, smiling. "Would you like to hear this story or not?"

"Of course!"

"Thank you. Now, where was I? Oh, yes, Abu Dhabi. I arrive there under the guise of an American student attending the same conference. I was quite young at the time, in my mid-twenties, and I wore a short beard and the round glasses of an intellectual."

She grinned, picturing it. He felt emboldened. There was that smile. He hoped for more.

"Is that so hard to believe?"

"It's the biggest bullshit you've told me so far," she said, then covered her mouth with her hand to hold back the laugh.

"Maybe I'm not saying this in Hungarian correctly. I was an *intellectual*." He used the word for *student*.

"Yes, you are saying it correctly. Continue, please..."

He pretended to be offended, but he had her now and he was pleased. He kept a half smile on his own face, as if his tale could spin into the absurd at any moment.

"So the conference is at the Palace Hotel, which is the most opulent building, let alone hotel, I've ever seen in the world. The ceilings are literally made of gold, and they even have an ATM machine in the lobby that will spit out gold bars instead of cash."

"You're kidding me."

"You have my word. So they have this enormous conference room the size of a football field, and I sit in the back with a notebook and a suitably bored expression on my face and wait for Zimmermann to speak. He's the third speaker, and his language is German, which I barely understand, and there's a translator but I forgot to pick up the headphones I see everyone else wearing, so I just nod my head and pretend to take notes like I'm fully absorbed in what he is saying. And let's face it, even if I did understand German, I'm not sure I would follow his talk comparing nuclear fusion energy and hydrogen energy or whatever the hell he's talking about.

"Out of the corner of my eye, I spot three Iranians—hard-looking guys with unfashionable short-sleeved buttoned-up shirts and khakis that say these guys belong at an intellectual conference even less than I do. And they're watching Zimmermann with these malevolent expressions, like really threatening postures. I recognize the one seated nearest me as a known terrorist who aided Al Qaeda in getting arms into post–Bin Laden Iraq. Anyway, dangerous guys.

"And you must remember, I'm new at this. I have no idea

if I'm sticking out like a sore thumb or if I'm blending in the way I hope. Maybe they've already made me and I'm a rubber duck in a shooting gallery. I have no idea. My mission is to dissuade Zimmermann, remember. It has nothing to do with tussling with Iranian hostiles, so I'd be wise to avoid them.

"So I look over again and the Iranians are gone and I breathe a sigh of relief. Zimmermann finishes speaking and I have to wait through three more equally boring, equally esoteric speeches before we break for lunch. Now, I know, because I've watched him, that Zimmermann is going to head back to his hotel room to eat by himself instead of joining the buffet for featured speakers. I also know the elevator to his floor is a good fifteen-minute walk from the conference room—this hotel is truly preposterous in its dimensions—and so I set out to tail him. The Iranians are nowhere in sight; I'm sure they were equally bored as I, and whatever money and information they'll be exchanging with Zimmermann is to be later that day. I wait for Zimmermann to step into the elevator alone before I follow him inside.

"I let him press the button for nine; then I press the same so he'll think I share his floor. We ride up in silence.

"I need more time than I would have on this elevator ride to properly convince him of the error of his ways, so I decide I will discreetly tail him to his room and then push in behind him and we'll have a little chat.

"So the doors ding nine and we disembark and no sooner do I slide out of the elevators than the three Iranians swing in behind me and I feel this knife in my ribs.

"I act startled, which is what you're supposed to do to maintain your cover, but the truth is I *am* startled. What the hell was I thinking, right? The one with the knife croaks at me in Arabic to move, and I pretend not to understand, but they're not amused and they push me into Zimmermann's room: 901. He's got a suite the size of an apartment and they shove me rudely down into this chair in front of a small table and two of these Iranian sons of bitches pull my arm out and hold it down so that the palm of my right hand is exposed flat on the tabletop.

"Zimmermann slides across from me, looking like the spitting image of Dr. Mengele, and he asks me in perfect English who I am.

"Now, I have a cover story. I am a PhD student at MIT, studying the ramifications of Haramein's paper on the Schwarzchild Proton or some shit I've completely forgotten now, and I think I'm convincing. I look the part; I sound the part.

"The doctor smirks at me, takes off his glasses, and starts wiping the lenses with the tail of his shirt, very slowly. 'Now,' he says to me, 'I'm going to ask you a few questions any student at MIT should know about physics, and if you get one wrong, I'm going to nod at Salaam here and he is going to chop off your hand, understood? Once Salaam is done chopping, perhaps you will be more forthcoming about who you are and who you work for, umm-hmm. Or perhaps you would like to tell us now, while you still have your appendages, hmmm.'

"I have spent the last three months learning all I can about Zimmermann and physics, but I'm no scholar, much less an MIT graduate. What can I do, though? Blow my cover and they'll kill me straightaway. Try to answer the questions and buy myself more time. That's the first thing they teach you at Langley: do whatever it takes to buy yourself more time. You just never know how the game will break, and time is as precious a commodity as gold.

"So I repeat that I'm telling the truth, I am who I say I am, and I beg for him to believe me, to call MIT, to call my roommates—and again, this is an Academy Award–level performance, but Zimmermann remains unimpressed.

"The two goons have my arm pinned down, that right hand exposed, and Salaam picks up the biggest, sharpest knife you ever saw and poises it over my hand like it's a guillotine.

"'If you are who you say you are, you have nothing to worry about,' says the doctor. I can't remember what I said then, but he keeps rubbing those lenses with his shirt. They must be caked in mud the way he keeps rubbing them. 'Ready?' he asks. I'm sure I begged him again to stop, but he keeps on.

"'The reason your head jerks forward when coming to a quick stop is best explained by what?'

"I look at Zimmermann, at Salaam holding that knife, at my right hand, which is about to say bye-bye. Then this answer pops into my brain; I don't know where it came from, what textbook I had pored over in preparation for this assignment, but my mouth is quicker than my mind and I blurt out, 'Newton's first law. Objects in motion stay in motion unless an external force is applied. Your head wants to stay in motion.'"

Marika started laughing and clapped her hands. "You knew the answer!"

"I don't know how, but I knew that one. It was basic physics, I guess. Really, I thought he'd try something harder, more germane to his field and why he was here speaking at this conference."

"And so you kept your right hand!" She looked as if she wanted to point to it, but his hands were in his lap, under the table.

"I'm not done."

Marika's eyes lit up, delighted there was more.

"So Zimmermann frowns and Salaam looks over at him expectantly, but the good doctor shakes his head. I think it's over, I've passed the test, but Zimmermann isn't finished.

"'One more,' he says. 'A fifty-fifty chance. Answer correctly, and you can leave here whole. Incorrectly and I'll feed you your right hand myself. True or false? For any pair of surfaces, the coefficient of static friction between the surfaces is less than the correspondent coefficient of sliding friction.'"

Marika sat up on the edge of her seat.

"Now, you have to understand, I have no idea what he's talking about. He might as well be speaking in Swahili. But I have a fifty-fifty chance of getting the answer right. And it's not just a guess, you see, because I do know something about the man doing the asking. I know he's the kind of man who is adept at lying. I know he's more likely to tell a lie than the truth. If I'm going to guess, and I am, then I have to guess with the only information I have: that this man is a practiced deceiver. And so I guess..."

"False!" Marika exclaimed.

"'False,' I said."

Clay paused, leaving the story dangling until Marika couldn't stand it any longer.

"What happened? Were you right? Tell me!"

Clay looked at her gravely, his eyes as serious as she'd ever seen them. "I had guessed..." He let the pause spread, his audience of one mesmerized.

"Wrong!" he yelled, and flung his hand up from underneath the table, where he had his table knife stuck through his fingers and a copious amount of ketchup dripping from his hand.

Marika shrieked and then burst into a fit of laughter that filled the whole room like a warm fire. Clay joined her, laughing hard himself, really letting go, and it was like a steam valve letting the pressure and the tension escape, and they continued laughing, drawing stares from the old Polish woman who stood next to the kitchen door, but they didn't care. The laughter felt good; it felt right.

He put his right hand flat on the table so the knife handle stood erect and the ketchup spread out and Marika laughed even harder.

"You...you are a terrible man," she said through the ripples of laughter.

Clay shrugged as if to say, "I am what I am."

The old woman next to the kitchen frowned.

CHAPTER ELEVEN

THOUGH THE announcement had not yet been made, Michael Adams was already enjoying one of the perks of his new position as head of EurOps; most notably, he had access to every personnel file within Central Intelligence.

He opened his laptop and performed the keystrokes necessary to pull up all of the information the Agency had about Dan Clausen, the head of District 1, headquartered in New York City. Adams hadn't spent a lot of time with the man, an occasional Washington summoning, an occasional cyberchat, and Adams had regarded his counterpart warily by instinct—Clausen had a quick mind but a wasp's disposition. Sting, sting, sting. Now the file on him filled in the details.

Clausen had started in the field, a rarity among the district chiefs; in fact, he was probably the only one. Field agents were tools, weapons; analysts were the schemers, the strategists, the wielders of those weapons. They saw the big picture, had greater territories at stake, focused on the macro over the micro. Field agents were on missions; analysts worked campaigns. Adams knit his brows and kept reading.

Clausen had operated in Eastern Europe and Asia, everywhere from Reykjavik to Tokyo. He was an adept killer, thief, actor, and planner, utilizing multiple covers, sometimes within the same city. He had distinguished himself on a variety of missions, and the DCI before Manning had brought him back to Langley and groomed him for a leadership position. He'd served as a deputy district head in Dallas and Seattle, and after September 11, 2001, had taken over the New York office, where he'd run District 1 for the last decade.

Adams was actually astonished by Clausen's rise. It was little wonder Clausen would expect EurOps for himself. His work in District 1, which covered pockets of Russia, Africa, and the Middle East, had been exemplary. He represented the best of both worlds: he ran campaigns as if they were missions, all-encompassing goals realized by pinpoint operations.

Adams reviewed the top of the file once more. Clausen was a killer. Adams had ordered men's deaths numerous times, but he had never killed anyone himself, with his bare hands, with a weapon. He wondered if he would have the nerve.

Clausen had no family, either. No wife, no kids, and the file made no mention of his sex life, which seemed an oversight. Or maybe it had been expunged.

Adams let his mind wander and return. He looked up at the clock. There were two hours until the meeting. They had reserved the conference room on the top floor of the Hotel Ambassador, overlooking Wenceslas Square.

He planned to show up five minutes late so the others would already be seated and he wouldn't have to pick his chair. He would try not to look at Clausen, lest he give away the purpose of the meeting. There would be plenty of time to judge Clausen's reaction when Adams had finished speaking.

His phone chirped and he looked at the number on the display. It was Laura, calling from their home line. He let it ring and go to voice mail. He wanted to keep his attention on the task at hand.

He could always talk to her later.

They arrived in Prague, tired and cramped but invigorated. The city spread before them like Oz. It was a gorgeous city, the hills, the river, the architecture. It more than made up for the stretch of abandoned warehouses, factories, and towns that littered the highway between Poland and Prague.

One thing nagged at Clay, and he knew he should turn his mind to the problem, but he was reluctant to do so. He should find the nearest bus stop and drop Marika off there. She was free, she could disappear, he could give her enough money that she could climb on a train to Berlin or Rome or Brussels. She didn't have papers, though, wouldn't know how to acquire them or whom to trust to do it for her, and would she be preyed upon, pretty innocent that she was? She wanted to go to Disneyland, she wanted to find a Hungarian community in Los Angeles, and he would make sure it happened. No one else would do it for her, would see it through to the end; it was up to him. At least, that was what he told himself.

They rented a room in a touristy hotel away from the bridge. Clay needed to go out, but he sat Marika down first.

"If anything happens to me and I don't come back, if you sit here for more than twenty-four hours without seeing me, then you need to dial the number 011-020-661-3992 and ask for a man named Andrew Stedding. You tell him you are Marika Csontos, you are all alone, and you need his help...."

"Nothing will happen—"

"011-020-661-3992. Say it."

"I didn't—"

"011-020-661-3992. Say it."

"Why are you being so ugly?"

"Because it's important."

"011-020-661-3992."

"Again!"

"011-020-661-3992."

"And ask for whom?"

"Andrew Stedding."

"And tell him what?"

"That the Right Hand is dead," she said.

He blinked once, then again, and slowly nodded. "That's right."

She got up, went into the bathroom, and slammed the door so it rattled on its hinges.

He bought a prepaid mobile from a cluttered electronics store and walked to the middle of the St. Charles Bridge. It seemed as good a place as any. The ability to laser in on phone calls and mobilize forces and have a predator drone in the air always played well in movies but took a bit more time in the real world. Not much, but enough. Besides, Stedding would break his own neck to cover for him, as any good handler would. At least, Clay hoped that was the case.

Stedding didn't wait for pleasantries to be exchanged. "Where are you?"

"Prague."

"What the fuck are you doing there?"

"I'll tell you when you get here."

"Dammit."

"How fast can you make it?"

"Two hours. I'm in Paris. I thought you might run here."

"I'm not running, Steddy. I need your help."

"What are you caught up in?"

"What have you heard?" It was a favorite tactic of both of theirs, to answer a question with a question.

"The version going around the Agency and the State Department is that you shot up the dignitaries bringing Nelson to the exchange...."

"They weren't dignitaries. They were FSB."

"They're saying you killed Nelson in the process."

"One of them got a lucky shot off. They were torturing him long before I got there, by the looks of him."

"They're saying State is furious."

"If they weren't, I wouldn't be doing my job correctly."

"The Director is personally covering for you, for the program, and he's told State to bugger off."

"You heard that?"

"I did."

"Two hours, then?"

"Yes. Where?"

"East end of the St. Charles Bridge."

"In plain sight, eh?"

"The best way to hide."

"See you then."

"And Steddy—don't tell anyone you're coming. I'm serious."

"Okay."

The line fell silent. Clay stared down at the water as it rolled underneath him, the current picking up silt and detritus from the bottom of the river and depositing it in another location, far away.

He waited out the time by flitting in and out of various hotels, looking for the telltale signs of Agency presence—black town cars or SUVs parked near side or back doors, guys in suits near elevators, groups looking more at people entering or exiting the lobby than at each other. He covered a quarter of the city, but he didn't see anything out of the ordinary. It didn't matter; mostly, he was getting the lay of the land, reacquainting himself with Prague. It had been years since he'd been there, and though he prided himself on his internal compass, it helped to scout for nooks and crannies that might come into play at an opportune time. He noted a parking lot, a hardware store, a side street that led to the train tracks. He clocked where a couple of small boats were moored on the river, where a cafe had a back door opening to a different street, where a footpath offered three different forks down three different avenues. He cleared his mind and focused on the work.

Stedding arrived at the appointed place at the appointed time. He wore his frown like a favorite accessory, put on whenever he traveled. It occurred to Clay that he knew nothing about Stedding's family—whether he had one or not. He had never asked. He wanted to believe it was because of the Agency's unwritten protocol; the less you know about your associates, the better it is for both of you professionally. He hoped he wasn't so far under as to make the answer the alternative—that he just didn't care.

"All right, Clay. Time to tell me why you're here, why I'm here, and why you haven't done one damn thing right since you left London."

"This is why it's better no one checks up on me. That way no one gets disappointed."

"They're checking now. Trust me."

"Did you know the six district heads are here in Prague as we speak?"

Stedding pursed his lips, so Clay pressed forward.

"One of them, Adams, is going to get punched by Russian Intelligence working in concert with a flipped American district head code-named Snow Wolf."

He could see Stedding's temperature rise as easily as if he'd been looking at a thermometer.

"I need you to find out where they're meeting, and I need

guns, pistols, ammo, whatever you can get me, but none of this Czech and Russian shit. I'm lucky I actually hit anyone back at the border."

"What happened at the bord— Never mind. The girl told you all this?"

"Yes, which reminds me, I also need papers for her and a plane ticket to Los Angeles, plus some cash, enough to get her started on a new life...."

"Anything else?" Stedding asked, his voice dripping with perturbation.

"Disneyland tickets too much? Forget that, papers, ticket, and money are fine."

"Why don't I just call an alert and clear everyone out of Prague? Especially Adams. Michael Adams, by the way, the head of District Two."

"Ahh, then it *was* my old handler."

"Why no alert?"

"Because I don't know who Snow Wolf is. If you want to blow it up and save Adams, that's your decision. But I think we're better off dangling him as bait and finding out which district head has claws. Otherwise, Snow Wolf goes to ground and maybe we get another twenty years of our business being their business."

Stedding rocked back and forth on his heels. He pulled out a handkerchief and spat into it. "I see your point."

"If I can save him, I will."

"I know you will. Okay. Where will you be in two hours?"

"Meet me at the train station. Track six."

Stedding walked away. Clay thought about telling him to

be careful, but what good would it do? He resolved to ask Stedding about his family the next time they were together.

It was a test, simple as that. The Director hadn't come to personally deliver the news because he wanted to see how Adams handled it, along with whatever fallout might come. It always seemed astounding that there was as much politics in the Agency as in the executive branch. No matter, he was ready. They would find him formidable or they would find themselves retired. He would make sure of it.

Adams left his room and walked the hallway to the bank of elevators running up the spine of the hotel. He absently pressed the up arrow, his mind elsewhere. He was thinking about espresso and that admonishment from Alan Fourticq regarding Dan Clausen.

He had no way of knowing there were multiple killers already in the building.

The elevator was empty, and he stepped inside and pressed eleven. The car stopped short on the fourth floor, and the doors opened to reveal Clausen. The man's lupine eyes sized Adams up as he stepped inside.

"Michael."

"Dan."

They stepped to the back of the car almost simultaneously and watched the digital numbers climb. After a moment, Clausen spoke.

"You know why we've been summoned to Prague?"

Adams thought about lying; he was certainly practiced in the art, but most likely Clausen already knew the answer to his question and was testing him.

"Yes."

Clausen's eyebrows arched. "Manning didn't tell me a damn thing."

"It's the nature of the beast."

"So what the hell is—"

The elevator car settled, the doors opened, and the conference room beckoned, interrupting his counterpart's question. Everyone was already seated. Clausen looked as if he wanted to finish the conversation before they stepped out, but Adams was tired of this particular dance. Fuck him, he could wait like the rest of them. Adams passed the four dark-suited men guarding the door and stepped into the room.

There were two chairs vacant. Adams chose the one just to the right of Fourticq, before Clausen could beat him to it.

Stedding hadn't shown up on time, and he was *always* on time. Clay felt his heart rate accelerate and forced it to calm. He'd give his handler ten minutes. It had been a difficult task on the shortest of notices, and maybe Steddy just needed a bit more of the clock to gather his intelligence.

Clay watched the entrance to the station but couldn't pick out Stedding's figure in the crowd. The place was teeming with people as trains from all over Europe arrived and departed at fifteen-minute intervals.

A Gypsy woman approached and thrust a clipboard toward his face. "Sign, please?" she said in Czech, but Clay waved her away. "Sign please, sir," she repeated, but Clay gave her his coldest glare and wagged his finger, saying "No, no," and the woman clucked her tongue before moving on.

His eyes found the big clock on the platform post. Five more minutes. Then where to look? He could walk toward the bridge and hope that—

The sound of an ambulance siren neared the station and echoed throughout the edifice. Pedestrians at the entrance pivoted and moved to gawk at something outside the doors, some accident. Police sirens joined the ambulance, a full choir of emergency alarms.

Oh, God, Clay thought. He walked briskly toward the crowd, quickening his pace to just short of an out-and-out sprint.

Bright sunlight spilled from the sky and threw him off-balance; it had been overcast an hour ago. He shielded his eyes with the flat of his hand just as the ambulance reached the scene, asserting itself through the semicircle of forty people. A woman shrieked and left the crowd, covering her mouth.

Clay pushed his way forward and saw Stedding lying on his back, half off and half on the curb, bleeding profusely from gunshot wounds to the stomach and chest. Clay forgot his cover, forgot his training, forgot everything and dropped to his knees, pushing the Czech paramedics out of the way. He cradled Stedding in his arms—and somehow the older man's eyes found his and focused. Police arrived on the scene, and one of them, in his hurry to size up the situation, accidentally kicked a black duffel on the ground near the wounded man. Four pistols spilled out, another woman shrieked, and the police and crowd started chattering in Czech at the same time, voices rising as if someone had spun a volume dial on a stereo.

Stedding pulled his mouth up to Clay's ear and whispered one word, "Ambassador," and then his eyes shifted away.

Clay stood, his handler gone. They'd worked together for three years, but that had ended today, in the sun-baked street outside the Praha Hlavní Nádraží train station. A policeman grabbed Clay's shoulder, but he shook it off and yelled, "This man needs help!" in English. "Ambulance! Ambulance! Help this man!" he continued to shout, until the police mistook him for the concerned and horrified bystander he pretended to be. The officers pressed past him to examine the body at the same time as the paramedics.

Clay took a few steps backward, until the crowd enveloped him and he could scurry away. At last, slipping around the corner, he broke into a sprint.

Whoever had put bullets into Stedding would be hurrying to finish the job on Adams, alerted and perhaps panicking, speeding up the plan. Stedding had given Clay a key piece of information before he died; Clay would make sure it wouldn't be in vain. "Ambassador," Stedding had whispered.

The Hotel Ambassador was in Wenceslas Square, less than five minutes away.

Adams waited for Fourticq to finish his preliminaries and introduce him. It seemed to take an eternity; the old man simply would not shut up.

"Finally, Michael Adams has a spot of news he would like to share with you all."

Adams rose and felt all eyes turn his way, inspiriting him. He cleared his throat, ready to claim his new position, not in flowery language but with crisp directness, which he hoped would signal to the others the authoritative way he planned to conduct himself, but before he could speak, alarms sounded throughout the hotel and emergency lights blinked on and off in the hallway.

"Fire alarm," Clausen said, and Adams looked to see whether Clausen's face gave anything away. Was he behind this? A last-ditch effort to control the outcome? What could he possibly be trying to pull?

The four guards outside stepped into the room. Their leader had thick white hair but a youngish face. "Gentlemen, I suggest we move to the street until this clears." The way he said it suggested poise and control. Adams thought he must remember to get this man's name.

"Unless you want to wait it out?" Fourticq offered, unperturbed by the alarms. Adams noted that the old man was already leaving the decision up to him.

But Clausen's voice interrupted that thought. "I'd rather not have my eardrums blasted into oblivion," he hollered into their ears, and strode for the door.

Adams had been in the game long enough to suspect any interruption. A sudden disturbance with this many high-profile intelligence officers gathered in one room? He didn't believe in luck, and he always doubted coincidence. He wondered whether Fourticq and Clausen felt the same way, and if so, were their poker faces as polished as his? A leader in charge of EurOps sure as hell better not show it if he's rattled. Adams shrugged and followed.

As they entered the hallway, the elevator doors swung open and the distinctive *crack, crack* of gunfire rang out. Two of the guards dropped immediately, shouting as they fell. The white-haired guard and the thick one to his right hit the floor and returned fire, but the assassin in the elevator refused to show his face. Instead, a hand holding a pistol swung into view and popped three quick shots, *crack, crack, crack,* which echoed throughout the hallway.

"This way!" yelled Clausen over the volleys of return fire. He had somehow dashed unscathed to the emergency stairwell and was holding the door open, beckoning Adams to follow. But Adams found himself crouched next to Fourticq, unsure, this moment not in any of the myriad permutations he had sketched out for how the meeting would go. And before he could seize on a rational thought, the older man made a dash for the stairwell. *Shit.* The white-haired guard kept on pounding the elevator with cover fire as that disembodied pistol intermittently swung out and coughed bullets.

Adams had to make a move. Now or never. Fourticq made it to the stairs, and Clausen continued to hold it open for Adams. The other district heads had retreated, had overturned the conference table, and were crouched behind it. Bad move. For guys who sent men out to their deaths, who sat with files and computer screens and maps and pushed men's fates around as if they were playing a game of chess, they were faltering spectacularly now that their own lives had been thrust from analysis into the field. Not the theoretical field, but a real-life, honest-to-God, bullets-flying battlefield. If the guards were to be overrun, they'd be sitting ducks. No, the best strategy was to stay mobile, extricate yourself, put as much distance between you and the shooter as possible. Adams might not have been a field agent, but he had studied their moves, pored over their reports, taken the time to learn their strategies.

He ducked his head and broke for the stairwell.

Clay had been to the Hotel Ambassador and knew its location on Wenceslas Square. The streets of Prague, which resembled more the cow paths of Boston than the reliable grid of New York, promoted walking and looking in windows rather than sprinting as fast as a man's legs could carry him. Clay did his best to anticipate the pedestrian movement in front of him and not miss a step.

Stedding. Stedding had asked the wrong man for help—the Snow Wolf had been alerted to the nosy handler, and he had bought two to the chest for his efforts. He had been left for dead, the killer not taking the time to finish the job, do it right. It was a mistake, had allowed Stedding to live just long enough to finish one last mission, give one last piece of intelligence to his field agent, and Clay would make sure it meant something, goddammit.

The Snow Wolf had tipped his hand, too, had certainly narrowed the mystery of his identity, and Clay would expose him whether he was too late to save Adams or not. He'd expose him or kill him. Maybe both.

Adams burst into the stairwell and joined Fourticq and Clausen on the landing, breathing hard.

"Are either of you armed?" Clausen cried, and Adams shook his head, too rattled to force a lie, not sure what good it would do anyway. The question seemed absurd, or was it? Keep moving. That was all Adams could really focus on... keep moving and maybe stay alive.

The stairs looked clear, and the sound of gunfire receded as they pounded down the first flight, single file, Clausen in front, Fourticq behind, and Adams sandwiched between, the most covered—and the most vulnerable, if he stopped to think about it. But he didn't think about it, didn't want to, he was flushed with adrenaline, and the floor numbers dropped as they reached a flight, turned on a landing, and spiraled down to the next.

Adams sensed that something had changed, the sounds of their footfalls had changed rhythms, and he turned to see Fourticq doubled over on the riser above.

"Are you okay, Alan?"

He hurried back up to Forticq.

Clausen called from below. "We've got to keep moving!"

"Just a second, dammit!" Adams yelled back, more loudly

than he meant to. Fourticq remained doubled over, and only then did Adams see the blood.

"My God, Alan, you're shot."

Fourticq grunted. "I don't think so. Just grazed. I just cramped up. Haven't run this much since the Boston Marathon. I was twenty then."

"Let me see it."

Adams guided Fourticq's hand away. His shirt was stained with blood. Adams pulled the shirt back and was relieved; Fourticq was right, it was just a scratch, probably from shrapnel. There was no bullet hole.

"You must've caught a splinter from all that wood paneling taking a beating."

"Do you get a Purple Heart for splinters?"

Adams had to smile at that, even in the midst of this pandemonium.

"Let's go, for fuck's sake!" yelled Clausen from the landing below.

Adams ignored him, spoke calmly to Fourticq. "I'll wait as long as you need."

"No, I'm fine. Let's go."

They started down the stairs again, Clausen leading the way.

Clay crossed Wenceslas Square without breaking stride and zeroed in on the Ambassador. The hotel looked the way he remembered it, a grand luxury job in the heart of the city. *Of course,* he thought. *Of course they would stay here.*

Sirens had been accumulating steadily behind him, or maybe his ears were just ringing.

He burst into the hotel's lobby, knowing how he must look, and he forced himself to slow, to walk calmly toward the elevator bank. The receptionist eyed him with suspicion. She was talking to a brawny bell captain, a kid who couldn't be more than nineteen and looked as if he might wrestle for the Czech national team. Clay tapped the up arrow again, hoping the doors would open or that perhaps the kid was approaching on a different errand, but neither happened, the kid approached and asked if he was staying at the hotel, and Clay nodded but pretended not to understand, and the kid asked again in English. Now the elevator doors were opening, but the kid moved between him and the car and asked to see his key. Clay didn't want to hurt him, but he couldn't afford any more lost time, and as the kid raised his hands to usher him away from the elevator they both heard the sound of gunfire—two shots—from somewhere nearby.

Adams turned down the landing to the basement floor and was following close behind Clausen when he stopped suddenly. A Russian FSB agent stood on the bottom platform in ambush, holding a pistol down low by his hip. He didn't wait for Clausen to protest, didn't wait for him to step closer, didn't wait for him to plead or fight or flee, he just shot him in the head so Clausen's blood sprinkled Adams's face as though he had been sprayed with a misting bottle.

Clausen fell straight down as though his legs had been removed, and for a split second, the Russian's gun was pointed at Adams. The man said something in his language that sounded to Adams's trained ear like "Do you want me to—" but then a second gunshot followed the first, this one from over Adams's shoulder, and it was the Russian's turn to have shock, surprise, and pain sweep his face. He squinted at the hole in his chest, disbelieving, and then his gun fell from his hand and hit the bottom step of the stairwell one moment before his body joined it there.

Adams was too stunned to move. His emotions were jangled, on edge, as if he'd been dangling over an abyss with only a shrinking step holding back gravity.

Fourticq stepped past him, fisting a stainless steel Beretta 92, a single wisp of smoke drifting from the barrel.

"I didn't—" Adams began to say, but found the words stuck in his throat.

Fourticq remained unruffled. He calmly stooped next to the dead Russian and fished the gun from under his body. He placed his own gun back in his pocket and pointed the Russian's weapon at Adams.

"I'm sorry, Michael," he said, and the Snow Wolf squeezed the trigger.

Clay smashed through the lobby's stairwell door, and the reverberation from the door smacking against the handrail sounded like an explosion.

He looked down to see a man he recognized as Adams diving out of the way as a second man below him fired a pistol into the spot Adams had just vacated.

In the heat of battle, in the world Clay had lived in since the moment his uncle had walked below deck and caught him breaking open the money jar, he had honed his ability to slow time down, to take in everything in his field of vision as if he were inputting data into a computer, and then to kick out a strategy, a plan, a mode of action, all in the blink of an eye. It was what separated him from his enemies, what always worked to surprise them because of his size, turned them from offense to defense before they knew how or why.

He knew Adams, and Adams was jumping out of the way. He didn't know the shooter, or the dead man lying at the shooter's feet, and Clay didn't wait for explanations or for everyone to identify himself; instead, he launched himself down the flight of stairs at the shooter as he'd done in Marika's stepbrother's apartment stairwell.

But Fourticq had positioned himself next to the basement door for a reason. He slipped through it before Clay could cross the distance. For just a moment, Clay turned back to his old handler on the landing above.

"You okay, Adams?"

"Yes!"

That was all he needed. Clay ripped open the door and poked his head out, and when no shots came, he ducked into the basement.

It was actually an underground parking lot—a large one. Clay heard an engine crank to life somewhere below, and it was followed by a shriek of tires. A BMW 5 Series banked around a turn, and Clay had a split second to lunge out of the way before Fourticq steamrolled him. Before the car passed, Clay was back on his feet, charging after it.

The BMW took out a wooden barricade as it sprang from the garage out onto an alley as if it had been shot from a cannon. Clay ignored the parking attendant, hurdled the debris, and kept up the chase. *You run until the car is out of sight, you keep chasing, you keep sprinting, and you hope your enemy makes a mistake.*

A row of cabs lined the street that crossed the alley, and Clay saw exactly what he needed, a cabdriver stepping out of his sedan to join the other smokers on the sidewalk outside an adjacent cafe. Had Clay stopped running, he wouldn't have had this opportunity, and one axiom he had found consistent throughout his professional career was: Luck favored the persistent.

He bumped the cabdriver out of the way, leapt behind the wheel, threw the sedan into gear, and took off after the BMW.

The driver ahead of him was skilled and in a superior vehicle, but Clay would not stop. The BMW jumped the median and bolted for the highway that ran parallel to the Vltava River. Clay forced the cab to make the same move and heard a crunch as his suspension raked the median. *Hold on, cab,* he thought. *I won't stop if you won't. Luck favors the persistent.*

He launched himself onto the highway, heading north, and weaved in and out of traffic, gaining on the BMW.

The BMW suddenly zipped across the road into oncoming traffic, and Clay followed, his accelerator mashed. He hugged the bumper of the BMW, sticking to it as if they were connected with a towrope, as cars honked and shot past them on either side. *If he gets hit, I'll run up his backside, but at least we'll both be stopped,* Clay thought. *Then we'll see what the Snow Wolf can do up close in a fight.*

The BMW swung back over to its rightful lane, and for just a moment, Clay was looking down a barrel at twin semis flying at him, but he yanked the wheel and the cab somehow responded, whipping back to continue the chase on the correct side of the road.

Traffic was lighter here, and, now in the open, Clay gained on the BMW. Just as he drew even with the back bumper, Fourticq tapped his brakes, allowing the cab to pull alongside, and then the Snow Wolf plowed the full weight, the full horsepower of his machine into the inferior cab.

The move surprised Clay. He should have realized that his car couldn't gain on a BMW unless the Snow Wolf wanted it to. It was skillful, tactical driving, and Clay would've been impressed if his cab hadn't hit the outside curb, flipped over the guardrail, and sent him spiraling through the air, down, down, down, until his world went black. He vaguely felt the sensation of suddenly becoming very cold and very wet.

CHAPTER TWELVE

MUDDLED SENSATIONS. Pain in his head. The taste of blood in his mouth. His lower half submerged and the water rising. His body took over, a deeply rooted survival instinct born on a boat his uncle owned, and he felt his body twist, his feet kick out the glass of the driver's door as more water rushed into the cab. He felt himself slip through the opening and pull toward the surface. He had spent countless hours of his youth swimming in the dark, swimming in the current, swimming by instinct. He was in the Vltava River; thankfully, the current wasn't strong, and the pull of the receding car wasn't enough to suck him down with it.

He kicked and pointed and swam toward the light, and with the last ounce of oxygen rattling in his lungs, he broke the surface. The river's bank was close, and a gaggle of Gypsies reached out and pulled him ashore. He wanted to keep moving, but his body wouldn't respond. He was tired.

He waited for the sirens and thought of Marika.

Clay said nothing in jail, nothing in the interrogation room, nothing when they threatened him and nothing when they coaxed him. When they allowed him a phone call, he dialed a number, said nothing, and returned the receiver to the cradle. When they put him in a cell with a garrulous American, a man placed there in a subtle attempt to get him to open up, he still said nothing.

He lay in his bed at night, long after the lights went out, staring up at a dark spot in the ceiling. It had been eight days since he'd been brought here.

Stedding was dead, so this might take some time to sort out. Clay had spent years in a cabin smaller than this cell, so he had no concern for his welfare. He used the time between interrogations to think over the mission, to analyze what decisions had led him to this spot. He hoped Marika had called the number and someone on the other end had found her, helped her, believed her, and had gotten her out of Prague. He had counted seven nights since they'd locked him up, and no one had mentioned a courtroom; that gave him hope. They knew he was part of an international game that had started at the rail station, continued inside the Ambassador, and ended with him being fished out of the river. Someone would put the pieces together soon; he hoped they would think him worth saving. Accounts in a ledger. Would his assets outweigh his liabilities? It depended on how much anyone knew of his actions, of his career. He knew one thing: he wasn't ready to turn his thoughts to escape.

The cell door opened in the middle of the night, clicking back in its track. He was trained to awaken alert, so he climbed to his feet easily. A man dressed much too formally to be a guard beckoned him to follow. They walked past sleeping drunks and petty thieves snoring in their cells and exited through a series of gates and locks that reminded Clay of the Panama Canal.

The man continued up a stairwell and held the door for Clay. He stepped onto a rooftop, the lights of the city spread out before him. Adams stood a few steps away, his hands in his pockets, waiting.

The suited Czech retreated through the door, and Adams waited to hear his footsteps recede before he spoke.

"They're calling you the Right Hand now."

Clay nodded. "And you did well for yourself, Michael. You look good."

"I'm happy to be alive."

"Aren't we all?"

"I tried to determine what you've been up to for the last few years. There wasn't much to read in your file."

"No, I've worked autonomously. Just myself and my handler."

"Andrew Stedding. Who died near the Hlavní Nádraží."

"Yes."

"The bullets in his body matched the ones fired into a Russian national at the bottom of the Ambassador's stairwell."

"Yes."

"Do you know who did the firing?"

"No. I have thoughts, but I would have needed more time to figure it out."

"What were your thoughts?"

"I knew the Snow Wolf was most likely an analyst rather than a field op."

"Snow Wolf?"

"His Russian code name."

"How did you know he was an analyst?"

"He shot Stedding but didn't wait to see him dead. A man can live a long time with metal in his chest, especially if he has information he feels compelled to share. A spy in the field would have put bullets in the head, not the body."

"I see. What else?"

"I knew he must be high-level within the Agency, someone whom Stedding would have trusted when he reached out for information as to where the division heads were meeting. Someone who had probably been there a long time."

"You're right. He was the head of EurOps. Or was until last week. His name is Alan Fourticq. Stedding reported directly to him."

"I see."

"I was to take his place, so he conspired to have me killed. Was going to use Russians to do it...that way he could cover his trail after it was done. He would probably have headed the investigation himself."

"He's been in bed with them for years."

"Yes. We're now learning to what extent. May I ask you something?"

Clay nodded.

"You knew about this from the nanny? Marika Csontos?"

A hint of pain creased Clay's face. He nodded. He didn't want to ask for fear of receiving an unfavorable answer, but he was compelled to ask anyway. "Do you have her?"

Adams read his thoughts and lowered his voice as if they were standing inside a funeral home. "She called and mentioned Stedding while we were still trying to figure out exactly what the hell happened. Someone in EurOps responded in a way that must have spooked her. When our men arrived at the location of her phone, she was gone."

Clay bit down his disappointment, his frustration. She had believed in him, and now she was more alone than she'd ever been. Without money, without friends, without a soul she could trust.

Adams waited for him to speak, and when he didn't, he offered, "I'm sorry."

It seemed to bring Clay back to the moment. "Yes, me too."

"What about Fourticq?"

"Well, that's messy. He's gone to ground."

"He's had a long time to concoct a contingency plan."

"Yes. Which brings me to you."

Clay looked up.

"It would be useful for Fourticq to be eliminated quietly, rooted out from whatever rock he's crawled under and exterminated. The Agency doesn't want to open it up across the field, a full assignment with dozens of agents and handlers poring over God knows how many files. Everyone would rather it be done... well, off the books."

"The left hand can't know what the right hand is doing."

"Exactly."

"I'm afraid I don't have a handler."

"Consider us reunited. You will report directly to me from now on."

"Wouldn't you want to delegate—"

"We'll get to that eventually. But I want you close to me, in my purview. I'll find you the right case officer for the ground work, but make no mistake, I'll oversee your work personally."

Clay thought it over. Did he have a choice? What was he going to do after this? Unlike Fourticq, he had no contingency plan in place.

Clay stuck his hand out, and Adams shook it. "I'll find him for you. But I'm going to need a couple of days to find someone else first."

Adams measured him, then nodded.

A helicopter's rotors started to beat down on them from above.

"Whatever you need," Adams shouted over the roar of the blades. The helicopter landed, and they both climbed aboard.

Clay stood outside the St. Vitus Cathedral, watching the door. He had spent the greater part of the last twenty-four hours fixed to the spot, watching as tourists entered and exited in groups or alone, talking in huddled clusters in English, German, French, and Czech, or taking pictures in front of the spires. He did not see her, and he saw her everywhere.

Every girl with dark hair, every faded jacket, every half-walking, half-skipping girl, he saw her. A clump of girls spoke Hungarian and he saw her. A young student walked around a corner, passed him, disappeared as quickly as she'd come, and he saw her.

Bells rang out, low and terrible, for Sunday Mass, and Clay went inside. It was his last chance; he was already pushing it. His new handler would lose patience quickly. He did not see her, and he saw her everywhere.

He watched as men and women dipped their fingers, knelt, and crossed themselves before finding seats among the pews. Clay didn't kneel. He took a seat in the back row, and his eyes drifted around the interior of the cathedral, its marble columns, its arched ceilings, the crisscrossed patterns high above him, the life-size statues affixed to the columns, the ornate altar at the front. Then his eyes found the stained glass behind the altar. Nine scenes were depicted, three scenes each for three people: a woman named Barbara being tortured and about to be beheaded; a man, Adulphus, riding in a boat reading the Bible, then being named pope; and finally Elisabeth.

It was a dull representation, the same one depicted in countless paintings of Mary, the mother of God. She stood with a halo around her head, her index and middle fingers pointed up toward heaven, robe around her; all that was missing was a baby in her arms. The scene was made of yellow, orange, black, and blue glass, cut into incongruous shapes, and there was absolutely nothing special about it. It was numb and flat and pointless and futile and stupid, stupid, stupid. A little girl's memory had romanticized it. Even had Marika come here, she would have entered, seen the stained glass, and felt only disappointment.

A priest was saying something from the pulpit near the altar, but they were just words with no meaning. Clay rose on wobbly legs and headed toward the narthex in a daze.

He felt sunlight on his back as the room warmed and dust motes whirled in the air around him. The sun must've broken free of some clouds, and now Clay understood why the cathedral faced east. He turned at the door, the stained glass now burning brightly behind the priest, Elisabeth shining—no, beaming, instilling peace, instilling beauty, my God, she *was* beauty, she *was* magnificence.

He went outside.

The street was empty.

He didn't see her, and he saw her everywhere.

A dog padded up to him and sniffed his hand. He stooped to scratch its ears and it loped off, uninterested.

He saw her then. She stood underneath a tree, thirty feet away. She was wearing sunglasses and had her hair pulled back, but it was her. He was sure of it. It was her. It had to be her.

"Marika," he called, more loudly than he meant to.

Trembling, the girl removed her sunglasses and dropped them in the street. She broke for him and he broke for her and they met outside the cathedral, with the sun shining brightly, and he scooped her up and spun her and he felt as if he were holding something sacred.

"You found me."

"Yes."

"I didn't know where to go."

"I know."

"The number you gave me. I was scared."

"It doesn't matter."

"You didn't come back."

"I couldn't."

"I know you would have."

"Yes."

"Are you okay?"

"I am now."

"Do we need to run?"

"We can walk."

"Really?"

"Really. Are you hungry?"

"Starving."

"Let's get you something to eat. Then I'll call a man and we can get on a plane. We'll have plenty of time for me to tell you how this all played out...how you fit into it."

"A plane?"

"Yes. To Los Angeles. And a new life."

She was in his arms again and he heard her laugh, a sound that penetrated his skin like a salve.

The Agency set her up with everything. An apartment in an area called Mid-Wilshire, walking distance from the shops and restaurants of the Grove. An allowance of a few thousand a month until she was on her feet. And a few pointed phone calls got her enrolled in the freshman class at USC for the following fall, after she'd had a year's worth of English lessons. She had an affinity for languages and would pick English up quickly, Clay was confident. She said she wanted to study linguistics, and Clay saw no reason why she shouldn't. The smiles came more frequently. He took her to Disneyland, and the smiles never left her face.

He imagined her meeting a young man at school, someone who'd had a childhood in which he was loved by both parents. Someone who could offer her stability and friendship and intellect and humor. Someone who knew nothing of bloodshed and hiding and lies and death. Someone who would get lost in that smile and never want to climb out.

"I'll drop by periodically," Clay said. "If you don't mind." He sat on a stool outside her kitchenette while she made coffee.

"I would like that very much," she said in English.

"That sounded great!"

She blushed and switched back to Hungarian. "Not so much, but you're being nice. It'll get better. Maybe you'll mistake me for a California girl someday."

"I'm sure I will." He stood. "All right, then. I think you're doing wonderfully here, Marika. I mean that. You fit in."

She nodded.

"I'm not sure when I'll have a chance to get back to see you. But don't worry. I'll find you."

Marika suddenly looked bereft. She put a hand over her eyes, and her body shook.

Clay didn't know what to do. "Come on, now." He moved around the counter and she leaned into him, let him hold her.

"You won't come back," she said.

"Marika..."

"I know it's true."

"You'll see me again."

She pulled away, and he could see she didn't believe him. But she wiped her eyes and nodded anyway.

"I really do have to go now," he said clumsily.

She crossed her arms, hugging herself, and nodded again.

He made it to the door and her voice stopped him. "Thank you, Austin Clay."

He turned, took one last look at her, and stepped out the door.

At first, Laura Adams had been apprehensive, but now, as the last of their possessions was carted out of their house to the curb, she was cautiously excited. The girls had embraced the news of the move to Prague, asking a million questions, exuberant. What would school be like? Would they ride on a train? Did Prague have grocery stores or corner markets? Did Czechs play sports? Would they get to go to France and see the Eiffel Tower?

Their spirit worked wonders on Laura. She believed that what Michael did for a living was important. Her own sense of adventure had been the reason he had courted her in the first place. She had not lost it; she was excited.

Adams draped his arm over her shoulder. "It was a good house."

"It was."

Most of their belongings would go into storage, but they would still fill a couple of containers with furniture and ship them across the sea.

The last of their boxes was loaded into the moving truck as their real estate agent approached. "Well—"

"I think we're all out."

"I'll let you know when we get a bite."

Adams shook hands with the woman, and he and Laura headed for the car. They'd pick up their daughters from school, spend one night in a hotel, and fly out of Burbank in the morning.

At some point, he did want to check into the LA district office before he left and see what progress Clay had made.

Clay returned to the windowless office he'd been using all week. Adams's assistant, a man named Warren Sumner, had helped facilitate the arrival of a crate of Fourticq's things, every single item from his office, from his desk, from his files. A second crate covered the small apartment he'd kept, but if the contents indicated the entirety of the Snow Wolf's possessions, the man had either rid himself of his things to cover his tracks or had lived the life of an ascetic. Neither option was encouraging.

Clay rubbed his eyes. The forensic work was usually a job for a handler, but Adams was busy preparing to take over EurOps, so Clay had volunteered to tackle it and get a head start. Truth be told, he'd rather shake the bushes and get information directly from the horse's mouth. But which horse?

Fourticq's computer had been scrubbed...there were no files that indicated anything beyond standard operations under his command. Clay read through them anyway, looking for any kind of flag. A couple of hours later, he had nothing.

"Want some coffee?"

Warren smiled from the doorway, holding a mug. Clay accepted gratefully.

"Anything?"

Clay shook his head. "He was careful."

Warren nodded at that. "It's bred into us." The younger man looked over his shoulder and smiled as his boss approached.

"He wasn't careful...he was cocky," Adams amended as he poked his head into the office. "He made a mistake somewhere. You'll find it."

Clay nodded. He was reminded how much he liked Adams's style.

"I have access to every personnel file within the Agency. If you sense he had inside help, I'll let you look at anything and anyone you need."

"I'm probably going to travel to Russia again. See if I can poke into finding out who Fourticq's contact was at FSB."

"I'll arrange it," Warren interjected.

Adams nodded at his protégé. "Warren's going to step into

a case officer's shoes as soon as I get my ducks in a row," he said, and watched Clay's face.

Clay gave him nothing. He'd need a new handler soon, but he certainly wasn't going to commit to anyone so green. Instead, he changed the subject back to where it had been.

"I'd much rather get inside the china shop and toss my horns around than sit in this room looking at a computer screen."

"We're opposites, you and me," Adams said. "I'd rather look at a spreadsheet than the wrong end of a pistol."

"Well, now you know I'll never be after your job."

Adams grinned, but Warren didn't. Adams said, "There aren't too many lines of work where office politics involve drafting the Russian service to eliminate your replacement."

"Why do you do it?"

"Work for the Agency?"

"Yeah. Someone asked me that, and I told her how I got recruited, without really answering the question."

"Why didn't you?"

"I don't know. Because the answer is I do it because I'm good at it. I belong. I spent a great portion of my life adrift, and this job grounded me. I get an assignment and I don't quit until it's completed. I've been around long enough to know my success rate is..."

"Unmatched."

"I was going to say 'pretty good.'"

Adams nodded, started to head out, then stopped in the doorway. "Maybe we're not such opposites." Warren followed him out.

It wasn't until he was alone again that Clay realized Adams hadn't answered his question.

Clay couldn't sleep.

Something was nagging at him, like a fly buzzing his ear. Adams had said that Fourticq was cocky and had made a mistake. But the mistake was obvious: Adams was alive and would run EurOps, while Fourticq was exposed and on the run. The mistake couldn't be more glaring.

The word *cocky* gave him pause. A cocky person, one as narcissistic as Fourticq, would not acknowledge such a mistake, because a cocky person would place blame elsewhere. *It's not my fault; I got screwed over.*

Clay rose from the sofa and went back to the desk containing Fourticq's belongings. He had stared at files until three in the morning and had finally submitted to sleep. Now the sun was turning the sky orange and the shadows were receding.

A thought struck him. There were two people the Snow Wolf would blame. Adams, definitely. But in his mind, Adams would have lucked out.

No, the person who'd proactively broken open his plot was Clay. Clay, who had found the girl and discovered what she knew and smoked out the leader of EurOps as the conspirator.

Adams had offered to let Clay look at anyone's personnel file within the Agency, and that meant access to every officer profile, both analyst and field. Fourticq would have had that same privilege when he held the position. Clay snatched up the desk phone and dialed a number at Langley.

"As head of EurOps, Fourticq had access to everyone's personnel files, right?"

"Yes, sir."

"Can you tell me whose files he accessed the most?"

"You got his laptop open now?"

"Yep."

"Hold on. Don't click on anything."

Clay could see the cursor move on the computer as the analyst in Virginia operated it remotely. The screen turned to coded gibberish. Clay could speak a number of languages, but programming wasn't one of them. He was thankful the Agency hired tech-heads out of MIT to run computer operations, and thankful he didn't have to rub shoulders with them very often.

"Checking...checking...you want it sorted by..."

"Most to least."

"Just their names?"

"Yeah. The people he most often checked out."

"Okay...here you go."

Names filled the screen. The one at the top surprised him.

The town car carrying Adams and his family pulled around to the back of the Burbank airport, through the security shack, and stopped at the private hangar used by the super-wealthy and by high-ranking officials in the government.

Adams had once seen a popular British action star waiting for his G5 to finish refueling, and he had been mystified at how small the man was in real life. If the actor spent five minutes with Austin Clay, he might rethink his portrayal of a spy.

The driver unloaded their suitcases and took them to a rack near the jet. *The greatest advantage of flying private,* Adams thought, *no security lines, no check-in bullshit, no waiting around a crowded terminal. The pilot comes to get you in the hangar and off you go.*

His phone chirped, and he excused himself.

"Are you in the air yet?" Warren asked, sounding breathless.

"No, what is it?"

"There's been an Echelon hit on Fourticq."

Echelon referred to the most advanced domestic surveillance technology the CIA had at its disposal. A hit would mean that tracking satellites had picked up chatter with pre-chosen buzzwords, either on cell phones, pay phones, email, or websites where terrorists might attempt to communicate. It wasn't an infallible system; a majority of data managed to slip past it every second of every day, but analysts worked to improve Echelon continuously and it had contributed to the prevention of major disasters on a number of occasions.

"What'd he say?"

"I think it was said *to* him. It's encoded within an obscure website that Snow Wolf—that Alan Fourticq—was using to communicate with his Russian counterparts prior to...well. He covered most of his tracks but wasn't aware we knew about this one."

"Get on with it," Adams said, annoyed. He looked at his family, standing on the tarmac near the jet, chatting with the pilot. They were happy, excited about the future. They would do well in Europe, and he was eager to get into the air and get started on the rest of their lives.

"Yes, sir. Sorry. It seems an address was passed on to Fourticq. An address in Los Angeles."

"Whose address?"

The girls were now tugging on their mother's sleeves. Laura looked at Adams again and started walking toward the plane with the pilot.

"55 Park La Brea."

Adams's face registered his surprise. That address meant Fourticq knew...but why would he...

"All right...I'm on it." He clicked off the phone and hurried over to his family and the pilot, catching them halfway across the tarmac.

"Laura!" he said as he reached them. "Why don't you and the girls head back to the waiting room for a bit?"

The pilot was a young guy with an aquiline nose jutting from a wide face. "We're ready to board, Mr. Adams."

"I understand, but I have to make a phone call."

"You're more than welcome to do it from the plane."

"I'm afraid I need to make it from a secure phone."

"I understand, sir," the pilot said warmly. His smile seemed awkward under that nose, as if it were spreading out solely to support its foundation. "But I've already filed a flight plan, and the tower's waiting...."

"Talk to the tower and hold until I say otherwise."

The pilot eyed him cautiously, as if he were contemplating his next move. Then the smile reappeared. "Yes, sir. Of course." He walked back toward the G5.

Laura gave her husband a concerned look. "What is it?"

"Probably nothing, but I need to call—"

The plane exploded, knocking Adams to the unforgiving tarmac.

A man with scars snaking across the back of his shaved head sat on a bench near the jogging trail of Pan Pacific Park, adjacent to the Grove, in the middle of Los Angeles. An elderly Asian couple passed him, doing that half-run, half-walk thing that old people like to do, and he watched them truck on by, indifferent.

In a shoulder holster concealed beneath his sports jacket rested a .40-caliber Glock 27, a gun he had carried for the better part of twenty-five years. He had not been carrying it, however, on a night in Colombia in 1993 when he had been closing in on Pablo Escobar and had walked into an ambush. He had taken not one but two knives to the back of the head, and in a true case of "you should have seen the other guys," he had emerged from the scene wounded but alive. He might have died on the side of the road if his friend and partner, Alan Fourticq, hadn't dragged him out of the dirt and into a doctor's house. The bald man would never be caught without his gun within arm's reach again.

Through his sunglasses, he watched the entrance of the

apartment complex across the street, a sprawling expanse of compact domiciles named Park La Brea. Soon enough, a young Hungarian woman with dark hair and a carefree smile, a young woman who knew how to speak Russian even though she had once lied about that ability to land a nannying job, emerged from the entrance and pressed the crosswalk button so she could walk over to the shopping center.

The bald man with the faded knife scars on the back of his head stood up and followed her.

Adams tasted blood, and his face felt as though the sun were resting on top of it. He opened his eyes to find that he could see as through a tunnel; dark smudges blurred the edges of his vision. *Laura!*

He saw her already climbing to her hands and knees, quelling the horror in his mind. His girls were also rising from the pavement; they had been behind their parents and had been shielded from the brunt of the blast. Adams had been looking at the jet, and that side of his face had not been spared.

He hurried to his family. "Is everyone okay?"

The girls were crying, but he checked them over and found only a couple of scraped elbows. "Your face, Daddy!" the younger one, Grace, squeaked. Her voice sounded muffled, as though she were speaking underwater.

He felt his face, and the heat seemed to be emanating from it, but his fingers didn't come away bloody. "Just a sunburn, I promise." It hurt like hell, but he was determined to keep up a solid front for Laura and the girls. His wife had a burn on the side of her cheek that gave him a sense of what his own face must look like, but she seemed to be fine.

"What happened?"

"I don't know, but we need to get off this tarmac."

The sun was beating down on them, which made the whole thing more surreal. It was an otherwise sparkly Southern California morning, the kind that appeared almost every day of the year, except this one was marred by the column of smoke rising straight up from the burning jet like a black finger trying to scratch the sky.

Adams tried to keep himself calm and resolute. It was the second attempt on his life in the same month, and the incident in Prague had forged a new mettle inside him.

He shepherded his family toward the private hangar, away from the jet's carcass. Where were the emergency vehicles? Who could have infiltrated a goddamn airport and put a bomb on a government plane, *his* plane? These questions jockeyed for position in his mind. He finally heard sirens as he opened the glass door of the hangar—it had been far enough away from the explosion to escape damage.

What was he doing before the blast? He had just received a call.

He looked down at his hand and saw his cell phone clutched in it, undamaged. He'd been about to call someone.

Yellow-and-green trucks raced their way. They looked like fire trucks, but he wasn't sure. Things were jumbled in his mind, as if a telephone operator had failed to connect the wires.

He looked at the faces of his family. They were terrified, in shock. Kate looked up at him, her eyes searching for answers. Her eyes. In that moment, they reminded him of another young woman's eyes.

And then it all came back to him.

Austin Clay answered the phone on its first ring. He assumed the techie in DC was calling to tell him he had decoded something else in all those bits of data floating around Fourticq's hard drive. But it was Adams on the line, speaking over sirens in the background.

"He has her address."

Clay stood up straight, as if he had been jolted with electricity.

"What? Who?"

"The Snow Wolf. Fourticq. He has her address. Marika's—"

"How—"

"He's here. He's in LA."

Clay didn't hear any more, because he was already sprinting for the exit.

The Grove was a sprawling shopping complex built adjacent to the landmark farmers' market smack-dab in the middle of Los Angeles. There was a Disneyland, movie-set feel to the shop fronts and stores that lined the long, curving paved street, complete with an old-timey trolley that ferried shoppers from one end of the complex to the other.

Marika stopped to look at the signs in the Apple store, announcing the latest smartphone, which seemed to be replacing another smartphone that had come out the previous year. The place was hopping, mostly with kids her age bustling in and out or mingling over the computer monitors. A young man stood near an iPad, explaining the newest features to a middle-aged customer, and something about the way he stood, the way he held one arm at the elbow with his other crossed in front of him, reminded her of David. She felt her throat tighten as the young man and the customer shuffled off and the feeling passed.

She had started to move west toward the farmers' market when an uneasy feeling that she was being watched struck her. Goose pimples rose on her arms. She looked around but didn't see anyone who stood out in the throng of shoppers milling around the Grove.

It was probably just the residual effect of the last year of her life, when looking over her shoulder had become an involuntary reflex. She told herself to relax. She was safe here.

She moved down the street but checked the reflections in shop windows to see if anyone was following her.

Clay drove his government-issued Taurus down the 110 freeway as if it had been launched from a missile chute. Five lanes let him weave in and out of slower traffic as though the other cars were standing still.

Cutting left, he easily caught the fork for the 10, saw an opening, and scooted up the shoulder. A stalled Jetta up ahead forced him to swing back out, and he nearly ran right up the backside of a slower bus. What the hell was it doing in the fast lane? No matter, he swept around it and shot down the freeway unimpeded, headed west.

With a little bit of room, he thumbed his phone, finding Marika's number. She answered on the second ring.

"Hello?"

"Where are you?"

"I walked over to find something to eat in the farmers' market. They have—"

"Find a policeman or a security guard and stay with him until I get there."

"What?"

"Five minutes."

He hung up and slid diagonally across three lanes, hitting the Fairfax exit doing close to seventy.

Clay banked a hard right, ran the next five red lights, and swerved onto Third Street, blitzing toward the farmers' market.

Marika heard the worry in Clay's voice and bit down her fear when the line went dead. She was in danger, that much was clear, and she cursed herself for not trusting her instincts when she'd thought she was being watched.

She looked around the market and saw only the usual mix of tourists and LA strangers—emphasis on *strange*—amid the maze of restaurants, trinket shops, candy booths, and coffee kiosks. The corridors were tight here, and the patches of sky glimpsed over the awnings felt close. Everything felt close.

Run.

Her eyes scanned the area for men in uniform, cops or security guards, but she didn't seen anyone except for a burly guy in a UPS shirt.

The jangle of smells accosted her—roasted pig, sushi, doughnuts, pizza—the market offered everything and nothing and she couldn't get her thoughts straight.

That was when she saw a bald man with hard eyes moving her way.

Run.

Her legs wouldn't move. The man didn't even pretend to look elsewhere. He was cutting a swath through the crowd, knifing toward her.

Run.

She turned and spun directly into the arms of the Snow Wolf.

Clay didn't bother to find a parking space. He peeled up to the outside of Du-par's deli in the corner of the farmers' market and sprinted into the sprawl of shops, leaving the car with the keys in it where it stopped.

The inside of the market was a madhouse, packed to overflowing with shoppers and eaters, and he scanned the masses for any sign of the girl. His eyes lit on a table of police officers eating tacos, and he hurried over. No sign of Marika, and as much as he wanted to ask after her, these guys wouldn't be sitting there stuffing their faces if a pretty girl had hurried up asking for assistance.

Cars were honking a symphony in the parking lot, most likely because of his illegally parked car blocking traffic both ways, and he must've been standing there looking like a lunatic, because all four officers were staring in his direction with disapproving looks.

Then he heard a high-pitched scream above all the other noise in the market, a young woman yelling the name "Clay!" and he broke for the sound.

She didn't think.

The man had a knife in her side and told Marika he'd finish her if she didn't keep her head down and walk quickly with him. His feet were already moving and she was matching his stride more or less involuntarily.

The bald man had joined them and was leading the way toward the parking lot like some sort of fullback opening a hole in the line of scrimmage. She found herself staring at the back of his shaved head and the carving-board scars that looked a nasty white against his cream skin. It was as though there was a pattern there that she couldn't quite figure out.

The sharpness of the knife in her side, the grip of the

hand on her arm, were like someone hitting a buzzer in her brain; she couldn't connect her thoughts and was only vaguely aware that her feet were moving. They were abducting her, she knew that. They wouldn't kill her in this crowd, she knew that, too. But if they got her into a car, then what?

They steered her toward the little alley that left the market behind, and as she walked toward it, she saw a man pushing an elderly woman—his mother?—in a wheelchair and she didn't think, she just reacted, twisting away with all her force from the man who held her, at the exact moment they were passing the wheelchair. She didn't know what she was doing, was just trying to prolong her abduction, trying to cause a scene, trying to bring other people into her mess, and she hit the wheelchair and toppled it so that she and the man and the elderly woman all became tangled on the path.

"What the hell—?" cried the wheelchair pusher, and the man who was abducting Marika said, "So sorry, so sorry," but was already snatching her back up by the wrist, his hand clamped like a vise.

In that instant, as she was rudely wrestled to her feet, a few shoppers moved a few steps out of her line of sight and she saw Austin Clay standing next to a table of policemen.

She didn't think; she just screamed.

Clay felt the policemen chasing behind him without seeing them, but it didn't matter, nothing mattered, only reaching Marika mattered, let them come.

He could see her jerked to her feet by Fourticq, and Clay was going to kill him as soon as he closed the distance, by breaking his neck. There wouldn't be a standoff, or a discussion, or a negotiation, he was going to pounce on the man like a jungle cat and snap his spinal column as easily as snapping a twig.

Fifty feet away and Fourticq had successfully untangled Marika from the man and old woman on the ground and was shoving her rudely toward the corridor that led out of the market. Forty feet. Clay sprinted recklessly, and men and woman hastened out of his way, or maybe out of the way of the cops chasing behind him. He didn't care. Nothing mattered and everything mattered. Thirty feet.

He closed, he was closing, and then a bald man stepped protectively between Clay and his target. The man had a gun in his hand, a Glock, raised it, and fired.

Clay saw the shot coming and somehow pivoted at the last second, shifting course as smoothly and quickly as a gazelle, and the bullet clipped the top of his shoulder and buried itself in the cop behind him. The bald man did not get off a second shot.

Clay erupted from his pivot and landed a fist in the man's throat with every bit of his torquing body behind it. The punch did what a pair of Colombian knives couldn't do. It collapsed the bald man's trachea, and the man went down gasping for air that would never find its way to his lungs.

The three remaining cops pounced on the bald man then, and thank God he was the one with the gun, he was the one who'd opened fire, because they ignored Clay in their haste to make sure the shooter was incapacitated. Clay left them behind and focused on the Snow Wolf.

It's not easy getting a woman into a car against her will. Fourticq decided he'd kill her right there. His chances of surviving this himself were diminishing steadily toward zero. He had a chance, however slight, and it was only if the animal zeroing in on him was preoccupied with saving the girl's life.

He'd love to say it wasn't personal, it was only business, but the two, the business and the personal, had intermingled like chemicals inside a bomb. The girl had cost him, the animal chasing him had cost him, and he might be going down into a dark hole in the ground, but he'd make them hurt before he did. His car was idling at the curb twenty feet away, but he'd never make it, never wrestle her inside and contain her and slip behind the wheel. No, the best chance he had was to end her life right then and there.

He spun her around so Clay would see, took the knife from her side, and raised it to her neck.

The sight of Clay jogged something in her memory, something he had told her a lifetime ago.

Eyes, groin. Eyes, groin. Eyes, groin.

The man holding her by the arm wheeled her around like a top and she saw Clay coming, saw the determination in his face, saw the panic rising. Then she felt the steel sharpness of the blade move from her side and she caught the flash of it moving upward, toward her neck.

She knew she should respond, should defend herself, but her limbs felt as if they were tied down.

Then a sharp noise surprised all of them, the *clang, clang* of the approaching trolley, pulling into the farmers' market, headed directly for them. It caused the man holding her to lose his concentration for only a second. It was all she needed.

She raised her arm and pounded her fist into the front of his pants with everything she had, and like a tornado, spun again and scratched at his face.

He was already countering, closing his lids to avoid her fingernails, raising his hand to swing the blade down in an arc.

Clay caught him.

The Snow Wolf's arm was raised and poised to swing down with lethal force, but Clay hit that arm right at its high point and damn near snapped it off. The shoulder made an audible pop as it flew backward, the knife banging uselessly on the pavement, and then the two adversaries came together and bounced off the front of the trolley as it braked to a stop.

It wasn't a fair fight from there. Fourticq crashed to the ground, his arm useless so he hit the pavement with his nose unprotected. It shattered.

A primal instinct within Clay surfaced at the sight of Fourticq's blood. He growled without realizing he was doing it and rolled onto the back of the Snow Wolf. Then he picked up Fourticq's head by the hair and smashed it back down into the ground, again and again and again.

Somewhere a young woman screamed, but Clay couldn't hear it. The sound of the ocean waves crashing on the hull of his uncle's boat drowned out the noise.

CHAPTER THIRTEEN

WARREN SUMNER ducked into the bathroom to wash his hands. He had prepared Adams's transfer to Prague down to the last detail, but he still had so much to do. That was the way it was with the best assistants: first they took care of their boss, then they took care of themselves.

The water felt good, cleansing. His kindergarten teacher had taught him how to properly wash his hands, first rubbing the back, then the front, then intertwining the fingers, and all these years later, he could remember her face, how it lit up when he did it right.

He was just turning off the faucet and reaching for the paper towel dispenser when the door of the bathroom opened and Austin Clay walked inside.

Warren swallowed but couldn't seem to get any moisture into his mouth. Clay wasn't moving toward the stalls; he just stood in the doorway, looking directly at him. Warren grabbed a paper towel and pulled, but it broke in the middle so he only got a small triangle from the dispenser. Absently, he dried his hands with that piece rather than try again.

"Is she okay, then?" He tried to put the proper amount of concern on his face.

"Marika? Yes."

"I was about to head to the hospital to check on the Adams family."

"Oh?"

"Yes. How this could happen here is—"

"How was it supposed to happen?"

Warren stopped. He could feel his eyes darting and wished they wouldn't, but he couldn't make them stop. He forced a smile.

"I'm sorry?"

"You heard me."

"How was what supposed to happen?"

Clay folded his arms across his chest and stepped closer. "I have a theory, and you tell me where I'm wrong."

"Okay?" Warren tried to suppress the rising panic inside him.

"I think you tried to pull off your first mission."

"I don't—"

"I think you looked at it like this. There were two dangling threads left over from the attempted assassination of Adams. Two threads that would keep him from starting his EurOps position with a clean slate. Snow Wolf and Marika Csontos. So you came up with a way to kill two birds with one stone.

You'd give Fourticq the address where Marika was staying, and then you'd make sure I got the news too late to stop him but in time to kill him. Fourticq would take care of the girl, and I'd take care of him."

"That's not—"

"What you weren't counting on was a bomb on Adams's plane."

Warren stopped trying to respond. His face felt flushed with blood. His eyes shifted again, and Clay's widened.

"Or... wait. Wait. Kudos, Warren. I didn't think you had it in you. You *did* know about the bomb on Adams's plane. Hell, you arranged it. And if it all went down the way you wanted, you'd have all your problems tied up in one swoop. Adams would be dead, leaving a vacuum in power that you could help fill. Snow Wolf and Marika Csontos would be dead. And you'd have me in your arsenal, unencumbered."

"That's... none of that is true."

"Do you know how many men I've gotten to tell me the truth over the years? How many men, bigger than you, maybe not meaner, maybe not more despicable, maybe not as evil as you, but bigger men nonetheless, who have told me their secrets?"

Clay stepped closer again, and Warren's eyes tracked to the door. Could he get around Clay? Break past him before the field operative could reach out an arm and stop him? Then what? Warren heard his voice come out squeaky, breaking like the voice of a teenager going through puberty. "What? You're going to torture me?" He couldn't keep the alarm out of it.

"No, Warren. You're going to confess to what you did. What your plan was. All of it."

"How did you—?"

"Because you and Fourticq were in contact before all of this. You were his inside man in Los Angeles long before Adams got on a plane for Prague."

"You couldn't know that. His files were all cleaned out."

"It's not on his hard drive. It's on yours."

Warren decided he'd just stick his chin up and blow past Clay, take a haughty air, act offended, and just...go.

"You're lying," he said. "And I don't have to stand here and listen to this."

"You got your loyalties confused, Warren. I don't know what Fourticq told you, or promised you, but you put your cards in with him instead of with the Agency."

"Absurd." Warren brushed past Clay and was surprised when the larger man didn't stop him. He breathed easier. He would walk out to the elevator, head down to his car, and drive away. He didn't know where he'd drive, but he would head south and then—

He opened the door to the corridor and shrank back when he saw the hallway filled with people. Twenty dark-suited men stood on either side of the door, blocking his way. He searched their faces until he saw one he recognized. Half of the face was peeling, as though the man had fallen asleep on his side in a lounger on a beach.

"You're going to tell us everything," he said.

"Michael. It's not what you think. I didn't—"

"Take him."

And then he was grabbed rudely under his arms and led forcefully away.

EPILOGUE

He needed a break.

Clay had spent the last four months in Berlin, tracking embassy staffers and reporting back to EurOps whom they met with, when they met, where they were headed, and why they were meeting. There was a reason these men were politicians; they were boring. They went to meetings, they wrote missives and reports, they glad-handed, and they failed to do a single thing that was interesting.

He met Adams at Sanssouci Park in Potsdam, near the obelisk that guarded the entrance. They looked like a couple of businessmen out enjoying an afternoon walk. The sun was high in the sky, and Europe was headed for another summer heat wave. They had both shed their jackets and draped them over their arms.

"I can see Prague has been treating you well," Clay said, and patted Adams on the stomach.

"What the hell does that mean?"

"I mean you look like you've put a tire around your middle, Patch."

He had taken to calling Adams Patch after the dippy clown Robin Williams had portrayed in a maudlin movie. Adams hated the nickname, of course.

"Don't call me that."

"But you've always filled me with such joy, such a will to live—"

"Enough," Adams said, now crossing his arms over his stomach. "What do you have?"

"If Berg and Eichel were sharing inside information with Nigeria, I found no evidence. These guys are clean."

"Hmmm," Adams said. "All right. If there's no fire there, there's no fire."

"There's not even smoke."

Adams nodded. "Okay…I'm going to need you in Dubai. There's a group of arms dealers—a consortium of American, British, and French—who might be trying to sell weapons to, let's just say, *unsavory* types in Syria."

"When do they meet?"

"You'll get the dossier this week. I believe they're flying into Dubai week after next."

"Perfect. I need a break."

"A break?"

"I just have to get out of here for a few days. Clear my head."

"And go where?"

"Where the left hand won't know what I'm doing."

Adams smirked and nodded. "Fair enough." He started to leave, but Clay's voice stopped him.

"How's the family?"

Adams turned, surprise on his face. He wasn't used to anyone in intelligence save the Director asking after his family. But there was no animus in Clay's voice, just genuine concern. "Great. Laura has found a group of expats in Prague who keep her busy. She's playing tennis again and feeling well."

"And Kate and Grace?"

Adams grinned, impressed Clay remembered their names. "They keep me on my toes. I don't think they've stopped smiling since we landed in Europe. We're going to take them to see Paris next week."

"I'm glad," Clay replied, and he meant it. "I'll report in from Dubai after I land. Take care of yourself."

"You too." Adams watched Clay disappear around the obelisk and head out of the park. He chuckled to himself, then raised his hand to shield his eyes so he could look at the hieroglyphics carved into the stone pillar, but he couldn't make sense of the shapes. Somehow, that struck him as apt.

Clay settled into his booth, drank his coffee, and gazed out the window. They made a strong pot at this diner, and when the waitress came, he asked for more. She topped it with a smile. "You in for the game?"

Clay looked back from the window and offered her a smile of his own. "No."

"Not a football fan?"

Now that he took a moment to look around, he saw that most of the booths were occupied by men and women in red-and-orange jerseys. They were all chattering excitedly.

"Not really."

"Well, you picked a busy time to come in…it's the first game of the season and we're gonna be hoppin'."

Now he knew why she was making conversation…he was taking up a whole window booth, just drinking coffee. She could've shuffled in a couple of families in the time he'd already spent sitting there.

"Tell you what"—he searched for her name tag—"Helen. You let me sit here and drink my coffee until I want to get up, and I'll give you a hundred-dollar tip."

"You'll get a piece of pumpkin pie and not another word from me."

"Can you make it apple?"

"I can make it anything you want, sugar." She waddled off, and he turned his attention back to the window.

She sat across the street at an outside table, cross-legged, peering down into a textbook. Her hair had grown longer since he'd last seen her and was shiny and clean. A single braid twisted down from her temple and dangled next to her mouth. She played with it absently as she read. Every now and then, she'd pick up a yellow highlighter and mark something on the pages.

The sun was reflecting off the window where Clay sat, so

she couldn't see him. He was adept at sitting in places where he could study people without their knowledge. He raised the cup to his lips as the waitress set down a steaming piece of apple pie.

He looked back out the window just as a young man about Marika's age approached and she moved a backpack so he could take the seat next to hers. The boy put his hand out on the table, and she took it. A smile stretched across her face so wide that it lit up the distance between the two cafes.

When the waitress returned to Clay's booth, she found a hundred-dollar bill there, but her customer was gone.

About the Author

Derek Haas is the author of *The Silver Bear*, the Barry Award-nominated *Hunt for the Bear*, and *Dark Men*. Derek also co-wrote the screenplays for *3:10 to Yuma*, starring Russell Crowe and Christian Bale, and *Wanted*, starring James McAvoy, Morgan Freeman, and Angelina Jolie. He is the creator of the website popcornfiction.com, which promotes genre short fiction. Derek lives in Los Angeles.

Visit his website at derekhaas.com or follow him on Twitter @popcornfiction.

In the shadowy world of hitmen,
one man stands alone.
His name is Columbus.
They call him the Silver Bear.

Read on for an extract from Derek Haas's
brilliant first novel.

'A thrilling page-turner – a cross between
the Jason Bourne movies and the classic
assassin film *Leon' Company*

CHAPTER ONE

The last day of the cruelest month, and appropriately it rains. Not the spring rain of new life and rebirth, not for me. Death. In my life, always death. I am young; if you saw me on the street, you might think, 'what a nice, clean-cut young man. I'll bet he works in advertising or perhaps a nice accounting firm. I'll bet he's married and is just starting a family. I'll bet his parents raised him well.' But you would be wrong. I am old in a thousand ways. I have seen things and done things that would make you rush instinctively to your child's bedroom and hug him tight to your chest, breathing quick in short bursts like a misfiring engine, and repeat over and over, 'It's okay, baby. It's okay. Everything's okay.'

I am a bad man. I do not have any friends. I do not speak to women or children for longer than is absolutely necessary. I groom myself to blend, like a chameleon darkening its pigment against the side of an oak tree. My hair is cut short, my eyes are hidden behind dark glasses, my dress would inspire a yawn from anyone who passed me in the street. I do not call attention to myself in any way.

I have lived this way for as long as I can remember, although in truth it has only been ten years. The events of my life prior to that day, I have forgotten in all detail, although I do remember the pain. Joy and pain tend to make imprints on memory that do not dim, flecks of senses rather than images that resurrect themselves involuntarily and without warning. I have had precious little of the former and a lifetime of the latter. A week ago, I read a poll that reported ninety percent of people over the age of sixty would choose to be a teenager again if they could. If those same people could have experienced one day of my teenage years, not a single hand would be counted.

The past does not interest me, though it is always there, just below the surface, like dangerous blurs and shapes an ocean swimmer senses in the deep. I am fond of the present. I am in command in the present. I am master of my own destiny in the present. If I choose, I can touch someone, or let someone touch me, but only in the present. Free will is a gift of the present; the only time I can choose to outwit God. The future, your fate, though, belongs to God. If you try to outsmart God in planning your fate, you are in for disappointment. He owns the future, and He loves O. Henry endings.

The present is full of rain and bluster, and I hurry to close the door behind me as I duck into an indiscriminate warehouse alongside the Charles River. It has been a cold April, which many say indicates a long, hot summer approaching, but I do not make predictions. The warehouse is damp, and I can smell mildew, fresh-cut sawdust, and fear.

People do not like to meet with me. Even those whom society considers dangerous are uneasy in my presence. They have heard stories about Singapore, Providence, and Brooklyn. About Washington, Baltimore, and Miami. About London, Bonn, and Dallas. They do not want to say something to make me uncomfortable or angry, and so they choose their words with precision. Fear is a feeling foreign to these types of men, and they do not like the way it settles in their stomach. They get me in and out as fast as they can and with very little negotiation.

Presently, I am to meet with a black man named Archibald Grant. His given name is Cotton Grant, but he didn't like the way 'Cotton' made him sound like a Georgia hillbilly Negro, so he moved to Boston and started calling himself Archibald. He thought it made him sound aristocratic, like he came from prosperity, and he liked the way it sounded on a whore's lips: 'Archibald, slide on over here' in a soft falsetto. He does not know that I know about the name Cotton. In my experience, it is best to know every detail about those with whom you are meeting. A single mention of a surprising detail, a part of his life he thought was buried so deep as to never be found, can cause him to pause just long enough to make a difference. A pause is all I need most of the time.

I walk through a hallway and am stopped at a large door by two towering black behemoths, each with necks the size of my waist. They look at me, and their eyes measure me. Clearly, they were expecting something different after all they've been told. I am used to this. I am used to the disappointment in some of their eyes as they think, 'give me ten minutes in a room with him and we'll see what's shakin'.' But I do not have an ego, and I avoid confrontations.

'You be?' says the one on the right whose slouch makes the handle of his pistol crimp his shirt just enough to let me know it's there.

'Tell Archibald it's *Columbus*.'

He nods, backs through the door, while the other studies me with unintelligent eyes. He coughs and manages, 'You Columbus?' as if in disbelief. Meaning it as a challenge.

I ignore him, not moving a centimeter of my face, my stance, my posture. I am in the present. It is my time, and I own it.

He does not know what to make of this, as he is not used to being ignored, has not been ignored all his life, as big as he is. But somewhere, a voice tells him maybe the stories he heard are true, maybe this Columbus is the badass motherfucker Archibald was talking about yesterday, maybe it'd be best to let the challenge hang out there and fade, the way a radio signal grows faint as a car drives further and further down the highway.

He is relieved when the door opens and I am beckoned into the room.

Archibald is behind a wooden desk; a single light bulb on a wire chain moves like a pendulum over his head. He is not a large man, a sharp contrast from the muscle he keeps around him. Short, well-dressed, with a fire in his eyes that matches the tip of the cigarette stuck in the corner of his mouth. He is used to getting what he wants.

He stands, and we shake hands with a light grip as though neither wants to make a commitment. I am offered the only other chair, and we sit deliberately at the same time.

'I'm a middleman on this,' he says abruptly, so I'll know this from the get-go. The cigarette bobs up and down like a metronome as he speaks.

'I understand.'

'This a single. Eight weeks out, like you say.'

'Where?'

'Outside L.A. At least, that's where this cat'll be at the time.'

Archibald sits back in his chair and folds his hands on his stomach. He's a businessman, talking business. He likes this role. It makes him think of the businessmen behind their desks in Atlanta where he used to go in and change out the trash baskets, replace the garbage with new dark plastic linings.

I nod, only slightly. Archibald takes this as his cue to swivel in his chair and open a file door on the credenza matching his desk. From the cavity, he withdraws a briefcase, and we both know what's inside. He slides it in my direction across the desk and waits.

'Everything you requested's in there, if you want to check it out,' he offers.

'I know where to find you if it's not.'

It's statements like these that can get people into trouble, because they can be interpreted several ways. Perhaps I am making a benign declaration, or possibly a stab at humor, or maybe a little bit of both. But in this business, more often than not, I am making a threat, and nobody likes to be threatened.

He studies my face, his own expression stuck between a smirk and a frown, but whatever he is looking for, he doesn't find it. He has little choice but to laugh it off so his muscle will understand I am not being disrespectful.

'Heh-hah.' Only part of a laugh. 'Yeah. That's good. Well, it's all there.'

I help him out by taking the case off the desk, and he is happy to see me stand. This time, he does not offer his hand.

I walk away from the desk, toward the door, case in hand, but his voice stops me. He can't help himself, his curiosity wins over his cautiousness; he isn't sure if he'll ever see me again, and he has to know.

'Did'ja really pop Corlazzi on that boat?'

You'd be surprised how many times I get this one. Corlazzi was a Chicago underworld luminary responsible for much of the city's butchery in the sixties and seventies, a man who redefined the mafia's role when narcotics started to replace liquor as America's drug of choice. He saw the future first, and deftly rose to prominence. As hated as he was feared, he had a paranoid streak that threatened his sanity. To ensure that he would reign to a ripe old age, he removed himself to a gigantic houseboat docked in the middle of Lake Michigan. It was armed to the teeth, and its only connection with land was through a speedboat manned by his son, Nicolas. Six years ago, he was found dead, a single bullet lodged in the aorta of his heart, though no one heard a shot and the man was behind locked doors with a bevy of guards posted outside.

Now, I don't have to answer this question. I can leave and let Archibald and his entourage wonder how a guy like me could possibly do the things attributed to the name Columbus. This is a tactic I've used in the past, when questions like his are posed. But, today, the last day of the cruelest month, I think differently. I have six eyes on me, and a man's reputation can live for years on the witness of three black guys in a warehouse on the outskirts of Boston.

I spin with a whirl part tornado and part grace, and before an inhale can become an exhale, I have a pistol up and raised in my hand. I squeeze the trigger in the same motion, and the cigarette jumps out of Archibald's mouth and twirls like a baton through the air. The bullet plugs in the brick wall above the credenza as gravity takes the cigarette like a helicopter to a gentle landing on the cement floor. When the six eyes look up, I am gone.

CHAPTER TWO

Lateral bursts of wind prick the side of my face as I walk into my building. By the time I hear the story again, the scene in Archibald's warehouse will have taken on Herculean proportions. There will have been ten guys, instead of three, all with their guns drawn and trained on me. Archibald will have insulted me by saying, 'There's your case, bitch,' or some other endearment. I will have danced around bullets, mowed down seven guys, and walked on water before the cigarette was shot out of Archibald's mouth. Advertising doesn't hold a candle to the underworld's word of mouth.

My apartment does not reflect the size of my bank account. It is eight hundred square feet, sparsely decorated, with only the furniture and appliances necessary to sustain me for a week, the longest I stay most of the time. I do not have a cleaning service, or take a newspaper, or own a mailbox. My landlord has never met me, but receives a payment for double rent in cash once a year. In return, he asks no questions.

On my one table, I open the case carefully and spread its contents in neat stacks. Twenty dollars to a bill, a hundred bills to a band, five hundred bands in the case. This up front, triple when the job is complete. Underneath all of the money is a manila envelope. The money holds no allure for me. I am as immune to its siren's song as if I had taken a vaccine. The envelope, however, is my addiction.

I slide my finger under the seal and carefully open the flap, withdrawing its contents as though these pages are precious – brittle, breakable, vulnerable. This is what makes my breath catch, my heart spin, my stomach tighten. This is what keeps me looking for the next assignment, and the next, and the next – no matter what the cost to my conscience. This . . . the first look at the person I am going to kill.

Twenty sheets of paper, two binders of photographs, a schedule map, an itinerary, and a copy of a Washington, D.C. driver's license. I savor the first look at these items the way a hungry man savors the smell of steak. This mark will occupy my next eight weeks, and, though he doesn't know it, these papers are the first lines written on his death certificate. The envelope is before me, the contents laid out next to the money on my table, the end of his life now a foregone conclusion, as certain as the rising sun.

Quickly, I hold the first paper to the light that is snaking through my window, my eyes settling on the largest type, the name at the top of the page.

And then a gasp, as though an invisible fist flies through the air and knocks the breath from my lungs.

Can it be? Can someone have known, have somehow discovered my background and set this up as some sort of a joke? But . . . it is unthinkable. No one knows anything about my identity; no fingerprints, no calling card, no trace of my existence ever left carelessly at the scene of a killing. Nothing survives to link Columbus to that infant child taken from his mother's arms by the 'authorities' and rendered a ward of the state.

ABE MANN. The name at the top of the sheet. Can this be a

mere coincidence? Doubtful. My experience has proven to me time and time again that coincidence is a staple of fiction, but holds little authority in the real world. I open the binder, and my eyes absorb photograph after photograph. There is no mistake: this is the same Abe Mann who is currently Speaker of the House of Representatives of the United States of America, the same Abe Mann who represents the seventh district of the state of New York, the same Abe Mann who will soon be launching his first bid for his party's nomination for president. But none of these reasons caused the air to be sucked from my lungs. I have killed powerful men and relish the chance to do so again. There is more to the story of Abe Mann.

Twenty-nine years ago, Abe Mann was a freshman congressman with a comfortable wife and a comfortable house and a comfortable reputation. He attended more sessions of congress than any other congressman, joined three committees and was invited to join three more, and was viewed as a rising star in his party, enjoying his share of air time on the Sunday morning political programs. He also enjoyed his share of whores.

Abe was a big man. Six-foot-four, and a one-time college basketball star at Syracuse. He married an accountant's daughter, and her frigid upbringing continued unabated to her marriage bed. He stopped loving her before their honeymoon ended, and had his first taste of a prostitute the Monday after they returned from Bermuda. His weekdays he spent at the state capitol as a district representative; his weekends he spent anywhere but home. For five years, he rarely slept in his own bed, and his wife kept her mouth sealed tight, fearful that intimate details of their marriage would end up sandwiched between the world report and the weekend weather on the five o'clock news.

Once elected to serve in the nation's capital, Abe discovered a whole new level of prostitution. There were high-quality whores in New York, mind you, but even they paled in comparison to the women who serviced the leaders of this country. The best part was, he didn't even have to make polite enquiries. He was approached before he was sworn in, approached the first night of his first trip to Washington after the election. A senator, a man he had seen only on television and whom he had never met in person, called him directly at his hotel room and asked if he would like to join him for a party. What an incredible time he had had that night. With the stakes higher, the women so young, so beautiful, and so willing, he had experienced a new ecstasy that still made his mind reel when he thought of it.

Later that year, after he had settled, he grew fond of a hard-bodied black prostitute named Amanda B. Though she argued against it, he forced her to fuck him without a condom, satisfying his growing thirst for bigger and bigger thrills. For about six months, he fucked her in increasingly public locations, in increasingly dangerous positions, with increasingly animalistic ferocity. Each fix begat the next, and he needed stronger doses to satisfy his appetite.

When she became pregnant, his world caved in. He crawled to her in tears, begging for forgiveness. She was not frightened of him until she saw this change. This change meant he was more dangerous than she had anticipated. She knew what would happen next: after the tears, after the self-flagellation, after the 'why me?' and the self-loathing, he would turn. His internal remorse would eventually be directed outward; he would have been made to face his own weakness, and he would not like what he had seen. And so he would destroy that which made him feel helpless. Even in the altered state that cocaine had made of her mind, Amanda B. knew this as surely as she knew anything.

But she liked the way the baby felt inside her. She liked the way it was growing, swelling her stomach, moving inside her. Her! Amanda B., formerly La Wanda Dickerson of East Providence, Rhode Island, formerly inmate 43254 of the Slawson Home for Girls, her! Amanda B.! *She* could create life as well as any uppity wife of a congressman, any homemaker in a big house on a big lot next to a big lake. Her! As good as any of them.

So she decided to hide. She knew he would come for her, and when he did, she would be gone. She had a friend back home, a john who had proposed to her when she was fourteen. He still called, long distance and not collect either! He would take her in, would hide her from the congressman when he came looking. If she could just get to him . . .

But she didn't make it to Rhode Island. Instead, she ended up in the hospital, her nose bleeding, her lungs exploding, her heart beating holes into her chest. The police had found her seven-months-pregnant frame in the basement of an abandoned tenement building during a routine drug raid, a rubber cord tied around her bicep, a needle sticking out of her forearm. She was checked into the hospital as Jane Doe number 13 that day. The next day, she went into labor and gave birth to a four-pound boy. Social Services took him from her before she had held him for more than a minute.

Congressman Mann saw her for the last time two months later. Having seen the error of his ways, having rededicated his life to his country, his wife, and his God, he had her forcibly escorted from his front yard as she screamed louder and with more vehemence than she had ever screamed in her life. Ten days after the police report was filed, she was found dead in an alley behind a Sohio gas station, a knife handle sticking at an awkward angle from her neck. The policeman on the scene, a sixteen-year veteran named William Handley, speculated the wound was self-inflicted, though the coroner thought the circumstances of the death were inconclusive.

It took me two and a half years to put all that together. I did not ask the clay's question of who is the potter until I had achieved adulthood, not believing I would survive long enough to care. Then, after killing my eighth mark in three years, achieving a level of professionalism few have matched, I started to wonder who I was. Where did I come from? Who could possibly have sired me? The past, for which I had held no deference, reached out its huge, black paw and batted me right in the face.

So I clawed and scratched and exercised the necessary patience and restraint, and slowly put the jigsaw puzzle together, starting with the edges and working my way toward the center. A newspaper story connected to a hospital report connected to a police record until it all took shape and became whole. Once the puzzle was complete, I decided to dismiss the past once and for all. The present would be my domain, always the present. Every time I had tried to befriend the past, it chose to have no amity for me. Well, no more. I would bury my mother, Amanda B., so deep I would never find her again. And so I would my father, Congressman Abe Mann of New York.

And then, here is his name at the top of the sheet. Seven black letters printed in a careful hand, strong in their order, powerful in their conciseness. ABE MANN. My father. The next person I am to kill, in Los Angeles, eight weeks from now.

Can this be a coincidence, or has someone discovered my secret past and put the jigsaw puzzle together as I had? In my line of work, I can take no chances with the answer. I have to react quickly, waste as little time as possible, for if this does prove to be just another assignment, I'll have to compensate for each minute missed.

I, too, have a middleman. Pooley is the closest thing to friend or family I have, but we prefer the noncommittal label 'business associates.' I take one more glance over the documents, stack everything back in the case, and head out the door.

A hotel a block away provides me with quick access to taxicabs whenever I need them. The rain diminishing, I make my way over to where the hotel's doorman can hail me a car. The driver feels like chatting me up, but I stare out the window and let the buildings slide by outside like they're on a conveyer belt, one after the other, each looking just like the one before it. Stymied, the driver lights a cigarette and turns up the radio, a daygame, a businessman's special, broadcasting from Fenway.

We make it to Downey Street in SoBo, and I have the driver pull over to a nondescript corner. I do nothing that will cause him to remember me; I pay a fair tip and move up the street quickly. A day from now, he won't be able to distinguish me from any other fare.

I buy two coffees from a Greek delicatessen and climb the stoop to a loft apartment above the neighboring bakery. I am buzzed in before I can even juggle the styrofoam cups and press the button. Pooley must be at his desk.

'You brought me coffee?' He acts surprised as I hand him one of the cups and sit heavily in the only other chair in the room. 'You thoughtful bastard.'

'Yeah, I'm going soft.'

I hoist the case onto his desk and slide it over to him.

'Archibald's?'

'Yep,' I answer.

'He give you any problems?'

'Naah, he's all bluster. What I want to know is: who's he working for?'

This catches Pooley off guard. Ours is a business where certain questions aren't asked. The less you know – the fewer people you know, I should say – the better your chances of survival. Middlemen are as common as paper and ink, another office supply, a necessity to conduct business. They are used for a reason: to protect us from each other. Everyone understands this. Everyone respects this. You do not go asking questions, or you end up dead or relocated or physically unable to do your job. But those seven letters at the top of the page changed the rules.

'What?' he asks. Maybe he hadn't heard me right. I can't blame him for hoping.

'I want to know who hired Archibald to work as his go-between.'

'Columbus,' Pooley stammers. 'Are you serious?'

'I'm as serious as you've ever known me.'

This is no small statement, and Pooley knows it. We go back nearly twenty years, and he's seen me serious all my life. This breach of professional etiquette has him jumpy. I can see it on his face. Pooley is not good at hiding his emotions, not ever.

'Goddammit, Columbus. Why're you asking me that?'

'Open the case,' I say.

He looks at it suspiciously now, as if it can rise off the table and bite him, and then back at me. I nod without changing my expression, and he spins the case around and unhinges the snaps.

'In the envelope,' I urge when he doesn't see anything looking particularly troublesome.

He withdraws the envelope and slides his finger under the flap as I did. When he sees the name at the top of the page, his face flushes.

'You gotta be shitting me.'

Like I said, Pooley is practically my brother, and as such, is the only one who knows the truth about my genesis. When I was thirteen and he was eleven, we were placed with the same foster family, my sixth in five years, Pooley's third. By then, I could take whatever shit was thrown my way, but Pooley was still a boy, and he had been set up pretty well in his last home. He had an old lady for a foster mother, and the worst thing she did was to make him clean the sheets when she shit the bed. Not a particularly easy job for a nine-year-old, but nothing compared to what he had to survive at the Cox house after the old lady passed away.

Pete Cox was an English professor at one of the fancy schools outside Boston. He was a deacon at his church, a patron at the corner barbershop, and an amateur actor at the neighborhood theatre. His wife had suffered severe brain damage four years prior to our arrival. She had been in the passenger seat of a Nissan pickup truck when the driver lost control of the wheel and rolled the truck eleven times before it came to rest in a field outside Framingham.

The driver was not her husband. The last person who could substantiate their whereabouts was the clerk at the Marriott Courtyard Suites . . . when they checked out . . . together.

Subsequently, his wife occupied a hospital bed in the upstairs office of Pete's two-story home. She was heavily medicated, never spoke, ate through a tube, and kept on living. Her doctors thought she might live another fifty years, if properly cared for. There was nothing wrong with her body, just her brain, jammed in by the door handle when it broke through her skull.

Pete decided to take in foster children, since he would never have children of his own. His colleagues felt he was a brave man, a stoic; they certainly would have understood if he had divorced his wife after the circumstances of the accident came to light. But not our Pete. No, our Pete felt as though his wife's condition was a consequence of his own sin. And as long as he took care of his wife, as long as he showed God he could handle that burden, then it was okay if his sin continued. And grew. And worsened.

Pete liked to hurt little boys. He had been hurting little boys on and off since he was eighteen. 'Hurting them' could mean a number of things, and Pete had tried them all. He had nearly been caught when he was first learning his hobby after he had sliced off the nipple of an eight-year-old who was selling magazine subscriptions door-to-door. Pete caught up with him in the alley behind his cousin's apartment – just luck he had been visiting at the time! – and invited the kid to show him his sales brochure. With the promise of seventeen subscription purchases, which would qualify the kid for a free Sony Walkman and make him the number-one salesman in his Cub Scout den, Pete got him to step behind a dumpster and take off his shirt. He had the nipple off in no time, but he hadn't anticipated the volume of the child's scream. It was so loud, so visceral, so animal, it excited Pete like a drug; yet, at the same time, windows were going up all over the block. Pete booked it out of there, and no one ever came looking for him. He promised himself to be more discreet the next time. And the next time. And the next.

By the time we came to live with him, Pete had hurt hundreds of children all over the country. He had thought his wife to be his savior, the only woman who had really, truly cared for him, and for a while after they were married, he had stopped doing what he did to little boys. But an addiction is tough to put away permanently; it sits in dark recesses, gathering strength, biding its time until it can unleash itself, virgin and hungry, again. It was a week after Pete had fallen off the wagon, had done an unmentionable thing to a nine-year-old, when his wife had had her accident. How could he not blame himself for her fate? The Bible spends a great deal of time explaining the 'wages' of sin, and what were his wife's infidelity and her crumpled brain but manifestations of the evil he had committed on that boy? So he took care of her, and four years later, signed up with the state to be a foster parent.

I don't need to shock you with the atrocities Pooley and I endured in the two years we lived in the Cox house. Rather, to understand the relationship we now share, I'll tell you about the last night, the night before we were sent to finish out our youth at Juvenile upstate.

I was fifteen then, and had figured out ways to make my body stronger, despite Cox's best efforts to keep us physically emaciated. When he went to work, I put chairs together and practiced push-ups, my legs suspended between them. I moved clothes off the bar in the closet and pulled myself up – first ten times, then twenty, then hundreds. I bench-pressed the sofa, I ran sprints in the hallway, I squatted with the bookcase on my back. All of this while Pete was gone; everything put back and in its place before he returned. I tried to get Pooley to work his body with me, but he was too weak. He wanted to, I could tell, but his mind wouldn't let him see the light at the end of the tunnel, so much had been taken out of him.

On this day, the last day, Pete had given his students a walk. He had not felt good, had started to come down with something, and when the dean of the department told him to go on home and rest, Pete decided to take his advice before he changed his mind. This is why he entered his house not at four o'clock like he usually did, but at two-fifteen. This is why he found me surrounded by books all over the floor, the bookcase lofted on my back, my taut body in mid-squat.

'What the fuck?' was all he could muster, before his eyes narrowed and he came marching toward me.

I tossed the bookcase off my back like I was bucking a saddle, and looked for the easiest escape route, but there wasn't one, and before I could move, his arms were around me. He hoisted me off the ground – I couldn't have weighed more than a hundred and twenty pounds – and threw me head-first into the wall. Instead of cracking, my head ripped through the plaster into a wooden beam. Dazed, I pushed away as fast as I could, shaking wall dust from my hair, but he was on me again, and this time, he held me up in a bear hug. His face was both angry and ecstatic, and he squeezed until I couldn't breathe and my eyes went bleary with tears. I think he would have killed me. I was getting too old to bully and he knew I was building up resistance. It would have been safer to kill me. To go ahead and finish this here and now. He still had one more little boy he could torture.

From up the stairs, Pooley found his voice. 'Let go of him, you stupid motherfucker!'

This got our attention, both of us, and distracted Cox enough to make him drop me. From *my* mouth, he was used to hearing such language, such resentment, such fury, but not from little Pooley. We both jerked our heads simultaneously and looked up the stairs.

The door guarding Mrs. Cox stood open. The padlock that usually kept it firmly closed was somehow forced, wood scrapings cutting claw scratches into the wall. Pooley stood just outside the door, his tiny body shaking, drenched with sweat, a glass shard in his hand, blood dripping from the end in large red drops.

Pete's face metamorphosed so dramatically, it was like someone had flipped a switch, turning from acid rage to sudden confusion and trepidation. 'What'd you do?' was all he could manage, and his knees actually wobbled.

Pooley didn't answer; he just stood there, trembling, his face strained, blood and sweat mingling on the carpet at his feet.

'What'd you do?' Pete shouted a second time, his voice marked with desperation. Again, Pooley didn't answer.

Pete launched for the stairs and ascended them in five quick steps. I was close behind, prepared to tackle him with everything I had if he went for Pooley. But he didn't. He took two more steps toward his wife's open door, peeked into the room fearfully, as though hands might suddenly reach out and grab him, and then collapsed inside.

I got to Pooley as tormented wails began to waft from the open door. 'Come on,' I said.

Pooley's eyes continued to stare off into space.

'Let's get out of here,' I added. The urgency in my voice snapped some life back into his face and his eyes settled on me.

'I had to,' he said weakly.

'I know,' I offered.

I put my hand on his arm, and he let the shard drop to the floor. The blood caught it, and it landed sideways, red flecks marring the beauty of the glass. We stepped over it and walked down the stairs. I picked up the bookcase again and heaved it into the living room window, somehow knowing instinctively the front door had been double bolted before Pete turned and found me there.

We climbed out of the window and tasted the air outside for the first time in over a year, just as the loudest wail rose from the dark upstairs. 'I'm sorry! I'm so sorry! I'm so sorry!'

All those months Pooley had been silent, pretending to be resigned inside himself, he had really been watching, studying, understanding the motivations of our Pete. Taking his beatings in silence, letting me take mine, but watching, waiting. Twice he had overheard Pete in Mrs. Cox's room, pouring out his penitence to her mindless eyes. Twice he had heard Pete begging for forgiveness, only to increase his savagery two hours later. So Pooley began to figure out that Pete needed her there to continue doing what he did to us. He needed someone who wouldn't judge him, but would sit passively and let him forgive himself so he could do it again. While I trained, trying to make my body stronger so I could one day fight back, Pooley cracked a mirror in the back bathroom, sharpened a shard on the side of the bedroom headboard, and waited. When Pete came home early and found me getting stronger, he knew he could wait no longer.

The police picked us up before we had gone a mile. We were indicted for killing Mrs. Cox, and my descriptions of our treatment seemed to fall on deaf ears. I had a petty-crime juvenile record in my past, and Pooley was done talking to adults for a long time. I can't say I blamed him; he saved my life, after all. Nor was I surprised when we were convicted. But because of some of the oddities that came out of Pete's mouth when he talked cryptically to the judge about swift, painful discipline – lending some credence to what I had said about our treatment – we were tried as juveniles and sent upstate to finish out our youth.

So Pooley was the first assassin I had known. When I decided to begin this life professionally – or you might say it was decided for me – he was a natural to be my middleman, though he wasn't my first.

CHAPTER THREE

Pooley agrees the coincidence surrounding my father is too odd to let pass without some digging. Since I need to head west without delay, he'll handle the shovel for me. We agree to speak again when I call next week from the road.

My rule is eight weeks out. I will not agree to complete a job in less than that time, and, as such, have turned down quite a few assignments, even when offers for more money have been dangled like grapes. I can flawlessly plan and execute a job in less time; of that, I have no doubt. But assassinating a target takes psychological preparation, and shortchanging yourself in that area can lead to debilitation long after the mark is in the grave.

I open the folder again and this time, study the contents without flinching. He will be traveling by bus, a 'whistle-stop' tour criss-crossing the country, culminating in Los Angeles at the Democratic National Convention. His path is strategically haphazard, planned randomness, with stops in most of the major television markets surrounding battleground states and enough small towns peppered in so that no economic demographic will feel slighted. Three thousand miles and a million handshakes in eight weeks. I will follow the same route, and will wait for him in the Midwest, allowing him to catch up, before I follow him the rest of the way to California.

The next morning, a rental car is parked out on my street with no paperwork to sign, no instructions to receive, the keys on the floorboard under the steering column. A beige car, a sedan, with nothing to distinguish it from the millions of other cars sprawling across American highways at any given time. With only a small duffel tossed in the back seat and a larger case lodged in the trunk, I head west, the sun at my back.

When I pull over to eat lunch at a small roadside dinette with the provocative name SUE'S NO. 2, I am approached by a prostitute. I had grabbed a booth in the back of the restaurant in order to avoid contact with the local denizens of this somewheretown, but this girl could care less where I sat. She homed in on me as soon as the bells jingled on the door.

She is dressed in a skirt that stops well above her knees and a white halter that exposes the baby fat around her middle. Her hair is stringy blond with burgundy roots and hangs away from her head like a web. She possesses a crooked nose but an uncommonly pretty mouth with perfectly straight teeth. Her eyes are sharp and intelligent.

'Hey there, mon frer,' she says, plopping down in the seat across from me. My guess is she cannot weigh more than a hundred pounds nor be older than seventeen.

I don't say anything, and she proceeds, unfazed.

'Here's what I'm thinking. I got dropped off in this shithole town, and I need a lift outta here.' This comes out between smacks of bright purple gum and the smell of grapes left too long on the vine. 'So I'm prepared to grant you favours in exchange for a lift.'

'A lift where?'

'Wherever it is you're headed.'

'What kind of favours?'

She drops her chin and looks at me from the tops of her eyes like I don't have the sense God gave me. Just then, the waitress approaches. The girl waits for me to order, and before the waitress can disappear, I find myself asking her if she's hungry.

'Fuckin' starvin', man.'

The waitress takes an order for steak and eggs and hashbrowns and bacon if they have any left over from breakfast. Oh, and some orange juice and some milk and that'll be it. The girl's eyes are merry now; there is a break in the storm clouds. I don't normally talk to people, but it's been an abnormal week and those merry eyes stir something inside me I thought wasn't there.

'How'd you get here?'

'This nut-rubber wanted some company for his ride over to Boston. He wanted me to jerk him along the way.' Hand gestures for emphasis. 'I gave him what he asked for and when we pulled over here to get something to eat, he split as soon as I stepped out of the car.' Matter-of-factly, as though she were telling me about her day at school. 'Stiffed me, too, the bastard. It's gettin' to where there's not any honest people around.'

'How old are you?'

'I lost track.'

I swear she's seventeen. 'What's the last age you remember being?'

'Let's not talk about me. Let's talk about—'

But she's interrupted by the food. We both eat in silence; I because I enjoy it, she because she can't get the breakfast into her mouth fast enough. The food is flying up to her face like a power shovel at full steam, and she is as unembarrassed as a hog at a trough. She devours all of hers, and when I proffer half of my plate, she attacks it.

After I've left money for the tab, she asks, 'So how about that ride?'

'What do you think?'

Smiling now with those beautiful ivory teeth, she puts one finger in her mouth. 'I think I've got a pretty good shot at taggin' along with you.'

She's asleep in the passenger seat, and I am pissed. Pissed I let my guard down, pissed I've committed a cardinal sin, pissed I've ignored every professional instinct in my ken to allow her to share this car with me. I can still kill her, can still pull the car down one of these farm-to-market roads, roll the tires against some deserted brush, and pop, pop, dump the body where it won't be found for weeks. She won't be missed, that's certain. Except, goddammit, people saw us at the diner, the waitress, the old man in coveralls at the counter, the couple in the booth at the far end of the joint. They saw her lock in on me, and they saw us leave together, and they saw us get into my beige sedan. People noticed. They noticed, goddammit. What is happening to me?

Bad luck. The name at the top of the page was bad luck, and now picking up this girl-whore is as black bad as it can get. My stomach is queasy with the blackness. I must be slipping.

'So, where are we headed?' She puts her bare feet up on the dashboard in front of her and blinks groggily.

'Philadelphia.'

'Yeah? Good. That's where I came from.'

'Originally?'

'Naah,' she snorts, finding the question funny. 'Originally I'm from a little hovel outside of Pittsburgh that you've never heard of. Recently, I'm from Philly.'

'That's where you . . . work?'

She snorts again, not at all self-conscious about the way it makes her sound like a sow. 'Yeah, work. Working girl.' She pauses thoughtfully, and then, as though she's struggling with the weight of her question, 'What do you think about that?'

'About what you do?'

'Yeah. I'm curious. You seem like a normal dude. What's a normal dude think about a working girl?'

'I think it can't be too good of a way to make a living.'

'You got that right, buddy. You certainly got that right.'

'So, why do it, then?'

'I don't know. I can tell you one thing, I'm rarely lucid enough to sit and think about it. You got any liquor in here?' She tries to swivel in her seat to look in the back, but when she reaches for my duffel, I grab her with my free hand and spin her around hard.

'Owww. Shit, man! I'm just looking to see if you got anything to drink!'

'I don't.'

'Well you don't have to be a cocksucker about it.' She's showing me the same mouth that can use words like 'hovel' and 'lucid' can spew vitriol as well. And she's testing the envelope to see how far she can push it. Was the way I spun her around portentous of a beating to come? Did she get a rise out of me with the severity of the way she pronounced cocksucker, the way she paused right before the word, collecting her breath and then pounding that first syllable like she hit it with a hammer? COCKsucker! We drive on in silence. I can tell she'd rather pass the time talking than pouting, but she wants me to make the first move.

After two minutes, she gives up. 'I was just looking to see if you had something to drink.'

'I don't.'

She decides to get off the subject. 'You like music?'

'I like silence.'

This seems to do the trick, and for a few minutes more, the only sound in the car is her nasal breathing, in and out, in and out, like wind through a cracked window.

'I need to pee,' she says suddenly, nodding at the approaching exit where a Texaco sign pokes just above the tree line.

I throw up my blinker and guide the car toward the exit. As we approach, I can't help but notice a farm road running directly behind the service station, leading off into obscurity. Maybe I can get away with it, with a little extra time. If I can find some soft earth,

I can dig a little hole to hide her body, and it'll be months, maybe years before anyone finds the remains. But it's broad daylight and I don't know this road and any dumb farmer could happen along at just the right time.

By the time I've rejected the temptation, she's opened the door. I watch her ask the attendant where the restrooms are and he hands her a giant block of wood with a key attached and points around to the back of the building. I watch him watch her all the way out the door, and when he catches me observing him, he quickly looks back down at the binder he had splayed on the counter.

What am I doing here? I should just gun the car and forget I ever saw this girl, but for some reason, I'm paralyzed. What is it about those teeth and that mouth? What do I see in them?

I turn off the ignition and head into the convenience store portion of the station where the clerk gives me a once-over and shuffles his binder down below the counter. I move to the drinks stacked like bricks up to the ceiling in the back of the store and withdraw a six-pack of Budweiser. For someone whose every move is performed to draw the least amount of attention – domestic over import in rural Pennsylvania – I realize I've already attracted notice just by parking the car and having this girl ask for the bathroom key. The clerk's once-over wasn't because he was worried I'd shoplift something from the store; he wanted to know what kind of man would pick up a girl like that. And he is going to remember who it was and what the man looked like when and if he is asked.

This is how it happens. In the game I play, you cannot give in to temptation, even if temptation is merely to hold a conversation with someone, to connect with another human being on a superficial level. And once you give in to temptation, even if you only do it one time, then the dominoes start to topple until the entire floor is covered with a dark blanket.

I pay for the beer and the clerk only grunts at me without meeting my eyes when he hands over the change. Maybe this isn't so bad. I've done a thoughtful thing for this girl, and the clerk is back looking at his binder before I even leave the store. Maybe I can pull this off, talk to this girl, gain some insight into her world and what she imagined she would be doing with her life. Find out where her life took the left turn instead of the right, where she missed the exit and eventually got lost and discovered that her map was terribly inaccurate. Maybe I can learn about someone for once, someone whose life had been like my mother's, with no hidden motives.

In the car, I slide back behind the wheel and put the six-pack on the seat so the girl will see it when she returns. It's as simple as that, buying her breakfast, giving her this six-pack of beer, and that smile will come to her lips again, and she will lean back in her seat, and she will be warm and rosy, and she won't have to say things like cocksucker and pee and we can have a normal conversation like normal people.

A moment exists in time – a flash of a moment – right before you realize how fucked you are. You can't explain it scientifically, but a shiver settles on the back of your neck as though someone placed an ice cube there. The fine hairs on your neck stand erect like they've been jolted with electricity. A rush of heat flashes through your body and your muscles all contract in unison. This happens instantaneously, when your mind hasn't quite caught up to your body's impulse. It is what I felt when I happened to glance in the back seat.

My duffel. She had reached for my duffel and I had immediately seized her arm and jerked her around hard. Therefore, there must be something valuable in the duffel. She must have taken it while I was in the store.

I bolt from the car and around to the bathroom, knowing instinctively the clerk's eyes are riveted on me. Nothing. Just a key stuck in the open door of a filthy bathroom and no trace of the girl or my bag. Behind the Texaco, a thick growth of trees, a country road leading to oblivion, and no sign of the fucking girl. Pandora has climbed out of her box.

My breath escapes quickly, four quick bursts, and then I'm off into the woods. I don't even know what goddamn name to call her, to call out, so I just stay quiet, a determined expression now blanching my face. I have to improvise, to hunt her quickly. How long will the clerk look at that rental car parked in front of the store before he calls the police with a declaration that something a little strange is going on down at the Texaco? He saw the girl. He saw me. He saw her go around to the back and then he saw me spring from the car after her. Had I even shut the door of the car? I'm not sure. Son-of-a-bitch, how had I let this get so out of hand?

I have five minutes, maybe ten to find her before the clerk ventures out to see if we're in the bathroom together. After that, who knows? Another five minutes to call the police? I'm fucked. That's all there is to it.

Trees everywhere, and then, a clearing, and I catch a glimpse of her just as she crosses into the growth about a tenth of a mile from where I stand. She caught sight of me, too, and I spot a panic in her face usually reserved for wild prey. Maybe she's seen what's in the bag and she's spooked. But she hasn't dropped the duffel either; I can see its yellow flash caught against her dark skirt.

I close the distance in no time. She's skittish, and she makes a mistake, turns and trips over a dead oak stump. Her hands go up as my footsteps crunch through the dead leaves, on her back, arms bent, scrambling, scratching the air, trying to get me off before I'm even there.

And then my foot comes down on her neck, twisting her face into the dirt so that those pretty teeth are smeared with earth.

'No, mister. Please. I don't want it. I didn't mean to . . . I didn't mean . . . I didn't mean . . .'

Fighting with everything she has, every inch of strength she can muster, her arms wailing at my shin, beating my pants leg, her eyes desperate with fear.

And then I step down harder until I hear the bones in her neck crack like wood.

* * *

The forest is silent in the peculiar way nature seems to go mute when a living creature is killed. I hesitate to say 'innocent' creature, because if she hadn't been so stupid, if she hadn't been so goddamn reckless, she'd still be alive and we'd be chatting on our way to Philadelphia, making a connection, talking about the normal things normal people talk about and her mouth would be smiling and sipping on a beer rather than silent and gaping and half-filled with muck, and leaves, and decay.

Or maybe the woods aren't silent at all. Maybe my ears are ringing so loudly all other sounds are drowned out. I am breathing hard and a bead of sweat has rolled from my eyebrows to the tip of my nose, but the silence is implacable, as thick as cream. Underneath my boot, the girl remains still, her energy as used up and wasted as her life.

I will need a little luck. I prop the girl on my shoulders as though I'm carrying a wounded soldier, and hurry back through the woods toward the convenience store. A little luck, a little luck. That's all I'm asking. My footsteps are firm, finding solid ground again and again, weaving in and out of the trees, the back of the store looming larger and larger through the brush. Her weight is slight, and her body bobs up and down on my shoulders, light as a backpack. Thirty feet, twenty, and no sign of the clerk. Just stay at your counter, friend. Keep marking in your binder, counting up that inventory, and you'll soon forget about us, just another couple of customers amidst a constant string of travelers.

I break through the tree line and I'm back at the store, the block of wood still dangling from the doorknob like a pendulum. In a quick step, I'm in the room with the body on my back and the block of wood in my hand and the door shut tight. Almost there. Stay with me, luck.

The smell in the bathroom is horrible, and stains splotch the walls like a foul mosaic. It doesn't take me long to work myself up. The stench, the agitation, the degradation of killing in this animalistic manner, her body propped across the sink, her head facing me, her lips curling back away from her teeth in a sneer that is accusatory and mocking and hopeless. I double over and retch until I can feel the pulse thick in my ears.

He knocks as I finish my second heave.

'Are you okay in there?'

Luck is a funny thing. I open the door, carrying the girl in my arms, quickly, out into the open. 'Do you have a hose?' I say, and his eyes immediately go over my shoulder to the bathroom, his nose curling.

'Awww, shit.'

'Sorry, man. She got sick.' I smooth the girl's hair with my supporting hand.

He doesn't even look at us, shaking his head. 'Don't worry about it,' he says, resigned, and passes me to survey the mess in the stall.

I don't wait for him to give us a second look. I am around the building and into the car before he can even hook up the hose, my bag and the whore's body laid to rest in the wide back seat.